"BRILLIANT . . . THERE IS A GOOD DEAL OF
HEART IN THIS NOVEL."   —*Los Angeles Times*

"COMPELLING . . . RICH . . . VIVID . . . STRONG."
                                —*Library Journal*

"It is the sure and delicate touch of Ms. Hunt which
makes her account of the dangerous etiquette of racism
so powerful."   —*Sunday Tribune*

"AMBITIOUS . . . POIGNANT . . . paints a graphic
picture of past horrors and the continuing bleakness of
sexual and financial persecution."   —*Publishers Weekly*

MARSHA HUNT was born in Philadelphia and attended
the University of California at Berkeley before moving to
London, where she starred in the hit musical *Hair*. Since
then she has enjoyed a successful career in music and on
the stage, including work with the Royal Shakespeare Company and the National Theatre. She won fresh acclaim with
her 1986 autobiography, and then with her highly praised
first novel, *Joy* (also available from Plume). Ms. Hunt cur-
rently resides in France.

By the same author

REAL LIFE
JOY

Marsha Hunt

FREE

A PLUME BOOK

PLUME
Published by the Penguin Group
Penguin Books USA Inc., 375 Hudson Street, New York, New York 10014, U.S.A.
Penguin Books Ltd, 27 Wrights Lane, London W8 5TZ, England
Penguin Books Australia Ltd, Ringwood, Victoria, Australia
Penguin Books Canada Ltd, 10 Alcorn Avenue, Toronto, Ontario, Canada M4V 3B2
Penguin Books (N.Z.) Ltd, 182–190 Wairau Road, Auckland 10, New Zealand

Penguin Books Ltd, Registered Offices: Harmondsworth, Middlesex, England

Published by Plume, an imprint of Dutton Signet, a division of Penguin Books USA Inc.
Previously published in a Dutton edition, and published in Great Britain
by Hamish Hamilton.

First Plume Printing, January, 1994
10 9 8 7 6 5 4 3 2 1

LIBRARY OF CONGRESS CATALOGING-IN-PUBLICATION DATA
Hunt, Marsha, 1946–
    Free / Marsha Hunt.
      p.   cm.
    ISBN 0-452-27061-8
    1. Afro-American men—Pennsylvania—Philadelphia—Fiction.
2. Friendship—Pennsylvania—Philadelphia—Fiction.   3. Young men—
Pennsylvania—Philadelphia—Fiction.   4. British—Pennsylvania—
Philadelphia—Fiction.   5. Germantown (Philadelphia, Pa.)—Fiction.
6. Race relations—Fiction.   I. Title.
[PS3558.U4678F7   1994]
813′.54—dc20   93-30341
                                                                          CIP

Printed in the United States of America
Original hardcover design by Steven N. Stathakis

PUBLISHER'S NOTE

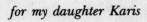

for my daughter Karis

FREE

I

Germantown, Pennsylvania
Saturday, August 2, 1913

Young Theodore "Teenotchy" Simms had been cleaning the Klebers' red-brick colonial house at the corner of Main Street and Schoolhouse Lane every Saturday morning since the age of seven and, twelve years on, reminiscing was as much a part of his routine as starting on the Klebers' top floor, like he'd seen his mother do, to work down to the parlor.

Tidy in his bib and suspenders, he was a slave to habit, thanks to fear, although he didn't know he was scared, sweeping the same worn-out memories from room to room along with the Klebers' old straw broom, which was nearly as old as he was. In and out, up and down on tiptoe, Teenotchy glided between the eerie silence of phantoms leaguing about. But no matter how many times he rummaged through his childhood, best forgotten, he couldn't remember his dead mother's face, though for some reason polishing the Klebers' Bavarian dining table invariably reminded him of her hands, which were a lighter shade of brown than that oak table. But whereas that imported monstrosity with its bandied legs and elaborately carved feet beamed like a mirror from Teenotchy's ardent buffings over the years, his mother's hands had been as rough as bark from scrubbing other people's floors in buckets of cold water laced with enough lye to cut grime.

It didn't matter that she'd been dead thirteen of his nineteen years; still his memory gripped the image of her lean, long fingers, nails bitten to the quick, wringing out stringy gray scrub rags or spreading a dab of grease on his knobbly knees when he was five . . . And back then it'd felt as good as a lover's caress to have her pick the sleep from his curly black lashes.

So as usual these time-worn images were replayed as if they'd happened yesterday while Teenotchy stood in the Klebers' parlor that hot, sticky morning. Not that any of them could help him recall his dead mother's face. Him with shoulders stooped as he eyed the jam jar of Mister Kleber's homemade furniture polish, which was as yellow as a withered daffodil and smelled to high heaven of the turpentine the old man used to thin it. Teenotchy's mother had sworn by that wax when she was in charge of cleaning the place, not that she was the only person who thought Mister Kleber should have marketed his concoction. But making his fortune was the last thing on the old Quaker's mind whenever she was around. So while he appreciated her compliment, he declined the temptation to get rich quick, like some of his Germantown neighbors.

Teenotchy was still eyeing the yellow wax as a little drop of his own perspiration plopped on to the jar. He used his stiff calico apron to dab at the slow stream of sweat making a trail from his temple to his chin, thinking all the while that he hadn't known an August like it.

"Hot as Hell," he mused to himself as he whiffed the clammy air, heavy with the smell of the wax he was meant to be spreading on Helga Kleber's Bavarian dining table.

His heart was outdoors in the blistering sunlight, and the four unadorned white walls closing in on him in the parlor heard him let out a sigh so deep it was practically a groan, helping him ease the tension he was feeling in the backs of his legs, which tightened any time he held that homemade polish in his hands.

When he'd been a lot younger, Teenotchy'd imagined that it was the sound of popping open the flat tin of wax which sparked the tingling sensation that crawled down his spine to the backs of his legs, making him want to kick them or, better still, jump out of his skin. But then Mister Kleber took to putting his wax into jars, and Teenotchy had to admit to himself that he still got that uncomfortable sensation down his legs whenever he unscrewed the lid.

In any case, one discomfort sparked another, and in addition to the creepy-crawly feeling in his legs, his breath got short and his ears would fill with the sound of his mother's voice screaming, "Run, Teenotchy! Don't stop!" like he had a safe place to run to. "Run, Teenotchy! Don't stop!" she'd wail, making him wish he could clamp both hands to his ears to keep the echo out. But what would have been the point when the voice was in his head, lurking in a dark corner where it'd slept since he was five and had first heard it?

"Run, Teenotchy! Don't stop! Run on, baby!" his mother's dark-brown voice railed every Saturday while Teenotchy tried to sneak up on the chore of polishing that table, hating the way his mother's screech managed to climb higher than a white woman's as it sailed from low B flat to scale a high C like the one on Helga Kleber's piano, which occupied a corner of the parlor but never got played in all the years Teenotchy had worked for the immigrant family.

It was no wonder the sound of his mother's voice made him shake even though he pretended on the surface not to hear it. And it was no wonder her wail gouged out his insides and churned his stomach upside down, because it lay in wait to recall that Teenotchy was a bad boy and didn't (or was it couldn't?) do as he was told.

Run?

Run to where, when no place was safe? No place to go but the memories, which is why he loved to replay the best of them, like remembering dark mornings, icy mornings back in '99 when he was five and stood watching his mother's hands carefully spoon out grits for him and his little sister, Atlanta, who was two years younger but acted like a big, bad baby, whining when their mother'd said there was nothing to whine about.

Teenotchy'd never whined back then—all of five and as stolid as an old man. As somber as Mister Kleber even if he couldn't be as wise, since his mother was always saying, "Nobody's wise as old man Kleber."

Teenotchy loved to recall how he and Atlanta got their steamy grits in chipped white enamel bowls, although their mother stood by the wood-burning pot-bellied stove and gulped hers straight from the pot, one hand on her hip, the other holding the spoon. Those rough hands that caressed him like no other.

Even the August heat couldn't stop Teenotchy from remembering back to those icy-cold winter days. He mused on how hot the grits used to be and pictured the curlicues of steam that used to rise from the bowl, winding around his nostrils like a charmed snake while the cold floor burned through his little black high tops, which were too big so his mother'd stuffed old rags in the toes.

It was easier thinking back than applying his mind to the task at hand, and it was sweeter thinking back than coping with the echo that his mother's voice left ringing in his ears. So Teenotchy avoided thinking about the jar of home-made wax and took the hard-tipped edge of his calico apron to blot at another trickle of sweat that was making its way from his forehead to his steel-rimmed glasses, which made his lead-gray eyes look smaller than they really were.

He strained to see the parlor, blanketed in dimness since

he hadn't bothered to pull back the dark-blue velvet drapes which cloaked the oblong windows that overlooked School-house Lane and had graced the Klebers' front room from the time Mister Kleber's wife, Ursula, managed to stitch them from her deathbed.

It didn't matter to Teenotchy that he hadn't known her. He knew her rocking chair and got a sense of her from her white crocheted shawl which lay draped over the back of it, like she'd only stepped out of the room and intended to return any minute. Like his mother's, Ursula Kleber's spirit knew how to hover and make a body feel that she was still around, like she'd managed to do since she died in '92.

And like his mother's, Ursula Kleber's soul was worth more dead than alive since her meekness had made her almost invisible.

Mister Kleber's son, Hans, had done a pencil sketch of his mother and it was that semiprofile which allowed Teenotchy to put a face to the woman who had been Mister Kleber's only wife.

Teenotchy looked over at her rocker, which sat opposite the piano and seemed to defy any other piece of furniture to dare change the place she'd created with its angular simplicity and uprightness. Everything placed at right angles to the wall and two pewter candlesticks sitting at either end of a fireplace which hadn't seen a fire since Mister Kleber's stroke relegated the old man to his bed long before his body was ready to lie down day in and out.

Though Ursula Kleber had never known Teenotchy's mother or him, Mister Kleber reminded them that the house was hers and they were to treat it with the reverence she deserved.

Aged five, Teenotchy was convinced he was privileged and living the high life whenever his mother was allowed to bring him to work, and he adored marching in the back door behind her, watching her put her apron on to settle down to business. By the end of her day there she would smell of bleach, although sometimes, when she cradled Teenotchy's face in her hands to ask if he was all right, he would faintly smell Mister Kleber's home-made wax, which left a workday perfume like the brass polish his mother let him use to clean those pewter candlesticks.

She knew how to please him and make him feel important. She knew just how he liked to hear her brag that his little five-year-old fingers could get at the bits that her long, lean fingers missed. Not that she missed much when it came to cleaning, whether it was dusting above the Klebers' doorsill or scrubbing their threshold on her hands and knees. House-cleaning proved she existed, which is why she held it in such high esteem.

She used to say, "Teenotchy, child, do just like you see me do and don't mess." And while she taught him this, the other thing he learned from her "Do as I do" message was to tiptoe through life, rarely speaking unless spoken to. This she thought was a good thing, since she dreamed that some day he might rise to be a butler and "do" for one of Germantown's first families. "Doing" for one of Philadelphia's first families, it being but six miles away, seemed beyond her wildest dreams.

Like any good mother, she was bent on preparing him for his future—what she called their "low berth on God's earth." And it was with this in mind that his mother, known as Dusty Simms to the Klebers, boxed her little son's tiny, perfectly formed ears some Friday nights though he did nothing to deserve it. Another one of her bits of "home training" which she dished out not through cruelty but more through the presumption that life would continue to be unfair and cruel to her boy and that she had a duty to prepare him for blows to come.

Not that Teenotchy would have remembered getting his ears boxed, because his Saturday reminiscing at the Klebers' and his memory generally blanked unpleasant details. For along with teaching him to clean, not to speak unless spoken to, hardly to breathe in the presence of white employers, Dusty Simms had also taught him to blot out ugliness in all forms. "When bad stuff happens," she would tell him, "you got to put it out your mind right quick." And he did just that, since he always did everything she told him, except that once in '99 when he was five and leaves covered the ground and he saw her murdered.

But then, Teenotchy didn't remember this incident any more than he remembered his mother's pretty coral-brown face.

That face, with its almond eyes, the color and shape of his, had graced the Klebers' parlor in the same way Teenotchy's did that hot August morning as he stood with his shoulders drooping for fear of standing as tall as his five foot six inches would allow. And it was in the stillness which Ursula Kleber had created in that room before he was born that Teenotchy finally mustered the strength to dip his rag into the yellow furniture polish and spread it caringly yet all the while carelessly on Helga Kleber's Bavarian table.

It almost made it all right in his mind to treat that oak table with disrespect since it was Helga's, her being kin to Mister Kleber only through her marriage to his son, Hans, also deceased, also with his spirit hovering among the inanimate objects in the parlor. Kinship by marriage didn't make Helga a real Kleber, Teenotchy's mother used to say, since it was her only defense against and explanation for the contempt Helga showed Dusty Simms any time she was cleaning the Klebers' red-brick dwelling.

Teenotchy stood back to examine the oak table and almost smiled when he spotted the bit that he'd missed. It was still glistening, as opposed to the rest of the table, which grew duller as the wax dried upon it. He thought about his mother saying, "Do like you see me do and don't mess," but still he screwed the lid back on the jar of wax, because even he,

Theodore "Teenotchy" Simms, was capable of insurrection
and rebellion. In fact, the older he got the more he relished
provoking Helga Kleber by doing less than his best.

Had Dusty Simms been standing at his elbow, he might
have had trouble explaining himself, since she considered the
most docile servitude necessary for survival. Indeed, she
might have called it a great talent, a gift, a blessing and an
asset no less important to her boy's future than the smooth
crinkle of Teenotchy's ebony-brown hair, which she'd refused
to cut even after he'd turned five. Because she thought if
little white boys in Germantown wore theirs to their shoulders, her son should do the same since he had what she
glowingly referred to as "good" hair, "growing" hair that she
observed and touched as one might the halo of a saint.

In fact, no matter what else Dusty Simms was required to
do in her day, she always found time to dress Teenotchy's hair
like he had some place special to go and somebody special to
see. And it didn't matter that she knew, like he did, that most
days he wouldn't get further than the desert of a yard that
surrounded their little dwelling which she called home.

Every morning before breakfast, Dusty Simms used to
perch as upright as a bronze Degas ballerina on the rickety
three-legged stool by the sooty pot-bellied stove to dress that
"good" hair of Teenotchy's. It was a labor of love and as
sacred to her as any communion, so she operated as a priest
in the throes of a holy ritual: silent, exact, reverent, slow,
Dusty Simms would set about to prepare her boy's hair.

Atlanta wouldn't get even a look-in, since the kink of her
hair made it a class below Teenotchy's in their mother's eyes.
And the little girl would watch her mother and brother from
under the kitchen table, since it was as safe from being
stepped upon as anywhere in their barren kitchen.

Atlanta would watch her mother point to the squat jar
of Doc Tatum's Green Hair Grow and, without needing more
of an order, Teenotchy would obediently fetch it and their
piece of comb by standing on tiptoe to take it from the corner

of the windowsill. Then Dusty Simms would gather her long black skirt and son between her legs, with ankles locked to secure all in place, and her deft fingers would begin their dance among the dark, crinkly strands of Teenotchy's shoulder-length hair.

Everything about her was graceful. Her spine was straight, her neck held just so, upright and erect as the index finger that would dig down into the jar of Doc Tatum's pomade and come up with a thick dollop which she'd rub between both palms before massaging it into Teenotchy's hair, never thinking that her rough hands had earned a dollop too before she had her fingers parting and twirling, twisting and curling, every greasy strand.

Teenotchy loved the attention and hated the pain; his gray eyes would fill with tears and he winced any time that piece of comb caught a snarl.

"Don't scrunch up that face. God'll leave you looking like that," Dusty Simms would warn her son. But he had no choice.

"Tender-headed," he'd hear his mother murmur under her breath, as though his inability to withstand the pain of her yanks and pulls was an affliction. But really she didn't mind, since it was all that wincing which helped him to hold back tears. It was important to both of them that he didn't cry, because "big boys don't cry" was not just her warning when his eyes welled but a threat that might have been followed by a smack if her patience was low. And Teenotchy never did cry, except that once in the woods by Lincoln Drive when he saw two men mount his mother like a bronco and twist her neck till it snapped.

Right up to her final year, those perfect curls his mother made brushed his shoulders and mattered to nobody but her—least of all to him as he played with Atlanta in the yard where Dusty Simms promised herself regularly that she would plant some zinnias, though she never had money for seeds. Not that they ever went without Doc Tatum's pomade at ten cents a jar, which was highway robbery to anybody who realized that it was nothing but petroleum jelly with a touch of green food coloring and a hint of bergamot oil to give a perfume.

And though Doc Tatum had long since gone out of business, with hindsight, Teenotchy treasured that rich smell of bergamot. It used to hang heavier than incense in their three small rooms, referred to by Dusty Simms as "home" though the few neighbors in their backstreet knew, like she did, that the place was just one of old Mister Kleber's converted stables, once part of his saddlery business.

"Least we not in the almshouse," Teenotchy's mother said when the cold turned the place into an icebox or the sun made it a sauna. Because she knew better than most what it felt like to live no place. So that hovel, with the so-called kitchen on street level and two boxrooms above which had once been grain stores for the horses, seemed more than ample. In fact, she may as well have been in a palace, albeit one at a dead end on the wrong side of Main Street, where the Rapid Transit trolley tracks connecting suburban Germantown and Philadelphia separated the haves from the have-nots.

What made the place more unbearable than the extremes of weather was that the soft-hearted, soft-spoken Dusty shared the cramped space with Aunt Em, whose mammoth hips took up more than her share of the three rooms. Not that the old woman ever dared to go up the rickety steps that Dusty called the stairs, constructed by Mister Kleber when he turned the dwelling into a space for humans instead of animals.

Aunt Em turned the place into a hellhole without even trying. Her farts and belches meant that the children stayed in the yard, weather permitting, and with their mother off doing housework all day, Aunt Em's employment as a washer-woman left her short-tempered. She ruled over them with glares and stares and the scary monumental silences of a slavedriver or a power-mad potentate. So nobody dared ask why she determined what Dusty and the two little children said and did, what they thought and ate. Aunt Em was law-maker and sheriff and she ruled like the two roles were designed as one.

Her moon-shaped face, jet cheeks and jet eyes told less about her toil than her gnarled knuckles, which had suffered the ravages of every kind of washboard, every kind of bleach and occasional bouts lost with tubs of boiling water. They looked like they'd been light-years slapping wet cotton against a washboard, and they would have probably looked worse had she got all the washing jobs she needed to help Dusty keep the children from starving and contribute to the rent.

Mister Kleber charged them five dollars a month back in '99 while Dusty was still alive, but it was probably too much considering that every time he came to collect his money, he'd stand at the door and tell Aunt Em how lucky they were to get such fine accommodation for less than the neighborhood's going rate. He would smile when he said it, and Aunt Em would almost smile back, because as she got older smiling came less easily to her.

Though Dusty Simms had been dead thirteen years, Aunt Em was going strong, although she was short of breath and found the rheumatism in her hips and knees hurt too much for her to work over a fire in the yard any more. But fat as Aunt Em had been when he was five, Teenotchy held a firm picture in his mind of the old woman in her more agile days, chasing stray cats from the yard with a broom or throwing scalding water at dogs that came to their yard to fornicate under the billowing sheets and long johns that drooped on the clotheslines supported by wooden props.

Some Saturday mornings when Teenotchy's mind lurched back to the old days, he remembered the time he asked his mother why Mister Kleber called Aunt Em "auntie," since it seemed impossible that the old woman was the Quaker's "auntie" as well as their own.

"Auntie ain't nothing but a nickname," Dusty'd explained, laughing all the while, although the scowl on Aunt Em's face had suggested that she didn't get the joke.

But then it did seem that Mister Kleber had odd names for Dusty Simms too, calling her his day girl although she was every bit of thirty-five when she died. Even aged nineteen Teenotchy still liked to recall the faded pattern of lilacs and bachelor buttons which adorned his mother's favorite bandanna, a gift from Mister Kleber, who was not one for gift giving. But the flowers were so faint the last time Teenotchy'd seen the scarf it was hard to believe the royal blue had ever been as strong as it was the first time she opened the box Mister Kleber'd handed her, with its layer of white tissue paper protecting the silk square.

Standing in the Klebers' parlor in the August heat, Teenotchy mopped his brow for the umpteenth time and set his mind to thinking about that scarf tied tightly about his mother's head, wishing his mind would just push itself from the edge to reveal her face.

Was she hovering about the parlor, fretting that he'd forgotten her sweet, gentle smile? Teenotchy could only worry and ponder.

At five, he never understood why she thought she amounted to more in other people's eyes because his button-down boots were spit-shined and his hair curled so that it had a patent-leather gleam. But he rightly sensed how important it had been to her that Mister Kleber saw that Teenotchy's knees were never ashy, even though the salary the old man paid her wouldn't allow her to buy her children long socks to stave off the bitter winter frosts. And at five, he even sensed that his mother had him on display, from the moment she guided him through the Klebers' back door until she marched him out.

It was a matter of personal pride to her that her boy could be seen standing statue-still in the Klebers' and hold his bowels for the hours she worked. Teenotchy was afraid to breathe while he watched his mother on hands and knees or preparing the Klebers' lunch, and he felt he could be looked through like glass when Helga Kleber walked into a room to give Dusty Simms orders.

Teenotchy remembered the relief he used to feel whenever his mother snapped her fingers twice in his direction, which was his cue to shift his feather weight from left foot to right and back again, though more than three quick shifts she called "showing out" and would be prompted to hiss at him, "Act your age, boy, and not your color!" through her clenched teeth, careful not to let the Klebers hear her sounding sharp.

Nothing Teenotchy did missed his mother's notice. Not even when her back was to him as she polished the ornately chiselled ivy-leaf legs on Helga Kleber's Bavarian table, which Helga said had to be polished just so since they were the handiwork of a skilled German craftsman.

Thirteen years on, those deeply engraved five-pointed leaves on the chunky oak legs of that table still reminded Teenotchy of being in the parlor with his mother, and that August morning, as he ran his own buffing cloth over them, he thought about how she'd trained him to say, "Have a nice weekend, sir," to Mister Kleber after she'd heard a butler say it in one of the fancy houses on Johnson Street where she did an odd day for extra food money if she was lucky.

Teenotchy had usually had to say it when they were leaving the Klebers' and came across the old man digging in one of the many flowerbeds which highlighted his sprawling garden. Dusty Simms even admitted to Mister Kleber that she had heard a butler say it when she'd worked for one of the Johnson Street families where Germantown's old money lived, even though she knew that he didn't hold much with the fancy ways of the community's better-heeled. Not that the Klebers were what Dusty would have considered white trash, but their quietude and sobriety prevented them from aspiring to the airs of a Johnson Street family.

With his buffing rag circling the center of the Bavarian table, Teenotchy rustled up his fondest memory, recalling the time Mister Kleber was digging intently in a rose bed, his craggy face browned by sun and his ice-blue eyes shaded by a black felt hat which he wore summer and winter, while his brawny white fingers brushed the black soil from his hands as Dusty approached him, holding on to Teenotchy's wrist.

Seemingly from out of the ground, Mister Kleber'd produced two minty-smelling sweets, peppermint drops, the scent of which mixed with the smell of honeysuckle on a vine near where he had been digging.

The old man had leaned back on his knees, resting his hands on his strong tree-trunk thighs before he removed his hat, saying, "That boy is a credit to thee, Dusty Simms. When thee tires of him, thee must leave him here with me."

Teenotchy remembered how his mother'd dropped her eyes on that occasion, like she did whenever Mister Kleber came upon her working in the upstairs hall passage and brushed up against her accidentally on purpose, making her nipples harden, though Teenotchy's five-year-old eyes missed this subtle change in her.

She was easily reduced to a bashful grin and a girly giggle would spill from her plum-shaped lips, punctuated by a high, thin put-on voice that Teenotchy heard from her lips only when she was talking to white people. And on the occasion when the two peppermint drops were produced, in spite of her dropping her eyes, that voice spouted forth to say to Mister Kleber, "That sure is thoughtful of you, Mister Paul."

"Mister Paul," Teenotchy said aloud to himself while he continued buffing the Bavarian table, with the sweat still pouring from his forehead and upper lip, dripping from his chest under his white stiff-collared shirt and running to his belly button. "Mister Paul," he said aloud a second time, smiling his wonderful broad-toothed smile as he thought of Mister Kleber being addressed by his first name as only Dusty

Simms dared to do on the rarest of occasions, though never in the smooth brown tone of voice she reserved for home and her own.

Like the five-year-olds who hear what is not meant for their ears and see what is not meant for their eyes, in those days, the little Teenotchy was expected to hear without hearing, to see without seeing. So back then, before the century turned, Teenotchy had witnessed certain improprieties that he automatically knew he was meant to erase while they were fresh impressions in his mind to allow Mister Kleber and Dusty Simms to go on pretending that there was nothing between them.

But there were greater subtleties back then that missed Teenotchy's comprehension. Like he didn't know that it bothered his mother that the Klebers' snowy-white parlor walls showed up the yellowness of the secondhand blouse she buttoned him into whenever she was allowed to bring him to the Klebers' for work. All that Teenotchy took in was how much the starched collar itched, aware that if he dared scratch his neck his mother'd be on him like an alley cat, flashing him a look which said, "Don't let me catch you scratchin' in these white folks' house, boy." Although if Paul, Hans or Helga Kleber was in hearing distance she'd sweeten her tone to the put-on girly voice to say, "Teenotchy, you too grown to let Sister see you doing that."

Sister. That's what she called herself. Sister. That was who Teenotchy remembered her as, Sister. Not mother. Not Dusty Simms. Not day girl.

Sister used to say that Teenotchy's puffy-sleeved secondhand blouse must have been tired of being boiled with Mister Kleber's long johns and socks, which Dusty toted home to be washed by Aunt Em—though Dusty always insisted that she do them herself since Aunt Em had a bad reputation f scorching things if she didn't like somebody. And she d' like Mister Kleber or Teenotchy.

Another one of life's subtleties which Teenotch

in his younger days was how his mother would stand over that boiling pan which held Mister Kleber's underthings and her son's secondhand shirt, praying all the while to herself that the old Quaker's cleverness in business and righteousness in faith would penetrate that blouse and bring good luck to her fatherless child.

Dusty Simms always seemed too grateful for the crumbs thrown her way by Mister Kleber. Whether it was a mundane "good day" or a peppermint, or his complimenting her on her exemplary work, Mister Kleber had a profound effect upon Teenotchy's mother, making her at once a little shyer than it was natural for her to be and yet bringing out a coy coquettishness that she had no control over which allowed the old man to turn her upside down with a word, a nod, a look that only she knew to be a look of love.

Once Teenotchy remembered the old man teasing her. "If a razor is what thee needs to cut thy boy's locks, thee'll find a sharp one in my workbox."

But Helga Kleber would have carved her initials in that Bavarian table quicker than Dusty would have chopped Teenotchy's fingercurls and the three of them knew it, which is why they all laughed when Mister Kleber said that. All at once. The three of them, with Mister Kleber's big-booted foot having crossed the threshold into the parlor and Sister and Teenotchy and him laughing simultaneously. Like it was correct. Like Mister Kleber was a colored man or like they were white.

This image of the three of them laughing was at the forefront of Teenotchy's mind while he stood in the dim parlor that August of 1913, buffing Helga Kleber's Bavarian table. But he soon wiped the grin from his face, jolted back to the here and now when he heard the imposing sound of her footsteps on the back porch.

Although anybody could have imagined Teenotchy's sudden swell of sweat to be due to the morning's heat, in truth he would have sweated as much at the sound of Helga

Kleber had it been a freezing day in February, because to hear her short, choppy steps clicking closer and closer along the passage was a sure indication that she was coming to the parlor to check that he was doing his work her way.

Teenotchy reached into his bib pocket, the one usually reserved for his harmonica, to pull out a clean buffing rag and he started rubbing that oak table down like he was in a frenzy since she raised less hell if she found him buffing.

"Theodore Simms!" He heard her spit his name as she got closer to the parlor door. His proper name from her lips was usually a death sentence. Not that she ever called him Teenotchy, but she was content to call him Theodore when in her normal state of ill-humor, saving Theodore Simms for the start of one of her full-blown tirades.

He got the jitters.

Helga Kleber should have seemed like the perfect remedy for that August morning. She was a cold breeze.

Teenotchy tugged at the bleached white sheath covering his forearm which she supplied every Saturday upon his arrival, but whereas he had remembered to put that on, his gray bespectacled eyes flashed to the closed velvet drapes . . .

Too late to open them with her hand turning the white porcelain doorknob. So he braced himself to take his medicine like a man, sure of what she would say, sure that she would scream the very second she entered the room.

As perspiration streamed down his temples, he didn't bother to stop buffing and hoped that she might think that the water on his face was a sign not of the day's oppressive heat but that he'd worked himself up into a good and proper sweat.

He let the perfect crescents of his smooth brown lips droop a fraction of an inch, trying to look glum since he'd come to realize that Mrs. Kleber liked him to be miserable. She assumed that he didn't take his work seriously if she caught him whistling, even if he was cleaning the barn or tending Mister Kleber's flowers in the garden.

Teenotchy had taken years to figure out which expression best deluded her. Dour, although he couldn't have put that word to it, was a look too close to her own domain to be satisfactory, whereas sullen was nearer what she liked, but his attempts always looked a bit sulky, as she justifiably complained. Teenotchy was nearly twelve when he finally realized that it was his broad, toothy grin which provoked her most. So he saved it to exasperate her on Saturday mornings, when even her snarl relieved the tedium and monotony of that day's drudgery.

Mrs. Kleber's Austrian accent regularly hacked through the peace of the red-brick house and that August morning was no different, which is why Teenotchy shook slightly seeing the doorknob turning (it also annoyed him to think she was leaving her handprint there so soon after he'd buffed the porcelain to a flawless shine).

Teenotchy didn't remember that he was also supposed to blink back the twinkle in his eyes before the starchy European thrust open the parlor door, making his heart pump too fast with her second, "Theodore Simms!"

He spotted a thick piece of straw jutting from her middle parting as she entered the room and concluded she'd been nosing around the barn before she swooped indoors. "Old witch," he was saying to himself, fantasizing like always about how he'd tell her that her blackish hair swept back into a tight knot at the nape of her neck made her look like a crow—a molting crow at that. But in fact Helga Kleber, with her simple high-necked mourning dress, looked perversely neat in spite of the intolerable heat, and he knew the drawn-out sigh she unleashed was meant to belittle and chastise him.

Her voice was sharp and mean when she said, "Boy, how many times have I told you not to work in the dark? Surely you're blind enough. You can't see what you're doing."

Teenotchy was used to the disparaging remarks she had been making about his eyesight ever since her father-in-law had paid for his spectacles the year before. But then, any time Mister Kleber did anything for Teenotchy she took it as a personal affront for some reason which Teenotchy failed to understand.

The parlor's stillness would have raised any sensitive soul above irritation, but even the quietude of that room, even now decorated to Ursula's specifications, with its white walls and stark, wooden furniture, couldn't coax her beyond agitation and she grumbled on, "How many times must I tell you?"

Teenotchy's apparent fear always fueled her to increase her attack and sap every ounce of his confidence, so she went on at the sight of him tense, hand visibly shaking. "You must, must, must open the drapes and window. Air is what the place needs. Air," she repeated. "Especially on a day like this with the house sweltering. Air!"

He hated her repeating things as much as she hated his fiddling with his round, metal-rimmed glasses. He dared not look at her, directly or otherwise, and kept his eyes on the floor, which was just as well since hearing her say, "You'll go blond as a bat working in the dark" would've made him laugh in her face.

"Blond as a bat!" He chuckled to himself and would've loved to have the courage to mock her aloud. He always felt momentarily superior when she mispronounced vowels, not that she did so that often but on those occasions when her mistakes made nonsense of the English, it kept him mocking her to himself for a week.

Teenotchy stooped to attention, adjusting his spectacles again. He knew what she said about letting light into the parlor was true—you could see what you were doing better with the drapes pulled back—but not seeing was important to him. He could reminisce best with shadows dancing around, and the apparitions were happiest too when spared the day's glare. Teenotchy balled up the dusting cloth in his hand, thinking that Aunt Em was right when she said the real problems at the Klebers' began when Hans Kleber brought a wife into his father's household who was low-born and didn't know that in summer decent people (including Ursula Kleber when she was alive) switched velvet drapes for linen ones to let air in.

Only the previous Wednesday when Aunt Em had arrived at the Klebers' back door delivering the wash she had tried to drop Helga, referred to by Aunt Em as "that Klabber woman," the hint.

"Miz Helba," Aunt Em smiled, although she smiled at Helga only while waiting to be paid, "y'all only got to say and I'll help put y'all's windows straight by pressing them linen curtains you got tucked up in the attic."

Having been Mister Kleber's washerwoman before his daughter-in-law came, Aunt Em believed she knew better than Helga what drapes the old widower had and in which attic chest she'd find them. So when she said, "Wouldn't take me but a couple days to get 'em back here, 'cause now them Chinamens done opened that there laundry round by Bringhurst, I don' be washing for riff-raff like I usta. Fact I got some free hours on my hands."

Aunt Em knew better than even Teenotchy that Helga Kleber didn't want the drapes changed, but sometimes contrariness gave her no choice but to provoke issues with "that Klabber woman."

"Miz Helba, lined velvets, dark blue at dat, still up de parlor windas? The sun's bleachin' the b'Jezus out 'em and tearin' 'em to shreds." She mournfully shook her bandannaed head when relating the confrontation to her neighbor, Tessie, who had long since given up saying, "Helga's name's pronounced with a *g*."

By Aunt Em's account, the Klebers' winter drapes hanging throughout summer were a blight upon the district's reputation. Helga's problem was breeding, she'd assured Tessie. "She proved she was trash when she went and set by the driver of that hearse that toted Mas'r Hans's body. A decent widow-woman woulda rid up to the graveyard with her daddy-by-law. Specially since Mas'r Hans dropped dead from the cholera. But see, when white folks is trashy, you know good as me they can't tell right from wrong."

Tessie agreed that as Aunt Em had been slave or servant to whites all of her seventy-something years, her knowledge of their intimate doings qualified her to classify them.

"It's ol' Mas'r Klabber I feels for, 'cause like he say," fabricated Aunt Em, "Miz Helba done shamed the Quaker nation more than once." Having heard of Indian nations, it was how the old woman referred to all tribes but her own.

"From the first I heard that Mas'r Hans was marryin' out his faith, I knew to expect the worse."

Over the years, Helga exceeded Aunt Em's prediction, first by refusing to use "thee" and "thou," and then by refusing to attend Quaker meetings. Although Paul Kleber was relieved by her Sunday absences, he could never have said so.

Through marriage, Hans had rescued Helga from indentured servitude, arranging to pay her passage from Vienna to Philadelphia before they'd met. She showed no gratitude and even tried to rule his father's house, still decorated to his wife's simple taste though she'd been dead twenty years.

Why English was spoken in their home was Helga's first challenge. Paul Kleber had to be uncharacteristically strident to ensure he did not become the guest.

"Why speak English in Germantown?" she argued.

As usual, Hans shyly but slyly colluded with her. On one occasion, he lifted the local German newsletter from the breakfast table to remind her to make an all-important point.

"Isn't it you who says reading English gossip is not worth the strain on your eyes?"

Paul Kleber couldn't deny that his newspaper and Bible were in German, or that he'd settled in Germantown because it characterized his Bremen beginnings. He relied upon mer-

chants who worshipped at the German Reform Church in
Market Square; he liked Günter Schlüss's black bread and
always ordered his lederhosen from Werner Kropp, who
gave his homemade dill pickles to regulars at Christmas.

Paul Kleber enjoyed hearing their German jokes but was
proud his English had no accent. At fifteen, boarding the
crowded Bremen freighter with his cousin Ursula, whom he
would marry a decade later, he believed as devoutly in
America as he did in God.

In this spirit, he scolded, "Had thee preferred things
German, Helga, thee should have emigrated to Germany."

As always he had the final say, but she defied him constantly by talking aloud to herself in German, as she did
sweeping past Teenotchy that Saturday morning to throw
open the parlor drapes.

He let no one know he'd remembered all the German
force-fed him during the year he'd spent with the Klebers
after his mother's death.

And there in that room, with the stifling heat outside
making the sidewalk into a skillet, Helga turned from the
window still muttering loudly in German. Not that this
stopped Teenotchy from hearing her long black skirt rustle
against her paper-stiff, white petticoats, which he could visualize billowing on Aunt Em's clothesline.

Even as a little boy, Teenotchy used to brush past Mrs.
Kleber's underslips and loved to see them blown up like bal-
loons as they caught the breeze before Aunt Em would take
them down to press the creases from their damp folds.

Mrs. Kleber would have burned them had she realized
that her petticoats and bloomers were as familiar to him as
his calico apron. And yet all the same she flaunted her body
when it suited her exhibitionist's bent. Like the times she
showed her bare shoulders or flashed her ankle. Not that
these titillations were a match for the time she'd demanded that
he unlace her from her rigid corset, which was a minor indiscretion when compared to what she did that summer of 1910.

Teenotchy should have easily been able to recall it as it had happened only three years previously when he was sixteen. But he had blanked this whole incident of being asked by Helga to escort her on a ride to Fisher's Hollow one Saturday since Mister Kleber was working away from Germantown. She used being thrown from her horse as her excuse to keep Teenotchy at the house all day, finally getting enough courage to demand he massage her bruised backside before he went home.

When she'd thrust a bottle of camphor liniment into his hands, he hadn't yet understood what she had in mind, and still he shook so much, he nearly dropped the bottle watching her fling herself on to the narrow cot she'd resorted to sleeping in after Hans's death.

It unnerved Teenotchy when it happened and he couldn't understand why she made so many throaty noises while he tracked her spine and rubbed in places which he considered too private to have mentioned by name. And naïve as he was at sixteen, he suspected more than the liniment made sweat pour down his forehead and the creased back of the widow's knees as his fine fingers kneaded to her demanding "Harder!"

His virgin eyes had needed to look away as he gave that massage, feeling her muscles spasm at his every touch and not realizing why she began to smell differently than he'd ever smelt her, his nose always being his most sensitive organ, even more sensitive than his penis, which he'd pretended wasn't getting hard as Mrs. Kleber sighed and sweated and generally made a to-do.

Teenotchy didn't realize back then that Helga Kleber's jelly thighs were colorless because they rarely saw sunlight. He'd hoped they were a sign she was coming down with the cholera that took her husband, then dead but six months.

Somewhat like him, Mrs. Kleber remembered only what allowed her dignity to prevail, so she would have flatly denied this gross indiscretion and had blanked it from her mind in

the same way he had, especially since she'd guided his hand
between her legs long enough for him to feel the furry wet-
ness there before he fainted from sudden light-headedness,
pretending when he'd finally picked himself off her bedroom
floor that the whole thing was a dream and nightmare, since
he was sure about one thing: boys his color got lynched for
less.

But three years on from that afternoon, stooped to attention like a schoolboy waiting for a caning, Teenotchy had
forgotten this occasion and stood in that August heat in-
wardly mocking her, though he knew better than to smile
about her saying "blond as a bat."

He knew better than to smile since the widow's tempera-
ment was bleaker than the faded black dress that she'd worn
since Hans's death.

Hans being Mister Kleber's only child and his living bond
with his beloved Ursula, the old man took his son's death
extremely hard and began to use his Bible as a hiding place.
It was almost understandable that he even lost interest in his
business, since he'd set up the saddlery with a dream of its
becoming a long-standing family trade to pass to his grandchildren. So it wasn't altogether surprising that he closed the
business down, retiring a month after they'd laid Hans to
rest. And at first it seemed that retirement was ideal for the
old Quaker. He was cheered by his morning buggy ride and
spent afternoons in the garden, and became more active in
church and civic affairs until he was felled by a stroke in the
middle of one of the harshest winters they'd known on the
Eastern seaboard.

Teenotchy rightly gathered that the old man only bothered to stave off death because Helga looked too content at
the mention of his dying. But bedridden, with neither son
nor saddlery, Mister Kleber's depressions mushroomed into
one extensive gloom that crept through the house and
drifted out to his garden, once the neighborhood's pride.

From the time he'd brought his wife Ursula to that salubrious corner of Germantown, that three acres of garden became his passion. And all the locals marveled at his fat yellow roses and the tree-size rhododendrons. Not that his Quaker brethren gave credence to the blue ribbons he won, but Mister Kleber excused this competitive side of his green thumb as acceptable.

Anyway, it was there in his beloved garden, just south of the avenue of oaks, where daisies battled dandelions for turf in spring, that Teenotchy had found the old man collapsed under a small snow bank, crippled up by a weak heart that pined after Hans. So it was Teenotchy Mister Kleber needed to thank for rescuing him that March noon, because he wouldn't believe that the old man had failed to come in for Teenotchy's chicken stew deliberately.

But trees were in bud before he'd rewarded Teenotchy for finding him. The narrow plot he gave the boy was too small to build on and wasn't nearly as impressive as the formal deed which went with it. "Grow whatever thee chooses," announced Mister Kleber with his new lopsided smile, a permanent reminder that his left side was paralyzed. But Teenotchy would have gladly returned the elaborately scrawled deed and the ten-by-thirty-foot plot that came with it to have the lanky old man looming about the house again with shoulders stooped and veiny legs still aching from half a century of saddle work.

Although the Bible had become the old man's solace after Hans died, Mister Kleber couldn't read it without help after his stroke. But he rejected anybody reading it for him in case they witnessed his inexplicable crying fits.

"Aw, don't cry, Mister Kleber, sir," Teenotchy would say if he found him in tears. But never sure what brought them on, he was more disillusioned about them than even the old man and would stand at the foot of Mister Kleber's bed with his head down, trying not to notice and praying the day would come when his old mentor would be striding about the house and stables again. "You'll be up in no time," Teenotchy would smile, polishing Mister Kleber's mahogany bedstead and pretending not to see the tears. But they upset him so much, he avoided the sickroom, electing to tend the old man's garden and tend his horses free of charge, though it was a job for two men, especially after Teenotchy planted his own narrow plot with vegetables to placate Aunt Em.

By the second spring that Mister Kleber was bedridden, Teenotchy knew more about those five horses than Mister Kleber did. They were the friends he'd never felt tall enough to make. And that garden also became an obsession. He snuck flower seeds into his plot, so many varieties that the strip vibrated with reds and blues and oranges and yellows. Even Mister Kleber marveled from his bedroom window, referring to that strip of land as Teenotchy's Patch. To Teenotchy, a boy whose mother had dreamt of a zinnia bed, that narrow stretch of earth was as good as an acre and whether he tended a seedling, added to his rockery or weeded his flowerbeds, the black soil was his holy water, those horses his family.

Teenotchy spent most of his spare time in Mister Kleber's stables and garden, where the paths to the circular beds of beet-red roses were lined with blue delphiniums. Pink and red impatiens covered the slopes to the pond where Emma and Rebecca, swans bought from a minstrel traveler, added to the serenity. Beside the meadow where the old man's sad-faced mare, Blossom, and Helga Kleber's chestnut horse grazed, wild lilies grew and vied with buttercups and daisies for space. They benefited from the breezy avenue of oaks Paul Kleber and his wife had planted, which shaded four benches Hans had built during boyhood.

As Paul Kleber expected, to be bedridden was to be damned. His speech still slurred a year later, he decided to sell even his beloved horses, keeping only Blossom. Teenotchy, heartbroken though he was, wore a brave face throughout and said, "I understand, Mister Kleber, why you can't part with a mare whose mother and grandmother you foaled." Not that Blossom hadn't become Teenotchy's favorite too over the years, but it was as if Teenotchy's own family had to be auctioned. He missed the pair of English hackneys and the two palominos after Mister Kleber'd sent them to the auctioneer, and he kept cleaning their stables for months.

Poor Blossom was goose-rumped and coffin-headed, but Paul Kleber had cared for her all her life, like he did his garden, where he'd taught Teenotchy to rise as a boy and to talk to the birds and flowers as though they were human.

The old man believed wild things had unchallenged rights to the land. He heard this from his father, taught it to his son and shared it with Teenotchy, who took his word as gospel after his mother's ceased.

Dusty Simms disappeared on a normal Wednesday in late September 1899, in the twilight of an evening warmer than usual when leaves crunched underfoot. And what Teenotchy's mind was too injured to recall is what happened that night after he excitedly watched her don her black knitted shawl. He knew her almost as well as she knew him, little though he was, and he knew if he quietly played near the door, she might think to take him for what she called her evening stroll.

She enjoyed his company and was always happy to have him along if Atlanta didn't take a fit and cry to go too.

Teenotchy knew as well as his mother that Atlanta was a chatterbox at three and too little to keep secrets, whereas he promised never to tell about the walks with his mother to meet Mister Kleber in the woods. And it was with special excitement that evening that they finally slipped out without Atlanta bellowing.

The little boy would have skipped across Main Street so happy was he not only to be going on the secret journey but also that Atlanta had actually waved them goodbye, thanks to a sock doll Dusty Simms produced as they left. She put it into her baby daughter's upstretched hands before the pretty child had a chance to cry.

Dusty said to her, passing the sock doll with button eyes, "This here is Sukey," and that was all Atlanta needed.

Once out of the door, the lean woman was soon in her stride and Teenotchy had to take three steps to her long-legged one. So he was often panting by the time they reached Mister Kleber, waiting in the usual place near the overpass above the Wissahickon.

The old man fussed the first time he saw her appear with her boy, but she protested. "Aw, Mister Paul, holding hands and kissing ain't nothing. He ain't gonna tell."

None the less, Mister Kleber insisted that he and she "talk" out of Teenotchy's view. And Teenotchy liked showing off that he was brave enough to wait that fifteen minutes alone while the noises of the wood got denser as the light turned to near-darkness.

Each time after, Teenotchy was left to wait at the stump near the overpass and Mister Kleber would ride off before Dusty reemerged waving a dollar.

Yet that September evening he never appeared and Dusty was on her way back to collect little Teenotchy when the rustle of footsteps caught up with her.

Teenotchy was running toward her as two hatted men blocked her path.

"What'ch'you wanting?" he'd heard his mother stammer before a booted foot kicked in her eye and split her nose open in reply.

"Run, Teenotchy! Don't stop! Run on, baby!" she sputtered from her knees as one stranger mounted her from behind, his burly mass crushing her to the ground. He was broader than the bearded one who'd first grabbed her skirt and clubbed her.

Both yanked and twisted her flailing limbs like two pit bulls on the same kill.

The one covered in a beard was beastlike in form and

face and his dirty claw wrenched her neck backwards to rip at her checkered blouse before he tore at her corset, then her breast.

She squealed, "Run, Teenotchy! Don't stop!" but his indomitable little heart knew not to obey. Just this once he couldn't do what she asked, because his soul refused to desert her long wail that filled the air like a gull screeching for its mother.

Fear froze Teenotchy into a crouch beside the faithful stump that had on so many trips to that place been his safety point. And with his mother's cry neither near nor far, he shivered and waited shaking as he heard leaves and men writhe and wrestle amidst his mother's skirt until they tired of it and ripped it from her.

"Bertram! This nigger's a real bobcat!" the hairy one cackled.

Teenotchy's warm pee rushed down his legs, bringing him greater shame than his terror and tears. He expected his mother to say, "Big boys don't cry and pee their pants," when she got him back home and to box his ears for not running like she'd told him to.

"The boogeyman comes for boys that can't mind," he expected her to scold.

But she didn't. And, as he waited, his eyes bulged to hold back boogeymen when dark crept in, making less noise than the night wind which paralyzed his limbs and chased the men off.

A bright moon braved the night air, but Teenotchy was scared to look for the Big Dipper or the Seven Sisters his mother used to show him. No Star of Bethlehem.

After his heart had run off, a tom-tom beat ten to the dozen in its place. Noisy clinks and clanks in the kitchen had jolted him from worse nightmares before, but that September night he cried and Aunt Em wasn't there to make him quit.

As morning broke around the five-year-old, birds laughed and gossiped and shadowy witches showed themselves as trees.

"Sister?" Teenotchy whimpered, somehow remembering he could speak. When his second call welled to a howl, he was no more frightened than the wild fowl that flew for safety.

Scrambling for the familiar folds of his mother's skirts, he stopped bawling when he could see her feet. Though rumpled and torn, her threadbare skirt was recognizable. So was her blue headrag and her black knitted shawl, though matted with dead leaves. But her face stifled his sobs. Her face. Her face, a swollen mask, a bloodied pulp of cuts and bruises. "The boogeyman!" Teenotchy screamed, but his spirit knew not to run. Filling his arms with brown leaves, he covered her.

Armful after armful, he piled a leafy sepulcher to help Sister on her way. But, having disobeyed, he looked to Heaven for nothing.

That night had flung him violently from the nest and his soul merely clung to him for refuge. While other fledgelings sang their morning's worth, he teetered and tottered from thorny bush to tree in search of the familiar.

Only a mile away Aunt Em, who was a master at shouting at home, meekly explained at the police station that Dusty wasn't the kind to stay out nights. The po-faced sergeant at the desk had his mind on other things. "I'm busy. We got a lot of work on getting ready for the Turn of the Century parade." But Aunt Em was thinking what she dared not say: had one of the women she took in washing for, or one of those Daughters of the American Revolution, or a member of the Women's Auxiliary gone missing, the whole of Germantown would have stopped.

Instead that afternoon Miss Brandauer complained to anybody who would listen in the general store that Dusty Simms hadn't turned up to do her morning's cleaning.

Two ladies in the store to buy fabrics looked up from their reams to sympathize with her. "Colored women get to running with men and can't keep their mind on their work," one whispered loud enough to be heard by all. "That's why

I keep a nice Irish girl nowadays. Straight off the boat and ready to settle down to work."

Not until Teenotchy was found wandering in the woods a couple of days later by two Boy Scouts did Paul Kleber finally come forward, as an employer of his community stature would have been expected to, to speak up for the family. But when he stepped into the police station, he looked drawn, his shoulders hunched and his voice quieter than normal as he asked and answered questions, admitting only, "Dusty Simms has worked for us three years. Always on time. Clean woman. Took care of her little 'uns. She would never have abandoned that boy."

So a half-hearted search for Teenotchy's mother began and Aunt Em resignedly accepted Paul Kleber's offer to take Teenotchy in temporarily since she had no time to deal with Atlanta, let alone Teenotchy, suffering from exposure and fright: his teeth were chattering so, he couldn't speak when spoken to, and his little legs, thin at the best of times, were as frail as bare twigs.

It was a week later when two policemen, full of themselves in new uniforms, interrupted Aunt Em in the middle of hanging out half of her Wednesday wash under a cloudy sky to report, "Dusty Simms's been found, Auntie, by the embankment where the footbridge crosses the Wissahickon."

Aunt Em could tell from the expression on their faces that there wasn't anything good to report and she stopped drawing breath and rushed to the stoop to scoop Atlanta up in her arms as the little girl was playing on the top step. It gave her some comfort to feel Atlanta's body next to her own while the youngest of the two policemen carried on. "Wasn't our fault we couldn't find her, see, 'cause somebody'd hid her body under a big pile of leaves. Hard to know how she died. Could've been exposure from the look of her, although looks like her boyfriend probably beat her up pretty bad."

What was the point in listening or refuting? No point. So Aunt Em put Atlanta back down and shook the anger off

herself before she went back to hanging the wash like nothing'd been said.

"We need to talk to her boy," the balding policeman said
as though he was about to ask for a cup of tea.

"Ain't here," was all Aunt Em replied, turning away from
them so she could turn away from the moment and from
herself and from the idea that Dusty wasn't coming back.
"You want to find him, you gotta head over to the Quaker's
'round by Schoolhouse Lane and Main. Klabber the name
is," said Aunt Em, putting three clothes pegs in her mouth
and looking up at the gray sky to ask herself whether rain
was on the way.

She didn't say goodbye when the two men walked off
and she paid no attention to Atlanta, who was playing with
the sock doll that Sister had given her the night she walked
out the door with Teenotchy in tow. Aunt Em wondered why
anybody would want to talk to the boy. But in any case the
old man refused to let Teenotchy be questioned.

"That child doesn't know the meaning of the word rape,"
Mister Kleber insisted, when he'd heard the details. "If he
saw anything, in time I expect he'll tell me," he said, hoping
his kindness could buy the orphan's permanent silence.

From the moment Paul Kleber took Teenotchy upon his lap
in the buggy and let the little boy snap the reins, Teenotchy
honored him as his son, Hans, never had.

But it was Helga who huddled in angry whispers with
Hans because Teenotchy was still living in the house a year
later.

When Mister Kleber asked them one Sunday before
going to meeting if he should enroll the boy in Germantown
Academy before starting him as an apprentice in their business, Helga railed, "And do please tell us the rest of your
plan, Pater. To raise him a Quaker!"

It had been a beautiful morning and Mister Kleber sat
calmly drinking his chocolate in the kitchen as if she weren't

addressing him as she threw her head back to gargle a spleen of laughter. "Well, be sure to let me know when you get the coloreds to sing God's praises at your meeting house. I want to be there to see the deacon's face."

She stormed out with Hans at her heels, but not before turning her butcher's knife. "That boy! Yours will never accept him and he'll be cast out by his own."

Within a week, a carpetbag of Teenotchy's clothes, including the leather apron inscribed "Twentieth Century" which Mister Kleber'd made to match his own, were tucked beside the child in the Klebers' buggy.

Aunt Em mocked his short hair when Helga delivered him. But the old lady agreed she'd send him back Saturdays to clean and polish once he'd settled at a school.

"It will help you keep up with the rent." Helga took credit for Paul Kleber's insistence that Dusty's children be spared the almshouse. But Aunt Em still fretted about how she would feed them. She shook her head. "Even with the rent down to a dollar a week."

After those thirteen years, Helga Kleber still resented Teenotchy's relationship with her father-in-law and found any excuse to needle him, as in the parlor that Saturday morning. But Mister Kleber's was as close to what other people thought of as home as Teenotchy had known. To leave it never entered his mind.

He tugged at the metal rim of his glasses, which bounced a sunbeam on to the jet button of her high neckline.

"I certainly hope those spectacles aren't greasy with fingerprints like last week." She had a master's voice. Placing them in her outstretched hand, Teenotchy was sorry they were clean and wished he had his sister's nerve. Somehow Atlanta came to work when it suited her and then did as little as she pleased.

The time Helga reprimanded his sister's sluggishness he had expected Atlanta to plough back, but he wanted to hop like a pogo stick when his sister reared up from scrubbing to say, "I'm not breaking my back for a measly twenty-five cents and that broken-down place that's nothing but a stable with some steps. Lincoln freed the slaves, you know."

Atlanta, though two years younger, stood several inches taller than Teenotchy. But why he got their mother's gray eyes and his sister got her height vexed them both. Atlanta's blackish brown eyes were pretty enough, but she coveted Teenotchy's. Like he did her five feet eleven inches.

"There's still growing time. You're only nineteen," Mister Kleber had consoled Teenotchy the previous weekend. But, impatient to stand shoulder to shoulder with boys his age, he begged Aunt Em to mix a potion that would have him shooting up, since her homebrews for toothaches, headaches and fever blisters worked. But she refused. "It's the Lord's punishment," she concluded. God as tyrant was the only savior she could perceive.

To suffer both that Saturday morning's humidity and Mrs. Kleber's humiliations was more than Teenotchy could bear, and seeing her close the parlor door behind her was a heavenly relief.

He went back to buffing and a memory of his mother's hand displaying her dime-store engagement ring made Teenotchy laugh to himself. He had been three that year Derwent Simms gave it to her and Teenotchy recalled the little jig his mother did in the kitchen, after Mister Simms vowed that a solid gold wedding band would follow.

No sooner than he'd proposed, Dusty took his name and gave it to her children, placing a daguerreotype of him looking wooden in a borrowed three-piece suit and bowler on their only table.

"Don't matter age got him all bent up," Aunt Em had advised her at the time. "And so what if we got to move yonder to Pittsburgh," she added when Dusty asked if they could marry right away.

But ten days after, Aunt Em was holding her bandan-naed head in despair when Dusty explained that Mister Simms had demanded the paste ring back and was hitching back to Pittsburgh on his own.

"It would've been a sin to marry Mister Simms and not tell him everything," wept the abandoned Dusty with three-year-old Teenotchy in her arms. Baby Atlanta was on the floor, sucking a fistful of her mother's hem.

Aunt Em hardly let Dusty finish the sentence before yell-ing, "You swore you wouldn't tell! Nobody with good sense is gonna want you and them children after they hears your mess."

II

As Teenotchy shook his flannel dust rag from the parlor window, an eye-catching old phaeton rolled by. It was half a century behind the times but as immaculately preserved as its owner, Jonas Calvin Tewksbury, who was in the driver's seat wishing that his wife's nephew beside him looked cheerier. But Alexander Blake, visiting from England, was unaccustomed to such heat and humidity. And he was also too distressed by his uncle's waxing Confederate sympathies to smile.

His questions about Germantown's darker contingency were persistent and meant to provoke, but his uncle was giving nothing away and merely complained, "Always asking about the doggone darkies. Why don't you get you some of your own?"

Had the white-haired man waited for an answer, Alexander would've been forced to admit that his grandfather employed only English staff, not even allowing for the odd Scottish scullery maid or Welsh footman.

But in any case, Mister Tewksbury couldn't have cared less. What he really wanted to talk about was the Civil War skirmish he'd survived before the black cat spooked his path and his horse. And he was annoyed when Alexander's lack of interest in his war tales became too apparent. Not that Mister Tewksbury realized he was talking to his nephew's deaf ear anyway.

Reminiscing was about as regular to Mister Tewksbury as it was to Teenotchy, and the old Kentucky tobacco planter didn't even have the trauma of trying to remember his mother's face to use as his excuse like Teenotchy did. Not two days could pass without some talk about Confederate fighting days, and Alexander was to be the perfect audience, Mister Tewksbury had assumed. He was finding out all too fast that he was incorrect about his wife's nephew.

Alexander was practically asleep by the time they reached the thicker flow of traffic on Main Street, where shoppers milled about or moved in clusters, shifting from one huckster to the next in the square to sell their wares.

When a Rapid Transit trolley car clanged behind the phaeton, Mister Tewksbury's mare was near to being spooked again and the old man chastised his horse. "Delilah, I didn't pay four thousand dollars for you to be scared by some midget of a conductor. Take no notice of that little red-faced Polack."

It wasn't the first time that Alexander noticed how money was foremost in the old man's mind.

But Mister Tewksbury had already resumed talking about the war. "I was twenty, same as you Al, when Robert E. Lee surrendered."

Alexander found "Al" unacceptable, but the good manners he required of himself as his uncle's summer houseguest didn't leave room for him to say so—which spared him several confrontations he'd been tempted to engage in with this uncle, who was merely the aged husband of his mother's youngest sister.

Mister Tewksbury carried on. "That war, my boy, was way uglier than books or men claim. But I reckon you ought to burn those old ledgers from the Revolution that I see you nosing in and get facts about fighting straight from your old Uncle Jonas here."

That Alexander's only war interest was the Revolution, and that even that interest on his nephew's part was academic, perturbed the old Confederate. For a start, reading was not on Mister Tewksbury's agenda socially or workwise, and when he noticed that his young English guest had arrived from England with two cases full of books and only a small one with clothes, Jonas Tewksbury felt betrayed, having expected Alexander to share his passion for suits, guns and fishing in that order.

Along Main Street the immaculate gray phaeton drew nearly as much attention as the curbside ensemble who were singing and banging their tambourines to a chorus of, "We'll Advance If We Fight in the Spirit of the King." Mister Tewksbury felt compelled to raise his shout to a holler, harping on, "That junk you read about sabers and trumpet majors on thoroughbreds ain't nothing but book stuff. But then, who am I to tell you to burn your books? No, I'm as good as the next fella at minding my own business," he cackled above the racket of Main Street's Saturday noontime din. "But what a man sees with his own eyes of war, now that's real and worth talking about, and what I saw of it was too real for my liking and about as gallant as two Irish drunks in a Saturday night fisticuffs outside the Buttonwood, where I'm taking you for lunch."

Mister Tewksbury licked his frosty whiskers again, though the handlebar tips on them were needle hard, having been rolled to a point that morning as always by Ezekiel, his valet for thirty years.

Alexander wrongly assumed that it was Uncle Jonas's marriage to his young Aunt Julia which encouraged this studied foppishness, but the man had long adored his wardrobe and was happy for the world to know that he had so many clothes that he needed three servants to maintain his closets.

Alexander wasn't impressed by Mister Tewksbury's parading a different ensemble every day, although the history student noticed and admired the gold watch which adorned every change of clothes, saying merely, "Very handsome watch, Uncle Jonas."

"That's solid gold, son!" his uncle explained, demanding more of a compliment, but Alexander's gentle nod reflected his worldliness. Having been born to wealth and traveled with his mother and grandfather to exotic shores, he'd concluded that men brandishing the most gold usually suffered from the meanest spirits.

Sitting beside his uncle in the phaeton, Alexander seemed as well matched to Jonas as a dove would have been to a cock. The younger man tended to understate everything in both clothes and manner, looking a little worse for wear in a crumpled linen suit and bow tie that had, been in his trunk throughout the two-week cruise from England, whereas Uncle Jonas's salmon brocade waistcoat beneath a white summer suit broadcast noisy taste.

"What especially galls me," the Confederate banged on, "is codgers bringing out their old yarns about how they fought beside this great general So-and-So or whipped the hindparts off that one."

Mister Tewksbury was a human megaphone and Alexander was as much awed as put off by his volume.

The old man carried on. "If your aunt can keep you here till Thanksgiving, like she's hoping to, you'll meet the worst example of one of these fellas: Colonel Danville from Saunders, Mississippi. But to tell truth, a man's got to respect a soldier like him who can think back on rats rampaging over the dead and still be able to suck the marrow out a turkey bone all the while he's talkin' 'bout it.

"War," he continued in another vein, "reminds me of something my dear mother, rest her soul, told my first wife." Mister Tewksbury usually tried to sound solemn whenever he said "rest her soul" but somehow still made a mockery of the phrase. He then carried on in a brighter tone, "Mother always said that if anybody'd warned her that childbearing would ruin her eighteen-inch waistline for life, husband or not, she'd have steered clear of the whole mess."

His loud laugh was supposed to be contagious and it annoyed him that Alexander sneezed instead, due to all the dust they were kicking up as they made tracks beside the trolley heading west on Main Street.

Alexander was too fascinated by the homogeny of dark faces dotted among the many white shoppers. He scrutinized how they tarried and toddled, rambled and struggled. None looked as foreign to him as the Amish couple with their brood of children or the two nuns who glided as one with their black habits trailing the dusty pavement.

One blue-black Nefertiti balanced a bundle of laundry on her head as a stray dog sniffing at her skirt refused to be shooed away.

They were like nothing he'd seen, but they brought back memories of his grandmother reading him *Uncle Tom's Cabin* when he'd been eight and too ill to read himself. Her ladylike renditions of Topsy and Harry, little Eva and Uncle Tom, sometimes got the little Alexander too excited to sleep. And what he'd dreamt of, treacle- and toffee-colored characters, came to life on Main Street.

He wanted to leap from the phaeton, but instead he solemnly caught the end of his uncle's lament while flags were patriotically unfurled from several houses.

Stars and Stripes drooped more than the red geraniums

in the window boxes as the stifling heat brought in the midday, and Mister Tewksbury's agile monologue dodged and darted to stretch every point as Alexander stared about him.

The Buttonwood Inn didn't stock the best bourbon, but the proprietor, Wolfgang Gambicini, reserved his back room for guests wanting seclusion from the saloon's gaud and sin.

Mister Tewksbury swore by Mrs. Gambicini's apple strudel and her Saturday special—roast pork and mashed potatoes whatever the weather.

What pleased Alexander most about the pale, square dining room was that they were the only customers.

The hearth was spotless, though the scent of wood fires from previous winters was as strong as the aroma of roast pig creeping between the floorboards from the kitchen below. Crude jars of wild flowers were centered on each round table, repeating the maroons and blues of the faded Persian carpet.

Before settling with his uncle in an alcove opposite the open window, Alexander studied a large portrait above the fireplace. But it didn't bear scrutiny. By comparison with the rest of it, the sitter's hands were naïvely crude and the skyline like a child's work. The artist merely signed himself Bertram.

Mister Tewksbury answered the question he knew Alexander, always brimming with questions, was about to ask. "Mister Gambicini says he paid that fella to paint it from a miniature of Mister Gambicini's great-grandfather for a big shindig here to celebrate the turn of the century, but the bandit took all the money and ran off before he was finished, so Mrs. Gambicini tried finishing what he'd left.

"Called himself a traveling artist. Gypsy, if you ask me. But this country's been filling up with riffraff since the war.

"Anyway, like I told Mister Gambicini, his wife best stick to cooking." Mister Tewksbury lit his pipe. A few hard draws soon filled the room with smoke. "The minute me and your Aunt Julia collected you from the port, I racked my brain trying to think who you reminded me of, and blow me if it ain't that painting! Wouldn't it be a turn-up for the cards if you were related somehow to Mister Gambicini?"

The dark-eyed Italian on the canvas had Alexander's angular profile and high cheekbones. Being indifferent to his own looks, the intolerably handsome Englishman never understood why he made girls giddy. But no doubt they smiled because his gentle brown eyes smiled, even at his most serious, which was too often for somebody with everything. Over breakfast that morning, his aunt demanded the secret of his ruby cheeks.

"Diphtheria," he quipped, taking her off guard.

"Diphtheria!" tooted Uncle Jonas to his wife, as though Alexander wasn't there. "He was eight . . ."

Aunt Julia blanched, asking Jonas to pass the sugar while she riffled through her mind for something kinder to say.

"As your mother always said, Alexander, diphtheria may have weakened your body, but it strengthened your resolve."

"He's *healthy*," insisted Mister Tewksbury. "Apart from being on the thin side. You confounded women keep fussing over the boy. I think you wanna keep him an invalid so he'll never leave your daddy's estate." Alexander silently agreed but would never have said it. "All he needs is some of this good American air and fattening up," he heard his uncle go on.

The Buttonwood's platters of pork garnished with peas and a mountain of potatoes, which Mrs. Gambicini's daughter set before him and his uncle, were intended to do just that.

"I'm ravenous," admitted Alexander, surprised to see his uncle bib his napkin at the neck. "Who'd think this infernal heat could give anyone an appetite?"

"Now, 'member that strudel I told you about."

As thirsty men herded into the Buttonwood's saloon, the German Reform Church pealed another noon, and a drunk's version of "Blue Tail Fly" rose from outside the dining-room window.

Mister Tewksbury grabbed a chunk of crackling from his

double side order and resumed his version of the Civil War. "I wasn't your age when I left our place for the nearest camp. Boy, was *I* brassy when I rode into Jacksonville toting a twelve-gauge and a couple of six-shooters." His big laugh was to imply that he'd changed. "The first thing to cut me to size was a sore gut from the snake stew."

Alexander's ear tuned to the drunken serenade.

> *When he'd ride in the afternoon*
> *I'd follow after with a hickory broom,*
> *The pony being rather shy*
> *When bitten by the blue tail fly . . .*

"The blue flies that varmint is singing about stung us worse than the mosquitoes. But neither got us like the rain. Try nightwatch in a swamp with a chest cold on top o' a head cold and no whisky. And that's not the only way fellas died before they saw a battle."

While the singer hammered the chorus, "Gimme crack corn and I don't care, Master's gone away . . ." Mister Tewksbury crunched pork rind.

"Take Charlie Donnelly. The first night we moved camp, Charlie's old Pinto stumbled in the dark and that kid rolled off backwards and snapped his spine. A man with a broken back is a pitiful sight. Happened to one of our niggers when I wasn't but knee high."

It was only during breakfast that Alexander finally appealed to his uncle not to call Ezekiel and the other servants niggers. But, hot and hungry as he was in the Buttonwood, he let Uncle Jonas plunge on without interruption.

"In our poky outfit, all we had for pain was some hemlock and a bit of morphine. Charlie got his ration of that but still cried louder than a barn owl after we laid him out on some bullrush."

In between this monologue, the minstrel sang:

He died and the jury wondered why;
The verdict waasss, The Bluuuuee Tail Flyyyy.

"I was only half sleeping," Mister Tewksbury continued, "when somebody crawled over to Charlie. I heard a muffled shot and some ignoramuses grabbed rifles, but the sergeant said, 'Back to sleep. It's only Rufus.' Rufus was Charlie's kid brother. Fifteen at most. We used to tease him 'bout dying before he shaved."

Mister Tewksbury's memory lingered while he chased peas around his plate.

"Word went 'round Rufus'd shot Charlie, realizing somebody'd have to. For days after, Rufus went sort of mousey, so one morning I went to slip him a bit of my jerky, 'cause farm boys only had army grub. Anyway, Rufus couldn't raise his head, so I run for the lieutenant—Croxley, he was called. He told Rufus, 'Being paralyzed is just in your mind.'

"We all knew Rufus idolized his big brother," Mister Tewksbury explained to Alexander, "but Croxley'd witnessed soldiers going off their heads before and couldn't spare a man to see the boy home five miles."

The yodeling outside the window rose as Mister Tewksbury said, "So when darkness fell, the lieutenant shot him. It was the Fourth of July that happened, and doesn't one pass that I don't wonder how the Donnelly boys' mother imagined she'd lost both sons."

Alexander was too disturbed by the story to sample the strudel when it came, but his uncle had appetite for two and was lapping spoonfuls as the drunk soared into a version of "Yankee Doodle."

Yankee Doodle, who's the noodle?
What wife were so handy
To breed a flock of slaves for stock?
A blackamoor's the dandy.

> *Search every town and city through,*
> *Search market, street and alley,*
> *No dance at dusk shall meet your view*
> *So yielding as my Sally.*

Seeing his uncle's face redden, Alexander assumed strudel had blocked Jonas's windpipe and rushed to thump him on the back. But his uncle upturned the table, hurrying to draw his palm-size pistol from his breast pocket.

Mister Tewksbury's bark outshattered the crash of dinnerware. "When he insults Jefferson, he insults the South, and when he insults the South he insults Daddy."

Oblivious to all, the songster carried on:

> *When pressed by loads of state affairs*
> *I seek to sport and dally . . .*

Alerted by the ruckus, Mister Gambicini rushed in to witness Alexander grapple his uncle to his knees.

"Hey, whatsa matter?" Mister Gambicini scowled, more concerned about his broken plates than the two men tussling. He bent to pick the bits up, trying to avoid the strudel and wild flowers in a sad little puddle of water.

Mister Tewksbury reddened, wrestling himself from Alexander's grip while the songster waffled on. "Sorry. But, of course, I'll pay for everything. But when that fartsmeller . . ." Disheveled, he looked older than his sixty-nine years. "When that drunk started singing about . . ."

Mister Gambicini looked more appalled and perplexed than Alexander.

"Bastard carpetbaggers," his uncle swore. "I told your Aunt Julia it was a mistake moving north."

"I run a nice establishment, Mister Tewksbury, and we don't allow no swearing. S'pose my wife . . ."

"He was singing about *President* Jefferson siring niggers. Surely you'd expect me to stand up for . . ."

Suddenly remembering the great persuader, Mister Tewksbury drew his billfold. Seeing him peel off the two tens restored the color to the proprietor's cheeks.

Pocketing the bills, Mister Gambicini scurried to shut the window. "Gitta outa here," he squalled at the drunk, before slamming it. "Sorry your lunch was disturbed and don't worry, my wife can clean this up in no time. If it weren't for men like you, there's no telling what these rogues would get up to."

An elephantine silence wedged itself between Alexander and his uncle as they headed for the phaeton in Market Square.

Odd automobile honks unnerved horses that thudded along Main Street's cobblestones, veined with silvery trolley tracks, and Alexander, trying to forget the Buttonwood incident, was starting to enjoy their walk among the shoppers despite the heat. But no sooner had they reached the German Reform Church, than Jonas Tewksbury suddenly let out a shout.

"I don't believe it! I won't believe it! But by God, it's staring me in the face."

Slowly dabbing sweat and dust from his brow, Alexander realized more was to come.

"This is your aunt's doing! Her and that bunch of battle-axes in the Women's Auxiliary will have our town crawling with niggers." To the amusement of passersby he yelled out, "Emancipation Jubilee be damned!" and tore down the flyer on the Civil War Monument announcing the Auxiliary's celebration picnic. FIFTY YEARS OF FREEDOM was as much as Alexander could read before his uncle balled up the flyer. "Julia should know better! But she doesn't think."

Across town in her study at Holybrook Manor, Mrs. Julia Tewksbury was actually thinking very hard, trying to decide which of the three high-school applicants she'd interviewed during the past hour would best assist her with her duties as Auxiliary vice president.

The third applicant, Atlanta Simms, watched for signs as Mrs. Tewksbury scanned her reference. But the latter's expression gave nothing away.

"Well, Miss Simms," said Julia, feeling magnanimous that she'd called a colored girl Miss, "your home economics teacher says you're her best dressmaker, as well as punctual and careful with the school's equipment." What she was thinking as she spoke was that Atlanta's light wool burgundy dress was too heavy for the clammy weather and wrong with her pert straw hat. She paused. "But something from your stenography teacher at Germantown High would have been more appropriate. You are taking the commercial course?"

"Yes, ma'am." Atlanta had been in two minds about applying for the job since the Women's Auxiliary included the principal's wife. But as soon as Mrs. Tewksbury offered her a seat, Atlanta's interest grew, although she was expecting satin chairs and gold mirrors and was sorely disappointed that the study was so plain.

Her friend Beulah, whose Aunt Ophelia had once worked in the kitchen at Holybrook, swore it was the fanciest house in Germantown. Pointing to a drawing-room illustration in a dog-eared *McCall's* magazine, Beulah had told Atlanta, "I bet it's like this, because Aunt Ophelia has cooked for some of *the* richest and doesn't lie." But sitting in Mrs. Tewksbury's study, Atlanta wondered, because the white room with white gauze curtains at the tall windows and simple wooden furniture was anything but fancy. She found Mrs. Tewksbury's green suede shoes far more impressive.

Julia, equally quick to judge on footwear, concluded that Atlanta's rundown high-tops, though shined, were the girl's only pair. But not wanting to be swayed by her looking poor, she asked, "Are you learning shorthand?"

"Yes, ma'am." Atlanta fluttered her lashes and forced a smile. She was imitating Ingrid and Marta, the Norwegian

twins in her domestic science class. They too cocked their
heads when they spoke and always sat with their hands
folded in their laps, and Mrs. Tewksbury did notice that Atlanta's manner and speech were decidedly different from all
the Tewksburys' Southern domestic staff.

"The Auxiliary only pays two dollars per week." Unsure
how her husband would react to a colored secretary, she was
hoping something she could say would put Atlanta off.

But Atlanta liked her and sat a little straighter for it and
knew she was closing in on success when Mrs. Tewksbury
asked, "You wouldn't happen to know someone who could
work in the stables, would you?"

"My brother! Teenotchy loves horses and knows . . ." Atlanta broke off, uncertain whether she was being too forward
and not sure it was a good idea to tell Mrs. Tewksbury that
her brother'd been riding horses since he was six thanks to
Mister Kleber. And while Atlanta was usually the last to compliment Teenotchy on anything he did, even she boasted
from time to time about her brother's horsemanship and how
much he knew about saddles, having been as near to Mister
Kleber's apprentice as Hans had allowed.

But before Atlanta could carry on, Julia interrupted.
"Two problems solved at once!" she enthused in an effort to
gun her own courage, deciding she could convince Jonas that
a secretary was a domestic of sorts.

Following Mrs. Tewksbury out, Teenotchy's sister eyed
the flock wallpaper. "Now this is more like it." She was beam-
ing to herself in the entry as she was shown to the front
door. Atlanta raised her nose to the servant who stood ready
to open the door for her, but just as her airs were about to
overwhelm her good sense, Mrs. Tewksbury brought her
down. "I know you people enjoy spending all day Sunday in
church . . ."

"You people" cut to the bone and Atlanta, though accustomed to such, stopped smiling as she listened to her new
employer finish the sentence.

"Tell your brother to see our stable boss tomorrow morning." Something suddenly made Julia wonder if she was making a mistake. "I'll need you at four on Wednesdays," she said, knowing that during school it would be impossible for anyone to walk from Germantown High to Upper Germantown in half an hour.

Atlanta pictured herself running. "Oh, that won't be a problem, ma'am," she lied. She could hardly contain herself. She cast a smug look at the immaculately turned-out servant who attended her, his white-gloved hand still poised to turn the doorknob.

Mrs. Tewksbury's damp smile was short of diplomatic. "Use the back door when . . . no, use the servants' entrance when you come Wednesday."

Even that couldn't stop Atlanta high-stepping like a Tennessee walking horse to Main Street. "Thank you, Lord! Thank you, Jesus! I have scrubbed my last floor," she yelped. "*Miss* Atlanta Simms is a sec-re-tary."

III

A sunbeam fondled its way into the L-shaped room overlooking the south lawn which Mister Tewksbury bestowed upon his wife because it was the best appointed in the grand house. There was an amber glow from the stained-glass window and Alexander was relieved to find near peace there.

"Did Jonas drive you to the Buttonwood in an open carriage?" Julia asked her nephew, noticing how he'd browned since breakfast. She was at her desk addressing envelopes.

A meadowlark preening itself outside her study had Alexander's attention, though minutes before he'd been comparing the Tewksburys' fancy hedging to Germantown's wilderness. But they were no more poles apart than his aunt's stark study in a house decorated with her husband's bawdy taste.

Julia carried on. "I'm glad I didn't join you for lunch. I

would have burnt to a cinder with the hood down." Dressed for dinner in sky blue, she'd made a point of wearing the cameo brooch Alexander'd brought among offerings from home.

He'd arrived laden with gifts, including a pair of Charles Rennie Mackintosh tables from his mother, who'd remarked, "Poor Julia must need everything, probably hasn't seen any decent pieces since she left home." Since her sister had married a man twice her age, Irene regularly referred to her as "Poor Julia."

Two overfed King Charles spaniels were asleep on one of the new tables, having scratched the other the day Alexander presented them. Childless, Julia had introduced the spoiled dogs to him as his cousins.

He turned from the study window. "I'm pleased you're wearing your cameo and I love your hair swept up." Compliments were meant to sweeten the way to discussing what had preoccupied him since lunch. He didn't feel familiar enough for the direct approach. "You're so like Granny with your hair that way."

Had Julia liked her deceased mother this would have been worth mentioning. But she had detested her and abandoned England to get as far from her parents as possible.

"Do you think she would have got on with Jonas?" Alexander blundered on, assuming Julia had doted on her mother like he had.

"I've never given it a thought," lied Julia. In fact, she'd hoped that her mother, who'd lavished support on abolitionist causes, was turning in her grave. "Ma was so peculiar. There's no telling who she would have liked. Did you have a nice lunch?" she asked, abruptly changing the subject.

Anxiety flung Alexander into the heart of the Buttonwood incident although he tried to sound nonchalant. "Uncle Jonas was going to shoot a man."

Julia reddened, but her spaniels looked up and yawned

as if they'd heard it all before. "He draws that ridiculous little pistol at the slightest thing."

"But over a song!"

"What song?" she asked, as if one in particular might excuse Jonas.

"A childish thing about Thomas Jefferson's slave wife."

Having said nothing during breakfast when Alexander challenged her husband saying nigger, Julia advised, "Just close your eyes and ears to ugliness." Her own humanitarian leanings played safe. "Decent people do."

"If I refuse to . . ."

The heavy smell of cigar smoke crept into the study before he finished his sentence.

"Are you goin' on about our niggers again?"

Only the spaniels seemed happy to see Jonas. "Two hundred and fifty head we owned. *Owned*." The tumbler of bourbon he always downed in his dressing room while Ezekiel groomed him for dinner often gave Mister Tewksbury a jagged edge. Though in his wife's presence he usually spoke softly and watched his diction, even she couldn't make him mind his tongue.

"Owned. Want me to repeat it again?" Alexander's jaw was rigid. "Family property. No different from your grandaddy's thoroughbred stock."

Crushing his cigar in the ashtray, he added, "And as a son of the great South, I would take up the sword again if . . ."

Maybe his wife's quivering bottom lip stopped him. Alexander also looked to his aunt, feeling that it was up to her to silence her husband.

"We've had all sorts in our family," Jonas said. "Pirates. Loafers. Drunks. Thieves. Even a couple of Australians. I proudly claim 'em all. But we never had to abide a nigger lover." He let the phrase take a low bow before saying, "Negrophile, if that sits better with you, Al."

Julia's pale complexion, a barometer for contretemps,

had already deepened to rose. So Alexander swallowed his rebuff.

"Laura, Georgia. C'mon, doggies," quipped Mister Tewksbury sweetly so that they leapt from the table to waggle off at his heels. "Ezekiel says dinner may be served, Julia, when you and *your* nephew are ready."

IV

Across town in that dusty dead end where the sun was less happy to shine Aunt Em was in a rage. "You been to school with them white crackers so long, you gettin' lazy like 'em," she ranted. But Atlanta hardly heard. In an effort to taunt, Atlanta was singing "fat tub of lard" under her breath and had both hands cupped over her ears.

"Heifer! Who you callin' a fat tub of lard? Don't you know I'll take and maul your head against the wall?"

As they normally had a major stand-off early Saturday evening, Atlanta was ready for threats, insults and minor shoving. But since a lifetime battling Aunt Em had taught her the danger of shifting her resolve, she knew better than to let up. "Fat tub of lard," her murmuring singsong went on.

"Sitting there like the Queen of Sheba with your good dress on!" charged Aunt Em.

After the interview with Mrs. Tewksbury Atlanta hadn't changed out of her Sunday best.

"And I told you last time you slipped out of here without going to do for them Klabbers."

"Klabber," hissed Atlanta. "Their name is Kleber! So ignorant you can't even talk right."

Such disparagements riled Aunt Em more than anything else. But she was deafened by the sound of her own voice. It ricocheted off the kitchen walls over the issue which had started the fracas. "Talkin' 'bout you free and it's a free country. The only thing a nigger's free to do is die."

The "fat tub of lard" singsong rose in blatant challenge; Atlanta's fear of Aunt Em made her so crazy she was incapable of backing down, though she knew Aunt Em lacked her usual bluster, having missed a night's sleep listening to a barking hound.

The old woman's rabble-rousing belied her homespun image. Wide as a barrel, wrapped in a navy skirt which was supposed to reach her bare feet but stopped above the ankle, Aunt Em looked motherly. But that didn't stop her saying, "Don't come in my face with no mess, 'cause I'll ram a knife in your gut."

With her two hundred pounds leaning against the aluminum sink, she jutted both hands on her hips to rant, "I done four shirts while you got the nerve to set with your head in a book . . . Claimin' you read one page and I done heard you turn don't know how many." The ABC had been her master's exclusive code and she couldn't abide it in her kitchen. "Next you be telling me you late for somebody's choir and ain't gonna cart that bundle to Miz Holloway's."

As it was, Atlanta had managed to slip through an entire week without scrubbing or ironing. She'd been trying to soften the skin on her hands, in the hope that Hernando Lopez might grab hold of one. Since he'd moved to town, she'd refused to be seen in the streets balancing washloads on her head.

"You ain't good for nothin'," accused Aunt Em. "Talkin' 'bout school this and school that." Tired or not, she was a steel-driving man when her dander was up. "Girl, don't you know I'd ruther see you dead in the gutter than let your narrow behind slip out this house without hitting tap at a snake."

Atlanta turned the page.

Her face was as stony as Lincoln's on Rushmore. But underneath the table, her right hand nervously twisted her petticoat around and around. Around and around, practically cutting off the circulation in her forefinger.

Her dream was to speak softly, change the tablecloth twice a week and be included in some pastor's social rounds. Other girls she knew hadn't been raised among smelly socks constantly boiling and strangers' long johns strewn around their kitchen floor.

In fourth grade Atlanta began claiming that her father was an elevator operator, and all through fifth she'd prayed that her real parents would come for her. When she was ten, being so much taller than Teenotchy made her able to convince herself he wasn't her real brother. But by the sixth grade she had to accept that they had the exact same noses and stubby toes and arched eyebrows. And he could remember their mother nursing Atlanta and imitate the way he remembered Derwent Simms hobbling with his cane.

Aunt Em saw Atlanta's mind drift from the book, so she reared. "I let you get away with your mess last Sat'day 'cause Tessie was laid up, but I'm ready for you now. I'll beat you till you black and blue!" She parroted every threat her slave owners had hurled at her. But whereas she only struck with belt or birch switch, she'd survived whips and the cat o' nine tails.

However provoked the old woman was, her rages were simply tornadoes that whirled up from past hurts and furies. They left a deathly hush within her once they'd passed.

Atlanta noticed the vein throbbing down the center of Aunt Em's forehead. It was the sign that any minute she would quit shouting to calm her nerves. So Atlanta closed her book upon the stained tablecloth. Having made it in her home economics class, she'd vowed never to make another for Aunt Em to ball up in the windowsill. Trying to turn the Klebers' converted stable into a home was impossible, she'd concluded, because Aunt Em refused to notice and Teenotchy refused to help.

"You ready to tote these things to Miz Holloway's?" Aunt Em asked in her normal voice. Sparrows could be heard again in the yard.

Atlanta stood to unravel her long limbs. "Guess Teenotchy's over in his plot." To share the news with Aunt Em about the Women's Auxiliary job and possible work for Teenotchy at the Tewksburys' would've been like passing secrets to the enemy. So she was saving it for him or Beulah . . . or Hernando Lopez, assuming she could think of an excuse to start a conversation with him at Glee Club.

Teenotchy'd advised Atlanta about her crush on Hernando Lopez. "Doesn't matter that he's as black as my boot. He's still over there on Coulter Street. And anyway, I saw him walking with Erlethia Robinson!" Erlethia's father had his own catering business and for two generations both sides of her family, so she bragged, had been born free.

Until Hernando arrived in Germantown, Atlanta'd resolved on a spinster life teaching, she was so sure that nobody decent would marry her. But standing behind Hernando in Glee Club and studying the way his hair grew down the back of his neck resurrected her passion for boys.

With her contralto rising above his bass, she could think only of running her fingers along the rim of his collar while their "Onward Christian Soldiers" sang out in descant.

Hernando's black eyes galvanized Atlanta and talking

about him constantly to Beulah let her believe that his failed attempts to explain himself in English were practically marriage proposals.

With him on her mind, she bounded upstairs blurting, "I need to change." Her plan was to slip out to Glee Club before church bells chimed seven.

Aunt Em huffed over to her curtained-off corner where she slept to avoid the rickety stairs. In a jar on the dresser was a chunk of bread pudding she'd been hoarding. Careful not to make a sound, she unscrewed the jar and, hearing Atlanta tiptoe out, she gobbled an edge, relieved to savor it in peace.

"You ain't so slick," mumbled Aunt Em, with her mouth full.

Her swollen feet shuffled to the door. "Teenotchy'll have to take them things 'cause I ain't studdin' her. One o' these days I'll stick her and her rags in the street."

Staring out at the three clothes-lines sagging with dried sheets, her mind was on the bread tin, where she kept the stale bakery goods that Tessie brought her Thursdays.

Although she regretted that Tessie suffered diabetes and couldn't have sugary treats, Aunt Em was grateful for the broken three-day-old cookies and other items Tessie got free, working for the Jewish baker. These large crumbs, exchanged for laundry services, found their way to Aunt Em's tin. Without them she could never have appeased her belly god.

Some nights, no sooner than she'd collapsed on her cot, belly god would nudge, "Feed me," and drag her from her bed in search of something, anything, to nibble. Wednesdays were the worst. Wednesdays Aunt Em needed more night feeds than a newborn, since on Thursdays she collected Miz Llewellyn's things. Not that Miz Llewellyn complained or short-changed more than the others, but she always searched Aunt Em's face for clues. "You sure, Auntie, that I don't know you from somewhere? You look *so* familiar to me.

Where you from?" she'd pry. "What's your last name? Who'd
you say you worked for?"

Aunt Em hadn't said, having vowed to live a lie from
the day she laid eyes on Teenotchy's grey ones, which
haunted her and made her remember what she needed to
forget.

"You ain't Emma no more," Aunt Em recalled the straggly
haired young mother informing her the day she bought her,
aged thirteen, plus a sick cow, from the dairy farm by the
river.

"Emma can't be a nigger's name. It's my name. Miz
Emma," she'd accentuated.

So the African girl who'd become Emma with her first
slave master wept under her horse blanket that February
night without name or number.

Next morning Miz Emma said, "Lottie, the baby needs
to be changed," and passed her a beefy one-year-old with a
big head and big feet, grinning to show off his baby teeth.
"This here's your mammy, James," she announced to her
son. "Her name's Lottie."

Until then Aunt Em had spent her hostage years cow-
herding and milking. She wasn't good with words, having
spent all her time with the animals, and had never been
trained for housework, having never been inside a house.
But Miz Emma believed a good hiding was the surest way to
train slaves. She expected a switch of birch to show "Lottie"
the way to iron and knead bread and fold back the corners
of the bed. And when that didn't work she tried the cat o'
nine tails, only relying on the old horse whip as a last resort.
"Don't make me beat'cha till ya bleed," Miz Emma used to
warn the girl, as if baby minding came easy and mending
wasn't a science.

"Lottie" waited for spring to try to find the dairy farm,
but Miz Emma's dogs soon tracked her on the road by morning. Beating her back to the barn, where the hatchet waited,

Miz Emma said, "This time I'm taking a finger, but you try to run off again and it'll be your big toe."

Aunt Em, remembering, opened and shut her four-fingered left hand. One less for her rheumatics, she always told Tessie, but it didn't make the washing any easier.

"Lottie," she said, shaking her head on the way to the cookie tin. But the Lottie in her refused to be buried. The piles of stale cookies and bread puddings couldn't shake off memories that clung like a noose.

V

Upper Germantown
Sunday, August 3, 1913

Before the sun got a chance to turn their hovel into an oven
the next morning, Teenotchy was taking his time to get over
to the Tewksburys' place. Along the three miles he ambled
past Sunday believers dressed to seek their redeemer. His
was the sun, casting a halo upon Holybrook Manor, where a
brawny man in freshly pressed navy-blue overalls examined
a wobbly stable door.

Teenotchy greeted him. " 'Scuse me, mister, d'you know
who I see about the stable job?" His hand, crammed in his
pocket, gripped his harmonica, his index finger caressing
each little wooden square.

The stern-looking man glanced up, removing his tooth-
pick. "Schoolboy?" he asked, giving Teenotchy the once-over.

"Finished high school in June," said Teenotchy, blushing
with pride.

"There's two of us sees to the horses already and Miz

Julia's only wanting an extra while her nephew's visiting,"
said the man as he stood upright to deliver the door bracket
a precise kick. "Don't need nobody else that I can see, but
then I ain't paying wages. Not to say I ain't the boss. 'Cause
you want the work, it's me you got t'see—Edison Edwards,
Jr. And I don't want nobody with less sense than a mule."

Teenotchy knew how to be silent and still when the situation called for it. He hardly drew breath.

"I've seen boys like you here, there, everywhere, after
stable work." The stable boss wasn't in the mood to give
Teenotchy a chance when only the day before Edison had
been thinking that his own position was growing precarious.
But it irritated him when his jealous streak got the best of
him and though he knew he was giving Teenotchy a hard
time, he couldn't have explained why, but he was trying to
ease up when he said, "Stable hand and you got some educa-
tion? Next year or the one after, stableyards'll be lined with
automobiles, like they got hooting all 'round Independence
Hall. That's why a young fella that reads oughtn't to be foolin' with no horses. I saw fifty last month and I'm right over
there on Rittenhouse Street, every minute I get. Over there
at Duke's Garage. Readying up for what's coming. Not that
there ain't gonna be no horses, but Boss won't be payin'
nothin'. 'Fact he don't wanna pay fair now . . ." He was as
much lecturing himself as Teenotchy, who still hadn't said a
word and had hardly looked up, though he could hear the
stable boss scratching at the days and days of stubble that
accentuated his heavy jawline. Edison Edwards, Jr., kept talking. "You want to start learning about these automobiles.
'Cause in a minute won't nobody find a post to tie a horse
to with automobiles lining the sidewalks."

He smiled and ran the tip of his tongue along his
chipped front tooth. His dark-brown face threatened to be
cheerful, although his black seedy eyes still examined Teenotchy with a hint of contempt. "What you say was your
name, kid?"

"Teenotchy, sir. Well, really it's Theodore. Theodore Simms." He wasn't sure whether to extend his hand or to wait for Edison Edwards, Jr., to extend his.

Edison set his tweed cap further back on his gray head to scratch his scalp with his baby finger. "What was that first? 'T. Nicey.' Betcha that's something they call you 'round these streets." Trying to look Teenotchy in the eye, Edison suddenly realized that he was shy, not silent and superior like the other two high-school graduates that had sauntered about the yard the previous week looking for a job. He wondered if he could get Teenotchy to crack a smile and thought about how boyish he seemed.

"You can't have no gals lollygagging by that fence waiting round for you. 'Cause one bad apple will sure rot the rest. T. Nicey, heh? Can you saddle good?"

"I guess so."

"Guessin' won't get you further than the corner store. Anyway, only a fool would take your word for it."

Teenotchy followed him to the saddle room, which had the comforting smell of polished leather and sweaty horse blankets. It was a smell that Teenotchy remembered too well from his days of working in Mister Kleber's saddlery, where he'd spent some of his happiest hours that year after his mother died, making string for the old man out of the best hemp. Teenotchy'd loved standing at Mister Kleber's elbow, half watching the old man stitching up leather using two needles at once, one in as the other went out.

"Seen one of these kind?" Edison asked Teenotchy as he hauled down a dark-brown saddle.

"Yessir," was Teenotchy's meek reply. Why didn't he say that he could have repaired every strap, replaced every buckle, stitched every stitch on that saddle if asked to? But he just kept his head down, remembering how Mister Kleber used to tell him that he had a real talent for leatherwork. Born to it, was what the old man liked to tell him any time he showed Teenotchy a trick of his trade, and Teenotchy was quick and determined to master it, because he so liked to please the old man.

Edison Edwards gave Teenotchy a long, hard look. "Lookahear, boy," the stable boss began, for the first time sounding half friendly, which was more his nature. "Call me Edison, 'cause sir is for ol' fogies or somebody I don't have no time for."

He pulled down two horse blankets and Teenotchy smiled as he grabbed the saddle. He knew it bore a tiny brass plate inscribed "Made by Paul Kleber."

Edison's bowed calves rolled his high behind from side to side as he led Teenotchy past a row of stables with a horse in each. They stopped at the last and a bay whinnied.

"Hey there, General Lee," said Edison. "Got a little whippersnapper for you to eat." The horse eyed Teenotchy with disdain.

"He ain't but four and just started with a trainer. We call him Gen'ral for short. . . . Speaking of which, you not big as a flea." Edison laughed. "You reckon you man enough to handle him?"

Such days always reminded Teenotchy of his first day at school, when the teacher made him stand all morning because he wasn't expected. It'd annoyed her that he knew the alphabet and could count. But Teenotchy saying "thou" made her frown and the room of brown-skinned children giggle. "Don't bring that Quaker mess in here," Aunt Em had yelled whenever "thee" and "thou" slipped out after his year with the Klebers. She soon beat it out of him.

Teenotchy stopped thinking back to that once the saddle was in place. He made a kissing sound and drew a carrot from his pocket.

"Don't let ol' man Tewksbury see," said Edison, looking over his shoulder to check no one was coming. "He don't allow nobody to feed these horses. Never," he accentuated, loosening the red kerchief tied around his neck. "But what he don't know won't hurt him . . . *this* time."

The goatee Edison was trying to grow was whiter than his kinky salt and pepper hair.

Teenotchy whispered something to the horse and General whinnied.

"What d'you say to him?" Edison asked, doubly amazed by Teenotchy's saddling technique.

"I told him that I grew that carrot myself and it's deee-licious," chuckled Teenotchy.

Any horse was his homecoming.

"Watch this one," warned Edison. "He can be a mean cuss when he wants to. Got a temper."

No sooner than the words were said, Teenotchy got a friendly nuzzle and Edison's mouth dropped open.

From that year with the Klebers, Teenotchy soaped saddles like the one on General and was given one on his fifteenth birthday. But pride in Mister Kleber's work was something he wasn't at leave to express.

Mounting the impeccably groomed horse, Teenotchy's head lifted and his spine straightened like a king reclaiming his throne.

"Let's see you ride," said Edison, slapping General's flank. Teenotchy started to canter but soon rocketed the stallion around the track until he remembered the cuffs of his good shirt. He slowed General to a dusty halt and Edison, fast for his chunky build, loped over. "I ain't seen enough."

"Sorry, Mister Edison." Teenotchy was convinced he'd already lost the job. "But maybe . . . can I ride with no shirt?"

"It don't bother me," said Edison, picking his side teeth with a long straw. "Ride without no shoes. I was a country boy myself once."

Teenotchy's perfect chest, chiseled in oak, contrasted with his five foot six inches. Smooth. Hairless. His muscles perfect and defined. In captivity they would have auctioned him as a stud.

"Please, would you hold my spectacles?" he asked self-effacingly.

"That's a quarterbred you saddled there, T. Nicey." Edison grinned, so Teenotchy did. "Best keep them bifocals on, 'cause you drive that racehorse into a wall and we'll both be a vulture's supper."

"I ride all the time without them. Honest."

Teenotchy crinkled his nose. Freed of the wire rims, his gray eyes readjusted to the morning. He was good and ready when Edison slapped General's rump the second time.

But the stable boss felt guilty as soon as Teenotchy and the four-year-old shot around the track. In his forty years of following circuses and running stables, he'd never known a horse as ornery as General and he wondered what made him test boys on that horse.

But Teenotchy Simms took to horses like his father and his father before him. James Van Zandt could ride a mustang bareback and mold himself into any horse so that he couldn't be sure where he stopped and the horse began. Teenotchy was no different, even though his frame was better suited to the fine saddle which he sat upon as he and that fancy thoroughbred shot past Edison, who pealed and hooted his revelation. "Niggah," he hollered, "you are sure one ridin' fool!" He was hopping with excitement when an English voice, clipped and precise, interrupted his own shrieks.

"That's not General Lee?" Alexander asked, having crept up, making a tall shadow beside Edison's there with the sun beating down on them from the east.

"Yes, Mister Alexander, sir." He put his cap back on to tip it. "If Mister Jonas had of had that boy down Kentuck, he might of won him a little something, 'cause we got the horses. Just can't get the riders."

Alexander, instantly seized by Teenotchy's sensuality astride that horse, said, "Let's see him take another lap."

"I think we got ourselves a jockey here," Edison beamed. His grin from ear to ear would have led any stranger to think he was Teenotchy's father.

Alexander was wondering why he hadn't seen the handsome rider before, and it annoyed him that he had to hold back a smile so overwhelming that he pretended to yawn to hide it. He felt it was unnatural that his heart did a headstand as Teenotchy darted past, but it was less easy to control his heart than his mind, which he checked by turning his thoughts to his uncle's pristine track, a great white elephant in that Germantown community where religion had always ruled the day.

Edison read Alexander's mind. "Mister Jonas told the missus he wasn't moving up north 'less he could have a little track. It ain't big like he's used to, but it's goin' to waste with the Quaker-this and the Quaker-that complaining that there oughtn't to be no betting and race tracking."

"Wave him in," Alexander ordered. "Why haven't I seen him ride before?"

"He didn't get the job till just now I found him," bragged Edison. "Miz Julia was wanting somebody extra for them two you bought last week."

As Edison spoke, Alexander's eyes stayed on Teenotchy, who slowed General Lee to a trot, patting him rewardingly with each step. Sweat dripped from them both and Teenotchy glistened more than the Klebers' Bavarian table.

Seeing the stranger in the creamy linen suit made him slump in the saddle, his pewter eyes avoiding Alexander's, whose heart thumped as a half dozen churches chimed a cacophony.

"Gen'ral," Edison chided, "ain't no need you getting skittish, 'cause them bells is the same every Sunday at nine and you ought to be used to it."

The horse was suddenly as anxious as any four-year-old anticipating a wordy Sunday service.

"OK, boy. OK," Teenotchy soothed.

"You've a way with him," smiled Alexander, removing his Panama to appear less formal. "Before seeing you ride General Lee I was beginning to wonder if he was part mule."

Teenotchy, with no cap to tip, drew in his shoulders and Edison grabbed the reins to lead horse and rider to the stable.

An hour later, on the shaded veranda with Uncle Jonas, who toyed with his ivory chessmen, Alexander asked, "That new chap at the stables, the one with gray eyes?"

"We got a white boy working in the stables *under* Edison?"

"He's not white."

"Worse still. A gray-eyed nigger. I didn't know we made 'em."

He got so sloppy with laughter, Alexander had to excuse himself, stopping Ezekiel in the hallway. "That fellow with the gray eyes at the stables . . ." hedged Alexander.

Ezekiel was prepared for the worst. "If somebody down there ain't pulling his weight, Mister Alexander, I'll go now and put him straight. 'Cause we don't have 'em cutting up and acting the fool at Holybrook Manor. Mister Jonas won't stand for nobody that ain't one hundred and five percent."

"Well then, he'll have no complaint with his new stable-boy." Alexander climbed the stairs two at a time.

"Looks like the air is finally doing that English child some good," Ezekiel told Ruth when he walked into the kitchen. "He just hopping up them stairs like a cock robin. Bouncing on his toes."

"That's funny, 'cause Miz Julia just said Mister Alexander was looking so miserable over his breakfast that I got to do his favorite dessert for dinner."

"Well, that child can stay long-faced if it means you got to bake another Boston cream pie."

"What you grinning like a Chessy cat for, Zekiel? I didn't say I was fixing it for you."

He was as good at teasing as Ruth. "I better find a bowl

of scrapings my side of the bed tonight," he laughed, "don't . . . you can find you another husband."

Within the hour, Julia passed Alexander's door and was surprised to hear singing. She knocked lightly and his bright-eyed welcome startled her.

"Are you feeling . . . ?" She stopped, because he hated inquiries about his health.

"I'm fine," he beamed, "and you'll be too when I give you the letter Mother wrote you."

"Have you been holding it back?" Julia guessed when he fetched an envelope from the secretaire piled with his research on the Revolution.

"Her instructions, I bet. Telling you how many blankets to wrap me in and how many steps I may take to the bath."

"Don't underestimate Irene's wisdom." The envelope was scented with honeysuckle. "Lovely Irene . . ." she mused, but could see her compliment fell on deaf ears. "I'd have thrown myself under a train to spite Father had she not convinced me to try New York first."

Alexander faked ignorance about his aunt's history but his mother's tales of Julia at twenty-two, running off to Manchester to join the suffragettes, had always intrigued him. To discover she'd given up causes for Jonas was a great disappointment.

With her husband still on the veranda, Julia wanted to strike a truce with her nephew. But, "I can see you regret coming," wasn't a wise start. "I suppose," she added, "you would've had a better time in Paris with Jacques." Jacques was her deceased sister Henrietta's son and Alexander's alter ego.

"We've spent summers together since forever. . . . It was time for a change. And anyway, I'll get lots done here."

"Work," she moaned, wondering jealously how Irene, no beauty who lived just for parties, had produced such a handsome, studious son.

Alexander's defense was, "I'm only snooping through old ledgers and log books. My history professor says I'm incurably nosy, so I'm trying to make the fault a virtue."

"You're not going to spend the entire summer in your room, reading?"

"No. In fact, I plan to take a long walk before lunch. Maybe I'll spot that red cardinal you've seen."

"Should you walk in this heat?"

"Walking's one of the few things I do all right," he joked.

"Irene said . . ."

"She prefers me as an invalid."

"She got you well!"

"Mother's just worried I'll die with no heir and everything will go to Jacques."

"Alexander!" She suspected, though, there was some truth in what he said.

"But like you, Aunt Julia, Jacques can't bear England, the stud farm or Grandfather."

She didn't flinch but knew better than to encourage such talk. "I can show you where I've seen that cardinal," she said, trying to get more time with him.

"But can you tell me about the new stableboy?" Alexander was thinking, though he knew better than to ask.

VI

While other Germantowners rubbed down their souls at Sunday prayer meetings that morning, Aunt Em shook herself from one of her daytime nightmares. She'd been catnapping in the kitchen until a blonde voice in her dream shrieked, "Lottie! I gotta take the whip to you ag'in. Don't look like you done that outhouse!"

Eleven o'clock, judging from the chorus of church bells that gonged. Not that it mattered.

By eight, Aunt Em'd pressed Teenotchy's good shirt for him (though he'd refused to tell her that he was going to Upper Germantown to see about the Tewksburys' stable job) and had already boiled a kettle of lacy handkerchiefs, a tub of Miz Brandauer's snuggies and the bank teller's white shirts.

The washerwoman's bunions ached worse than her knuckles, knotted from rheumatism and cracking them most of her life. So, snatching her clothes-peg bag, she could just about do a lead-footed shuffle to the door.

The line of dress shirts had to be taken down and ironed, which she did year in and out, never complaining that for all the men she sent to work clean not one had ever labored for her.

When she came north, Thanksgiving of '96, she'd considered it an honor that what she called "high-class folk" trusted her to wash their finery. She marveled at the crocheted doilies, delicate silk stockings and hand-embroidered collars. But she'd given up admiring other people's fancy goods. They didn't change her life. If anything they made it more difficult, since she was expected to note when they needed repairing.

Work to eat. Eat to work. Aunt Em was a washing machine, scared the three of them would end up starving in the poorhouse if she idled and believing she had no right to more.

Her soul sustenance had been an annual Good Friday revival meeting, until she and her neighbor Tessie went to one where the preacher, possessed of a great pair of lungs and fancy patter, damned all fornicators. That sermon convinced Aunt Em that God served only the sinless, so she refused to go again, telling Tessie, "I'm too crippled up to walk anywhere that I ain't *got* to." She knew she was damned and needed no reminders.

But even without revivals, her body and mind stayed too busy for reflection until the Chinese laundry opened on Bringhurst, taking some customers and leaving enough time for her memory to taunt her.

Whether she sidled back in daydreams or got jostled back in a nightmare, she couldn't forget the Van Zandts' decrepit homestead by the river, or her mistress, Miz Emma. Or Miz Emma's son, James, whose gray, almond-shaped eyes stayed the same though everything else about him, particularly the size of his hands and feet, changed in those seventeen years she was their hostage, or slave, as they called her.

*   *   *

James Van Zandt was three before he could say Lottie.

"Thick-tongued and dumb like his damned daddy," explained Miz Emma, never having a kind word for the Dutchman who'd abandoned her and the baby boy before Lottie arrived.

From the moment the thirteen-year-old African girl was purchased, baby James curled his plump toddler's arms around her birdlike black neck and burrowed his mass of straw-colored curls on her shoulders, because he could resist her innocence no more than she could his. And at seven, he still made her his refuge and she, starved of hugs, all but his, was glad to have somebody to hold. They made a handsome portrait, especially when he was perched on her shoulders, which was as often as not.

"You can't hang about all day on that wench," his red-faced mother would quip, resentfully noticing that her son had found comfort while she had none. "Time you got over to that schoolhouse, so they can learn you the alphabet."

But James wouldn't sit still in the brick room they called "school" unless he was sure Lottie was outside on the steps. Through all inclement weather, the scrawny figure could be seen shifting from one foot to the other beside the school steps. Her fingers were number than ice cubes in winter and her round ebony head would soak up sun and sweat in the long Southern summers.

The older schoolchildren were quick to tease and taunt once they realized that the frail figure was James's mammy, stationed to escort him. And they were quick to chant, "Jimmy Van Zandt's a mammy's boy," whenever they saw her walking back through the trees along the dusty old road that touched the Mississippi.

From time to time he'd demand that she show him where she'd planted her baby finger, but she couldn't remember where she'd buried it, and the stick marking its grave had been blown away by the years.

It was only due to the fact that his mother had nothing

to give James for his eighth Christmas that she handed over Lottie's papers to stop him whining. Lottie was chopping wood when the long-limbed boy rushed out, wielding her bill of sale.

"I own you," he said, and he danced up and down, slinging chickenfeed at her from a pail beside the rooster's pen.

"You won't never 'mount to nothing!" his mother chastised him two years later. "Ten and can't say your ABC." Not that she cared. Her denouncement was for Mister Rankin's benefit, him being the elderly suitor she'd finally collared. He was a traveling salesman who owned a two-storey house she called a plantation to make herself feel important.

"You gotta read to get a plantation like Mister Rankin's here," she'd advise, though she could barely write her name.

Her beer-bellied old boyfriend taught James to chew tobacco but showed no other interest, taking Miz Emma off for weeks on end.

So James grew up a vagrant woodsman. From swinging axes and mallets against the two-hundred-year-old oaks, at fourteen he had the build of a mountain man. He was proud his fists were clubs.

"When I get me a plantation," he would yell out of boredom, kicking at the chickens but seldom kicking Lottie, "we gonna eat white turkey meat every durn day." All his plans included his hostage, who'd refused to forget that her name had once been Emma.

James sauntered into the barn one evening while Lottie was cleaning the goat's shed. Fifteen, but looking twenty, he'd come to do to her what he'd seen Mister Rankin's horses do the time he was allowed to visit Rankin's place with his mother. Lottie was puzzled when he pushed her against the disused rabbit hutches where she was storing grain. "Bend down," he ordered, so that he could enter her from behind. But he was too tall. "Help me, Lottie!" he whined.

But, living fourteen years in isolation with only him and his mother, she knew less than he did. Maybe a boy from the next creek told him what to do after that failed attempt, because he was sure the second time. Laying his hostage on her back, he rode her so long and hard that her virgin insides were torn and bleeding from his frantic boy lust.

"I'm sore," he complained the next morning, finding her weeping in a heap at the back of the dark barn. But it was discovering she hadn't got his corn pone fried and waiting for lunch which really provoked. "Fix my food!" he threatened, kicking her. She could only cry louder when he grabbed the horsewhip. "I'll beat you, nigger, till you can't stand." Not that she could anyway. But his ten lashes laid her up until the next afternoon.

James was more her child than his birth mother's, so his shoving her to the ground to satisfy himself didn't seem right, but she couldn't complain with only him to complain to.

All she could withhold was her smile, and it took a lot of cherries, pecans and fresh catfish before James won back her grin.

Every balmy night that summer their bodies rolled into one. His sweat became her second skin and he wanted her more than tobacco. So when hoot owls ranted in the great oaks by the river, James, Lottie and the mosquitoes would be eating each other up, so that by daybreak she'd be worn out, hardly able to drag herself from that cot to get his breakfast after she'd been sitting on him all night. Back to front, front to back, he didn't mind how she got him wailing as long as she got him there, his long arms often stretched forth to hold her in place if he wasn't too tired. Not that he ever seemed to tire of her fast dance, which seemed less shameful to her than what he made her do to him with her mouth whether his backside was clean or not. She thought that was as wrong as him resting with his head on her thigh and staring hard between her legs like he could see something. Him just star-

ing like he could see straight into infinity or heaven or some
place that wasn't just another part of her flesh that had been
made his through that piece of sale deed that his mother'd
handed him the Christmas he was eight.

It wasn't within her to hate him. She'd known his great
long feet as soft baby feet that she'd often tickled to get him
laughing when he was a toddler round her ankles. Like she'd
known that deep belly button before swirls of dark hair grew
above and below it. And she'd washed his foreskin enough
times when he was a little boy not to faint at the sight of it,
though she never felt easy waiting for James to get hard
before she'd mount him that summer they took those frantic
journeys together to that primal place which had neither
name nor lights but got them as heady as a couple entwined
on a wild mustang.

There wasn't much else for James and Lottie to get up
to in that outback, so as the days grew shorter, James taught
her some play-acting games. Like evenings he'd make her go
out to the barn like she was being made to sleep there, telling
her that when the sky blackened and stars studded it, she
was to brave the icy ground to steal to the foot of his cot,
saying, "Mas'r James . . . Mas'r James . . ." She'd coo like a
lover, which was as much part of the game as him having
her in the petticoat his mother'd left behind, not realizing
his yellow stains splotching it from one end to the other
wouldn't come out.

"James Van Zandt!" his mother lambasted him when she
found it after her three-month absence. "That nigger was
bought to do more than whore." And indeed, when Miz
Emma was at home, the work never stopped; she would have
had "Lottie" picking leaves off trees rather than let her rest.

But when acorns fell from the massive oaks, Mister Rankin's brougham pulled into the Van Zandt yard, scattering
chickens and scaring the goat, to collect Miz Emma and her
two carpetbags. So once again young James could cast his
hostage as mule or minx.

*   *   *

Standing in the Germantown yard with Sunday church bells ringing in her ears, Aunt Em was trembling with contempt for the "Lottie" in her, who'd been too scared to run, too cowed to raise her voice above "Yassuh, Mas'r James." After fifty years Aunt Em'd forgot he could've chopped off another one of her fingers if the mood took him, or beat her senseless with the handle of the hoe with nobody to stop him. "Lottie," Aunt Em spat, as though her loathing was for someone other than herself.

Though a half-century had dulled her memory in certain respects, it was impossible for Aunt Em to forget the time James dragged her fishing and made her eat his worms because he couldn't get a catch. But he was only twelve then and his orders at that same bank five years later were harder to swallow. Pushing her down on spongy moss, he'd say, "Spread your legs for me, Lottie. C'mon . . . c'mon, nigger, you know you can get 'em wider than that!"

Aunt Em's tent of flesh masked the doe-eyed "Lottie" in her and hid the nineteen-inch waist which James measured to buy her a satin ribbon.

Staring at the clothesline, the old woman didn't want to remember giggling when he licked her cone-shaped breasts, stuffing himself deep in her until his heavy breathing rattled her brain.

Dropping a couple of clothes pegs as she limped into the house with the shirts, Aunt Em wouldn't pick them up, but all the while she was recalling the time James punched her into a stupor because he'd just heard about Lincoln's Emancipation.

She'd been washing clothes that morning too and he came rushing at her with his gray eyes flashing and his fists clubbed for a fight. "You ain't goin' nowhere!" he warned. Like he expected her to walk off that very minute. "I'm getting a plantation with a yard full of coons and ain't Lincoln nor nobody else gonna stop me. And you gonna be my house nigger!" He was yelling, pummeling her face and body and crying, like her pain was his.

But the States War drew James into battle with the rest of the country. He'd been gone two summers before "Lottie" heard a thunder of singing one afternoon. Hoping he was back, she grabbed their gray-eyed baby girl off the stable floor and ran out to see scores of brown faces with dark voices crossing the Van Zandts' lower pasture. "D'is the Exodus Day," their chorus swelled in waves. Remembering this always gave Aunt Em a rush.

She'd been barefoot and bouncing her baby girl on her hip. "Where're y'all headed?" she'd called to the tiny straggler who lagged behind the rest.

"We *free*," he called back. Like it was a place. Then his bandy legs ran to keep up with the long striders at the front. But a brown, gangly girl in a gunny sack dropped from the scores of revelers to yell, "C'mon, gal. We headed for Philadelphy. Goin' to the promised land. C'mon!"

Her toothy grin beckoned with as much enthusiasm as the kinky-haired blond boy in her arms who mimicked his baby-faced mother. "C'mon!"

And the voices sang on. "Exodus. Exodus. D'is the Exodus Day."

The girl was practically singing too when she said, "No more slavin'. You free."

But the excitement frightened Lottie, and her baby caught her fear and cried.

"Come on!" the girl called, eager to rejoin the rest.

"Waitin' on my master," Lottie answered.

"T'ain't no more masters! Lee done surrendered!"

"Surrendered" and "Exodus" sounded like flowers.

"See what I told you," Lottie clammered to her howling daughter as the revelers disappeared from sight, their voices still ringing above the trees. "I knew Rose wasn't s'posed to be your name." She blew into the baby's gray eyes, trying to get a smile. "I'm naming you Exodus."

But within days "Lottie" was calling James's child Dusty for short.

Aunt Em hummed "D'is the Exodus" over and over while folding the half dozen shirts on the kitchen table. Working on the Sabbath worried her but she was resigned to going to Hell, where she expected her daughter Dusty to be waiting.

As she prepared to iron the shirts, a slab of bread pudding hidden in the jar behind her head kept sweet-talking, "Iron me, Lottie! Please iron me."

VII

Saturday, August 9, 1913

That following Saturday, with tempers getting shorter as the heatwave hadn't let up, Helga Kleber was in her darkest mood while preparing lunch. She claimed it was to do with Atlanta not coming to work for the second week running. So Teenotchy slaved for two. But when church bells struck noon, instead of being ready to collect his quarter, he still had the parlor to do.

He was polishing the brass lantern when a tinny male voice whooped outside the parlor window. "Tee-not-cheeee!"

He responded in a loud whisper. "Not finished, Geronimo. Go 'way."

The skinny Indian standing in the noonday sun didn't budge; a change in plans was too much for him to comprehend. To be fair, it was a miracle he was at the right place and on time, but with Mrs. Kleber banging about in the kitchen, Teenotchy couldn't risk congratulating him.

It was also a miracle that Mrs. Kleber, already at Furies' gate, didn't storm the parlor when Geronimo cawed "Teenotchy" again.

As it was she'd blocked the back door when Teenotchy'd arrived without Atlanta at eight-thirty.

"Theodore Simms," Mrs. Kleber had railed when he crept up the garden path, looking sheepish, "you're half an hour late and if your sister's not with you, turn around and go home! We don't need your kind." She was evil, with her black eyebrows knitted and eyes narrowed to slits so the blue barely showed. "And when you get home, tell Aunt Em I want her." Insurrection from the staff, a bedridden father-in-law to care for and the hot sun still rising would have set even a gentle woman on the warpath.

Teenotchy was glad Atlanta wasn't there, because she saw stars whenever Mrs. Kleber called Aunt Em anything but Miz Van Zandt. "Our aunt is no aunt of yours," Atlanta'd dramatically say, stomping her foot to clarify, being as oblivious as Teenotchy, and everybody else, that the African washerwoman was their grandmother.

Out of mercy as much as respect, the generations born free allowed old slaves their secrets and dared not tamper with their silences. So while assuming captivity was too regrettable to discuss, Teenotchy and Atlanta had skated round Aunt Em's past, asking nothing and being told less.

But that Saturday, no sooner had Teenotchy turned on his heels to go, after suffering in silence Helga Kleber's tirade about him being late and Atlanta being absent, he was saved by Mister Kleber's three loud thuds on the ceiling. His summons for Teenotchy was only two, so Mrs. Kleber went up.

"There are better ways to deal with the boy," Teenotchy heard the old man chafe. After years of fencing with his daughter-in-law the flip side of Mister Kleber's mildness was a serrated knife edge. "How many times must I tell thee,

Helga? The Simms children will work in this house till I go. Now will thee please send Teenotchy up," he added politely to regain composure.

Similar outbursts encouraged Atlanta to take liberties, although her brother paid for it with Mrs. Kleber's wrath.

Teenotchy's heart pounded double time bounding past her on the stairs to Mister Kleber's bedroom. Though he'd planned what to say while he made the two-mile run from the Tewksburys', Teenotchy was as awed in the old man's presence as his mother had been. They needed a saint and made him theirs, unable to see his failings.

Indeed, propped in his four-poster bed, Mister Kleber was a calm sea. He had the quiet air of a country friar and the moment Teenotchy stepped into the bedroom he felt safe.

"I'm sorry I'm late, Mister Paul, but I've got an early morning stable job, over by Maiden Lane. They're not Quakers but they're OK and their horses . . ."

He spewed an excuse that Mister Kleber was ready to accept before it began, because in Teenotchy's eyes he saw Dusty Simms smiling in her gentle way, and he needed her forgiveness.

Teenotchy stumbled on. "I'm not planning to quit here. But you're always telling me to ride and although I love Blossom, I get to ride a couple of pure thoroughbreds."

"Nothing wrong with mixed breeds. Blossom's got four good legs like the rest."

"Better than most," Teenotchy said. "But these two'll get shipped to a stud farm in England at the end of the summer and—"

Mister Kleber interrupted him. "Why isn't Atlanta with thee?"

"It was Atlanta that sort of found me the job. She's working over there too, but she doesn't want Mrs. Tewksbury to know she cleans."

"There's no shame in serving others," said Mister Kleber,

who'd always worked for himself. He and Teenotchy adjusted their glasses.

"A secretary serves, sort of." Teenotchy apologized for his sister's ambition. He needed Julia Tewksbury's sophisticated argument, given when her husband discovered Atlanta sitting at the desk in his wife's study.

Mister Kleber said. "Tell Atlanta she's excused this week, but I expect her next."

With it being way past twelve and Geronimo still waiting for him outside, Teenotchy hurried to finish in the parlor and wondered if he could get away with not doing the mirror. He never understood why the room had to be cleaned every Saturday when it never got used after Hans died.

It was in the parlor that the Klebers spent time together when Teenotchy lived that year in their house. Mister Kleber used to keep his deceased wife's doll's house there, and on his sixth birthday Teenotchy had been allowed to touch some of the pieces since he was "family." The perfect miniatures were all made by Mister Kleber and Helga, who did the needlework. How Teenotchy longed to be one of the stick people that stood fixed in the kitchen.

When he'd come there with his mother, the front of the doll's house was always closed, but during the time he'd lived in the house Mister Kleber's bedspread was forever covered in the various bits of chipped wood and metal that he used to make the pieces; and although he'd always promised that he would teach Teenotchy the craft, the old man never did. Teenotchy unnerved him, unless they were in the open air, where his guilt could breathe.

While he polished the parlor mirror, Teenotchy vaguely recalled the time in September '99 Mister Kleber had carried him through the front door, with his milk teeth still chattering from his trauma in the woods.

"One blanket not warm enough?" Mister Kleber had asked, grabbing a folded shawl from the back of Hans's rocker. "Thee will thaw out soon enough with a pitcher of hot chocolate and a cinnamon bun," Mister Kleber'd said to Teenotchy, still in his arms.

"A few nights in the woods never hurt anybody," greeted Helga, as Hans smiled and said, "Why did thy mother leave thee?"

Though it wasn't likely Hans would get an answer, Mister Kleber'd whisked Teenotchy upstairs. Taking two steps at a time, the old man whispered, "Thee must never, never tell why thy mama was in the woods. Does thee promise?" He waited for the frightened child in his arms to nod. "Otherwise everyone will say she was evil . . . and evil girls burn in Hell." Slipping a peppermint between the boy's quivering lips, Mister Kleber wiped away Teenotchy's tears.

After tucking him in the guest room, Paul Kleber tiptoed away once the five-year-old fell into a heavy sleep. So Teenotchy woke, forgetting why he was flanked by the maple bedroom furniture he'd seen his mother polish only the Saturday before. He was petrified.

Used to the converted stable, noisy with life, he needed to hear dragging feet, his baby sister's utterings, the rub-a-dub of wet clothes slapped against the washboard, his mother's hum.

But from the Klebers' window that afternoon his little gray eyes watched grayer clouds speed by. The sky looked like it would never be blue again, and only a silly bunny stood huddled among the leaves and grass while thunder promised a storm.

Alone, Teenotchy'd waited, afraid to move left or right; he picked bits of crispy leaf from his matted curls, looking over his shoulder from time to time to study the three peppermints Mister Kleber'd left for him at the foot of the bed.

"Sister" had to say he could have them.

Shocked beyond tears, he needed a brown voice from the other side of town to explain how to get to tomorrow.

And he wondered about his mother. Had she told him to watch out for the boogeyman, knowing she was it?

Each time it thundered, that September evening quaked, but he kept his face pressed to the Klebers' window while a six o'clock torrent ripped the heads from the dahlias and forced the trees to dance obscenely, shedding leaves like snowflakes.

Being too little to call out, "Help me, God," like grown-ups in distress, Teenotchy finally cried, "Mister Paul, Mister Paul."

That Christmas, before the century turned, Mister Kleber bought Teenotchy a bristle brush. So the child imagined him to be the kindest man in the world, especially as Helga Kleber had scolded, "I'll feed you and teach you your alphabet, but I'll never touch your nasty hair."

Not even Mister Kleber could pretend, after Teenotchy's months with them, that there was any choice but to crop his nest of tangles. "Does thee think thy mother will forgive me if I cut thy hair?" asked Mister Kleber, sure Dusty's spirit was at her son's side.

"Hey, Geronimo!" Teenotchy called when he stepped outside the Klebers' side gate. He'd been rescuing lame birds since he could catch them, although he didn't consciously put Geronimo in that category.

The Indian had appeared after President Wilson's January inauguration ceremony, when the town's festivities drew strangers and stragglers from the countryside. Others went back to where they'd come from but, two days later, with snow falling, the Indian was still sitting amid the heap of flags and confetti outside the general store.

Teenotchy reported the homeless man to Miss Sullivan, an eighty-year-old spinster he chopped wood for, because she collected strays. Poor herself, she could offer only a bed in her one-room cabin west of Main Street. As the snow mounted, she insisted, "Somebody must need my spare bed. A good deed'll help me get to Heaven." Her age preoccupied her with the afterlife, although she managed to get to walk into town every month the weather allowed.

"Colored or not," Aunt Em had warned Teenotchy, "that old maid'll get her throat cut and they'll be looking for you." She refused to bet him a nickel that the dewy-eyed Indian was harmless.

But Miss Sullivan was eager. "I used to know a squaw when I lived in Oklahoma. The people I worked for said don't mix with Injuns. But she taught me to bead moccasins." Miss Sullivan had tales for everything, which was why Teenotchy liked to drop in on her.

Her bony elbow nudged Teenotchy when he brought the Indian for inspection. "He's handsome. But you know I love a chat. Seems he won't be good for that," she confided, because the Indian answered, "My country 'tis of thee," to all her questions.

But her heart found things to praise after she'd rescued him. "He's not wasteful. Won't let me throw away old matchsticks nor the last teency bit of candlewick. And that hair reaches his waist!"

He genuinely didn't know his name, tribe or age. "Could be Iroquois, Seneca or Algonquin," she guessed, grunting, "Ganono-o! Ganono-o! That's Algonquin for New York."

His blank smile assured her. "Can't be Algonquin," she'd said.

When a nail-biting census taker came with his sheet of questions that first week, she'd put him straight.

"My son? This boy's not colored and I'm a virgin."

"We can accept unnamed babies," the civil servant stuttered. "But not adult males."

So Miss Sullivan came up with "Geronimo" on the spot, taking the Indian's sudden smile as approval.

Though Geronimo accepted her offer to sit in her rocker from time to time, he refused the spare cot and slept in a corner, which is why Miss Sullivan brought a mute home from Main Street one Sunday.

"I've nicknamed the deaf man Chopper," she told Teenotchy beside a huge woodpile when he'd arrived to check her supply. "That one cuts down sycamore like it's pine. And long as they clean their own mess and don't expect me to cook, they can both stay. But so much company and nobody to chat with I take as a sign God's about to call me yonder."

With Mister Kleber bedridden, Teenotchy was glad for some place to go and hated Aunt Em calling Miss Sullivan's "the old maid's shack." The one-room cabin felt more like home than his own.

Although she'd long since burned the old pear tree for firewood, Miss Sullivan referred to her place as Pear Tree Lodge. But when Teenotchy carved her a sign bearing that name, she cried like a baby; like she did when he'd potted some red, white and blue anemones for her for the Fourth of July.

He openly spent Saturday afternoons with Geronimo, though Atlanta was mortified. "No wonder you don't have any friends! I'd rather be by myself than hang around with a halfwit." She was setting her hair in rags while she kept on at him. "Beulah told me she saw you plain as day walking down Main Street with an Indian. And right off, I knew who she was talking about since no other Indians would be mixing with you."

"You're supposed to be such a big Christian!" he'd said.

"Brotherly love is one thing," Atlanta retorted. "But the Bible doesn't say a thing about being friends! Beulah told me one time he followed her all down School Lane, farting and blowing a penny whistle."

Even Miss Sullivan complained about the Indian's lack of intelligence, although she didn't like anybody else to. It riled her every time Geronimo came back with head gashes from local roughs stoning him. "What he needs is a tommie-hawk," she'd say.

In time she'd made him presentable, with Teenotchy and Chopper's help, but Teenotchy identified the greater problem. "He doesn't look American enough. Maybe if we cut his hair, Ned Cleary's gang'll stop throwing bricks at him."

The ten or so young toughs met by Old Race and Floodgate, where they hung a skull and crossbones sign that had KILL KIKES, KOONS AND KATHOLICS printed neatly underneath.

Geronimo's black braids were obviously inside his shirt when he rushed up to meet Teenotchy at the Klebers' side gate that Saturday. "Hey!" Teenotchy's quick smile to his slow grin got to the point. "Suppose we just cut it to your shoulder. Betcha nickel Ned and them'll . . ."

Furiously shaking his head, tears welled in Geronimo's eyes.

"OK. It's OK," Teenotchy calmed him. "But it's gonna be your funeral."

A tear rolled down Geronimo's smooth cheek.

"You act like I've got the scissors on me," Teenotchy consoled, deciding to forgo a walk to town since Ned's gang hung about in Market Square at lunchtime. "Help me pick Miss Sullivan some daisies and we'll take them straight to her."

"Miss Naomi! Miss Naomi!" Geronimo repeated ten times before Teenotchy made him stop.

"All right, Miss Naomi." That Teenotchy had a different name for her agitated him, but Teenotchy thought it disrespectful to call her by her first name, even though she'd suggested it.

"You're like family," she'd said and, in time, he trusted her fantastic tales of pioneering with the Hochfield family. It was for her he'd kept an eye out for Geronimo in the beginning. But that responsibility is a two-sided addiction; both protector and protected get hooked.

"The youngest Hochfield was a simpleton like Geronimo," Miss Sullivan once explained. "And just as sweet-
natured. But with seventeen kids, nobody expects every one
to be right. That slow child was more work than all the rest
put together. But like their granddaddy said . . ." Her facts
were always tangential, and she was incapable of finishing
the main story.

Her tales of Utah were the highlight of Teenotchy's
week and he didn't dare guess which part was fabricated.
Though he noticed details changed: "Seventeen children and
the grandaddy more work than all of them. Real ornery he
could get, being from upstate New York. Fought Algonquins
in Schenectady and *shot* two redcoats in the Revolution," she
said as though she'd held the musket herself.

"It was him taught me how to read and write, old Mister
Hochfield," she'd mused. "He always said, 'Naomi, life's not
worth a broken bottle without poetry. So that's what you best
set your mind to.' Young and silly as I was, I didn't know
colored girls weren't supposed to write poetry, so I started
keeping my little notebook."

For all the time he spent cultivating his patch and Blossom and Mister Kleber's garden, Teenotchy still devoted the
odd hour to planting vegetables at Pear Tree Lodge, because
there were a lot of mouths to feed. He and the silent Chopper could often be seen digging back to back, with Geronimo
running between them during that spring of 1913.

VIII

Atlanta's whole week would have been ruined if she'd seen Teenotchy and Geronimo headed across Carpenter's Meadow for Pear Tree Lodge that afternoon. But she was on Main Street, having finished her work at Holybrook Manor while a gang of brown-skinned yardmen trundled the Tewksburys' grounds, their efforts sabotaged by the sun.

Cool at her desk with the overhead fan turning, Julia was contentedly making place cards for dinner. She didn't need to look up from her red-ink design when Alexander's rap opened her study door. "Boston cream pie's not on to-night's menu. Does that mean you won't be joining us for dinner?"

Her sarcasm didn't sting.

"Possibly." He smiled, while his aunt's spaniels wriggled in his arms. He was being eyed by one and licked by the other. "Either Georgia or Laura just disgraced herself on that Turkish carpet in my room. But I'm not sure which to smack."

"Don't you dare lay a finger on my darling girls," Julia warned. "Anyway, it serves you right for trekking off to Valley Forge when Buppy Phillips is bringing Wilhelmina for dinner."

"I danced with Wilhelmina at a New Year's ball two years ago and, though I'd cross the Yorkshire Dales for Ruth's pie, I wouldn't cross the Thames for Wilhelmina. She's dull."

"She's a princess."

"A likely excuse!"

Alexander's slight opened another of Julia's wounds.

"And refusing to join Jonas for lunch . . ." she began.

"So did you!"

"I don't like roast pork." Julia couldn't decide whether she liked her nephew either, but she actually envied his directness when nothing was at stake.

"Anyway," Alexander said, "last week's skirmish will hold me for a while."

"Jonas isn't grudge-bearing," Julia said, implying Alexander had been at fault at the Buttonwood.

"I couldn't possibly eat a full lunch in this weather and appreciate dinner tonight."

Julia passed him a small place card. "Proof that I had faith you wouldn't let me down."

"I love your calligraphy," he said, admiring the curlicues surrounding "Viscount Blake." "But . . ."

"No buts. It's taken time to make that."

He stuck the card in his vest pocket. "Just Alexander Blake will do on mine, please."

"I can't overlook your title and present Buppy's and Wilhelmina's."

"And what about yours?"

"I've been Mrs. Jonas Tewksbury for five years."

"Either your American friends treat titles as God-given or want to tiff about the monarchy. As if I care."

His aunt's genius was avoiding arguments. "We'll be ten

tonight. You've met everyone apart from Cornelius and William Cranford and their cousin, what's-her-name." Julia checked her guest list.

Alexander dropped onto a chair. "Another matchmake?" He sounded hard done by.

"Mrs. Orestes Adams is Jonas's age and my apologies for having only one young person, but Colonel Fullerton's grandson had to cancel," sighed Julia.

"Will the Colonel bring his granddaughter?"

She responded to his beaten tone. "Melanie Fullerton's not only beautiful and from a wonderful family, she's a sculptress." Alexander looked so unimpressed, Julia tried spice. "Dare I say she's taken a fancy to you?"

"I can guess exactly what Mother said in her letter." His outstretched hand was a demand. "I saw you lock it in one of those drawers last week."

"Had Irene meant it for you, she wouldn't have addressed it to me."

Julia couldn't understand why he refused to talk about his future as a husband and father and assumed it had to do with his youth.

"Do you want to know the seating arrangements?"

"As long as Melanie Fullerton's not on my lap, I'll be happy anywhere."

As they laughed, it was obvious they had nothing in common except the charm and charity of inherited wealth. She found him hard to read.

"You're at the opposite end from Jonas." Alexander's indifference made her cheeks pink. "I know Jonas should be kinder to the servants."

"Don't say it," Alexander injected. "But Jonas *is* a patron of the arts and built an old soldiers' home in Nagansett."

"You don't sound a bit like me!"

However, his mimicry was quite good, so Alexander carried on, "And *you* haven't seen him waltz."

"Well, you haven't seen him waltz."

"Surely you didn't marry for ballroom graces?" he said.

It wasn't the first time someone made her feel she had to explain her marriage. But few women admit to marrying money, so Julia claimed love at first sight.

"Love at first sight," she reiterated to his frown. "And Jonas was lighthearted in Kentucky with his racing chums."

"Speaking of racing . . ." Alexander leapt at her opening. "I was wondering if we couldn't organize a small charity race."

Julia found the idea so unlikely, she went back to making place cards. "Jonas is reluctant. The locals aren't at all sporty."

"I'll do everything. And cover costs. You two can sit back and have a laugh."

Julia took a deep breath. "You're just trying to be nice because you've heard we're canceling the Emancipation Day picnic. But it wasn't only Jonas. Some of the other ladies' husbands were livid too."

Alexander had overheard his uncle refuse her charity a contribution. "After Uncle Jonas and I had lunch at the Buttonwood last week, we saw a crowd of children gathered around your poster in Market Square." He didn't mention her husband's performance. Julia's long sigh was defeatist. "You're wearing Grandfather's expression when he's about to spoil one of Mother's social plans," he told her.

"Could the race coincide with Thanksgiving?" she put forward weakly.

"I'll be gone by then. Jacques expects me back for the start of the hunting season."

"He used to be the image of his father," Julia said, glad for any excuse to avoid talk of a race.

Jacques remained a family sore point, and her drooping inflection made Alexander defensive. "No one I know does as many things as well as he does. And I don't know why everybody's made such a fuss of his returning to France with Uncle Pierre after Henrietta drowned."

As estranged as Julia remained from her family, she'd
maintained, like they did, that her deceased sister's son was
as much family property as her father's country seat. But she
knew better than to voice this with Alexander ready to argue
the point. "What would've been gained by Uncle Pierre mop-
ing on about Henrietta like the rest of you?"

"Her grave was still fresh when Pierre married that tawdry Parisian girl!"

"You sound like Grandfather," her nephew reported.

"It's bad enough that I look like him." Julia's face creased
with laughter, which made Alexander giggle too. "Dinner'll
be the best time to propose that race of yours," she went on.
"Jonas'll be much more likely to agree if you suggest it with
Wilhelmina next to him."

The feast over at Miss Sullivan's later that same afternoon
was bean and tomato stew, and all the wild berries Teenotchy
and Geronimo had picked crossing Carpenter's Meadow.

Miss Sullivan's digestion required meals by five, so before
the light changed Teenotchy had cleared away the bowls and
settled on the cabin step, hoping to hear one of her tales of
Utah.

While Geronimo circled the small yard, collecting peb-
bles to bestow on Teenotchy, Miss Sullivan said, "I didn't
expect to have that Injun a week and it's coming two years."
Teenotchy smiled at the plain rock Geronimo handed him.
"What'll happen to him and poor Chopper when I go?" she
asked.

Teenotchy refused to think about it, though Chopper
made a few cents sweeping the saloon and might have managed. "Aw, Miss Sullivan, you'll outlive us all."

"You know better. Come Monday I want you by first
thing to take the deeds for this place to the bank."

"You think somebody'll steal them?" he wondered. She'd
long trusted them under her mattress.

"Course not. I haven' stole from anybody, so how could

anybody steal from me." But she had another purpose. "Chopper's not here as much as Geronimo, but if I leave the Lodge in both their names, he might stick around. At least they'd have each other."

Teenotchy saw death as ugly and brushed aside Miss Sullivan's preparations.

"God's up there all right," she asserted. "That's him cooking when you smell the evening's air. I can't wait to find out what he puts in that pot. Bet my appetite'll pick up." Her talk of Heaven had been angled that afternoon to ask, "Teenotchy, you want me to say something to your mama when I get up there?"

"No, ma'am." He reached in his pocket for his harmonica and hid behind its lonely whine.

"Lord, that's so pretty it's pitiful."

When he'd finished he said, "My mother ... used to hum it all the time."

Miss Sullivan wasn't self-serving enough to know how to nose in other people's business. She rarely got answers about Teenotchy's family, although he talked about Atlanta occasionally.

With Miss Sullivan's gentle questions he could pretend her place was the world and, neither pining for the past nor worrying about the future, he found peace abundant there, like that Saturday.

IX

While Teenotchy entertained Miss Sullivan on his harmonica, at Holybrook Manor the Tewksburys' dinner guests
nibbled duck in orange sauce while Jonas gnawed fried
chicken gizzards and addressed his nephew. "I've owned
'em all shapes and colors and you can't trust light-eyed
nigras to act right."

Having said nigras instead of niggers, he anticipated Alexander's best behavior.

"Act right?" Alexander was puzzled.

"Know their place." Melanie Fullerton tee-heed beside
him, as if he was being intentionally witless.

"Son," chomped Jonas, "as you get older, you'll learn a
man's soul is in his eyes." He leaned over and poked the
princess to get her full attention before he paraphrased.
"Eyes are the soul's corral, you might say."

"Exquisitely put," hailed Mrs. Orestes Adams, who'd established before dinner that she grinned too much and agreed too often.

"It's different for the blind, of course," Mister Tewksbury philosophized. "Nature having spread their soul to the fingertips. I saw that when I visited their school by the turnpike."

"Jonas donated a Braille printer there," announced William Cranford. The Tewksburys were the largest depositors with his family's bank, so the banker was always armed with Jonas's footnotes.

"Mister Tewksbury's so generous—a rarity these days," Mrs. Adams confided loudly to Buppy Phillips, hoping all could hear.

When Julia noticed Alexander gritting his teeth, she turned the conversation back to the race he was scheming. "But Jonas dear, if Alexander wants the new stable boy to ride for him . . ."

Jonas Tewksbury believed a wife's opinion should mirror her husband's and doubly so with cronies present. "I've agreed to this race," he informed William Cranford specifically, "and no gray-eyed nigras will ride for my family."

Ezekiel, elegant in tails, his ebony cheekbones accentuated by his white sideboards, bowed before offering Mister Tewksbury more champagne.

Reference to those serving cleared the way for Princess Wilhelmina to mention what'd been on her mind throughout the soup course. "Did anyone see Nijinsky dance the Silver Negro? In the Ballets Russes's *Scheherazade*? It was ages ago, but unforgettable."

Assisting Ezekiel and Ruth was Julia's maid, Marie Annette, and her daughter Candy. The quartet looked as striking as the guests because that evening Julia had the three ladies serving in long black linen dresses with white organdy smocks to match their frilly caps. Gliding from guest to guest, bearing platters and plastered smiles, their silent performance was as mesmerizing as any corps de ballet's.

But it agitated Julia each time the winsome, brown-eyed Candy offered Alexander anything. Suspicious that the sixteen-year-old was vying for his attention, the hostess finally snapped, "Child! There's no need to disturb Lord Blake again." Julia was equally annoyed with herself for not telling Ezekiel that Candy wasn't to serve because Melanie wasn't to be outshined.

Not that the Cranford brothers minded. They were only too happy to have the long-haired Candy beautify the party. Although he reserved his compliments for the ladies seated, Cornelius Cranford got gummy when Candy came around a second time with the rolls. He managed to brush her behind twice as she curtsied and the indiscretion was harder on Marie Annette than her fourteen-hour workday.

Alexander missed her flinch. He was too busy stretching his ear to catch the conversation between his uncle and William Cranford.

"They were supposed to be exported to South America," he heard Jonas say.

"No, William," interrupted Cornelius to steal away from Mrs. Adams's chatter about the poor quality of American lace. "Weren't they shipping them back to Africa?"

William shook his balding head. "Unlikely, Corny. Think of the extra cost." Only twins could have resembled each other more than the bleak, willowy Cranfords. Even their Virginian accents were softened to identical lilts after half their sixty years had been spent among Philadelphia's high society. But, nursed on mammy's milk, they remained pro-slavery.

With no husband to mouth her defense, their Bostonian cousin pretended not to hear their slights against Yankees. Smiling coquettishly, Mrs. Adams swallowed hard and wondered why Colonel Fullerton was so quiet.

He declined more of the orange sauce offered by Ruth. "We lost two billion freeing slaves." His "we" referred to the South.

"I get indigestion just thinking about it," added Cornelius.

"Speaking of wars," smiled Lady Phillips, as bored with the conversation as Princess Wilhelmina opposite, "your mother tells me you're interested in my grandfather's role in the Revolution, Alexander."

A matron who refused to leave the mirror until it said "too much powder, too many curls," Buppy Phillips was a gawdy addition at the table, but Julia welcomed the sound of her soup slurping because everyone important in Philadelphia called Lady Phillips a friend.

"Surely enough's been written about the Revolution," said William Cranford.

"The seedier motives are what I'm investigating," admitted Alexander.

"A bit of a sleuth!" joined Melanie.

"My cousin Jacques and I have a joint thesis planned. He'll cover the conflict from the French point of view."

Jonas had to get in on the act. He recited, " 'We hold these truths to be self-evident . . . that all men are created equal.' "

"When I was about ten I knew the whole Declaration," Melanie announced. Her cameo earrings and brooch were slightly paler than the ochre of her evening dress, and their engraved silhouettes might have been her own.

"How's that bust you've been sculpting?" Julia asked her, determined to remind Alexander that there was more to Melanie than a delicate face framed by platinum curls.

"There'll be an unveiling soon," said Colonel Fullerton.

But Melanie was more interested in Alexander's career. "How do you find time for all those history books Mrs. Tewksbury says you brought?"

"He reads too much," chimed in Jonas, playing up his uncle image. "Boys his age need the great outdoors . . . and an affair of the heart." He winked at Princess Wilhelmina, oblivious to the fact that his familiarity vexed her.

"I love reading," pursued Melanie. "What's your favorite novel, Lord Blake?"

"Uncle Tom's Cabin," answered Alexander without blinking.

Ezekiel cleared his throat and Marie Annette rescued the moment by rushing around with the platter of duck.

Melanie wasn't to be put off. "My grandfather must take you to Valley Forge."

"Not a shot fired, of course," the colonel told Julia, relieved to be back on a war that his side had won. "Three thousand Americans died for freedom."

Cornelius, a Civil War veteran, said, "Despair was the terrible tragedy there. Like we suffered at the Battle of Wilderness." He was a warehouse of Confederate war stories and his jaw was set to tell one when Lady Phillips yawned. She was already regretting the dinner and the seven-mile journey back to Philadelphia's Rittenhouse Square. She toyed with the three medicine bottles she'd brought to the table, determined that Ezekiel shouldn't open them. "There's a spell inside which only I must release," she explained to Jonas. "Not that I *believe* in such things. But mumbo jumbo is adorable. Two drops have to be stirred eight times and one mustn't miscount."

"What's that one for, Buppy dear?" asked Princess Wilhelmina, pointing to the brown bottle she knew was supposed to remove the large mole on Lady Phillips's chin.

"Wilhelmina, please!" Lady Phillips made a production of preparing the first potion and downing it in a noisy glug. "So sorry, Mister Fuller," she beamed at Colonel Fullerton. "What were you about to tell us?"

Only a mosquito on the chandelier benefited from the aerial view of the servants' ballet and the Tewksburys' dinner play performed simultaneously in the dining room.

Ezekiel's burlesque bows protected his lean pay and senior status in the kitchen. But his smile was less forced than Marie Annette's.

In her prime her step had been as light as Candy's, but years of demoralizing domestic work had hardened her heart to a Brazil nut. She knew that the men with pink lips encrusted with coffee and after-dinner cigars could steal her daughter's kisses. Anticipating Cornelius's lewd whispers at the back door made Marie Annette lumber to the kitchen like a ballerina in leg irons.

"Marie Annette, bring more duck for Mister Cranford," Julia ordered.

With a curtsy, the highly strung maid shuffled to the kitchen, cursing, "Heifer," under her breath.

From year to year, for Ruth's ears only, Marie Annette had charged, "Miz Julia likes to play blind. But she see what them mens get up to." For all her tough talk, fear pulled down the corners of her mouth. Marie Annette was a leaf quivering in a night wind, the branch she clung to being the Tewksbury job. She'd been employed for fifteen years by Jonas Tewksbury, giving him after-hour performances for that extra dollar when Candy was knee high. But he never knew how close to madness her humiliation brought her or how often she'd murdered him in her sleep.

The ten at the table were a sorry blend. Conversation was haphazard, so Melanie, schooled in rescuing dinner parties, made an extra effort. "I'll be taking the train to New York on Monday. I wasn't actually looking forward to it but now I'm going to order a dress there for this wonderful race of yours."

"I hope, Julia," interrupted Buppy, "you have better luck than we did at Epsom in June when that foolish Emily Davison threw herself under the King's poor horse and got herself killed."

"Fool women, messing in politics!" barked Jonas.

Mrs. Orestes Adams, in favor of the women's suffrage campaign and opposed to racing, voiced neither view and kept smiling.

The rhythm of the evening had never settled and Julia asked that dessert be brought in, knowing it to be her trump card.

As Jonas dipped his fingers into the finger bowl, introduced by Julia after she discovered he always ate greasy fowl with his fingers, he realized she hadn't smiled at him. Not once since he'd refused to allow Alexander to use the new stable boy as a jockey in the race. Flattery was his only option.

"I must say, Julia, you're looking ravishing this evening," he told her.

"Truly," agreed Mrs. Adams. Proud of the Calvinist sensibilities passed to her from her grandfather, she was relieved that Julia was covered from head to toe in a dark beige silk, as opposed to Princess Wilhelmina, who was in a black low-necked dress too daringly Parisian for Germantown.

After four glasses of champagne, the princess's charm was thinning. Like Buppy, she was more accustomed to a dinner dance with a monarch or two on the prowl. Lady Phillips normally introduced her to fabulously rich, flamboyant Americans and she felt her friend had failed her on this particular evening.

"Tell me more about Valley Forge," she asked Colonel Fullerton, to avoid the lull in the conversation which could prompt another invitation to the race from Julia.

Ezekiel approached Jonas with a silver plate of pickled pigs' feet, but Jonas waved him off, beckoning Candy. "A neck and the parson's ass," he whispered. He couldn't understand why his tastes (which had been his mammy's) distressed his wife, but Julia was convinced that his favorite after-dinner savories, chitlins or pickled pigs' feet, made him snore.

When Lady Phillips marveled at the first bite of Ruth's lemon meringue pie, Julia blushed like she'd baked it herself.

Alexander was all the dessert Melanie wanted.

"When you fall in love . . ." she began.

He wanted his aunt to hear. "I don't plan to."

"You'll have to produce an heir," Julia said matter of factly.

"Heritage is everything," contended Buppy Phillips, since her ancestry, traceable to the thirteenth century, was the basis for her claim to wealth and fame.

"Even the Bible fusses about bloodlines," said Mrs. Orestes Adams.

The group hadn't been in such agreement all evening. But against Alexander they could unify.

"Well, however you came by your title, Lord Blake, not many are born to your privilege," winked Colonel Fullerton as though he could already see a great-grandson with Melanie's blue eyes bearing Alexander's title.

"No," Jonas laughed. "Our dear nephew won't be driving an omnibus." He insisted Princess Wilhelmina try a gizzard.

Before anybody else could interject, Cornelius Cranford said, "Passion lures us all on hot nights. Once I fell in love in Polynesia ... those native women ..." But that was as much as he could get out before Julia stopped him.

"Cornelius dear," she said, with Candy flooding her mind as the girl approached, "you haven't touched your tart."

"There's also a tart?" Lady Phillips asked greedily, still swallowing pie.

At that moment, the mosquito on the chandelier, wanting the bluest blood that clammy night, sniffed everyone in the dining room before biting the red-headed Ruth. Born on one of Virginia's grandest plantations, she served wearing gloves so the brand on the back of her hand wouldn't offend appetites. The mosquito didn't care why Irish blue blood was in her veins. It was just happy for the bite.

An evening of toing and froing had loosened Candy's braid to a fetching angle and, as she passed him, her uniform looking like a ball gown, Cornelius Cranford's sigh had more to do with her than his forkful of meringue.

His brother, who also had a penchant for Tahitians, had an equal lust for Candy's intercontinental blend. He smiled anxiously as she served Mister Tewksbury and, overcome by desire, William Cranford, the image of gentility, squeezed her backside. Her pale complexion reddened, but she curtsied and smiled.

Her mother, at attention by the kitchen door, spotted what Alexander saw, Cornelius envied and Ezekiel expected.

A stranger to the rules of this parlor game, Alexander squawked, "Mister Cranford!"

That instant, his aunt's satin slipper jabbed him hard on the shin. Nobody could miss his venomous look as he rose. "Please excuse me. I've a slight headache," he announced, throwing down his napkin and omitting to bow to the ladies.

"How long's Alexander been with you?" Lady Phillips asked as he stalked out.

"Two weeks," sighed Julia, rising to follow him.

"You didn't see what he did," said Alexander.

Julia's color rose. "Candy's used to it."

"You would have slapped his face."

"Air will make you feel better," she said.

"Humidity's not the issue," he fumed.

"We'll be having coffee in the conservatory, Alexander."

While Melanie attempted Beethoven on Jonas's baby grand a rift also opened in the kitchen between Ezekiel and Marie Annette.

"Lickin' their behinds is part of the job," sniped Ezekiel. "And after all these years I'm sick of the smell, same as you, but that don't give you rights to bring your sass in my kitchen."

Marie Annette rumbled on. "If I'd of had me a knife, I'd of rammed it straight in his gut."

"Keep your voice down!" Ezekiel ordered.

"Let the so-and-so hear," challenged Marie Annette, knowing she jeopardized her job.

"Momma," began Candy, afraid for her mother to start trouble that could land them both in the street. "It's OK."

"Sure it is," Ezekiel agreed.

Ruth hummed and ran champagne glasses under the tap.

"That wasn't your baby he was putting his hands on," said Marie Annette.

"Candy ain't no baby. Nor did the man tar and feather her, nor hang her from a tree."

"Uncle Tom!" Marie Annette hissed, her nerves rattled with rage.

"This job keeps me and Ruthie, and put two of our nephews through Howard. So they can call me Uncle Tom. I do what I got to do to get by." He picked up the tray of chocolates and petits fours and repainted his smile. "Bring the coffee, Candy," he ordered, heading for the conservatory as Jonas played the crescendo of "Ich Scheibe."

"Darling, that was divine," clapped Julia. "Liszt is so dark and complex. It always reminds me of waterfalls."

"Truly remarkable," lauded Mrs. Orestes Adams.

"Calm down, dear," Princess Wilhelmina said under her breath. "He didn't compose it, and we all play dots."

William Cranford, seated on the other side of the princess, declined the petits fours which Ezekiel served gracefully from one to the next.

"Mister Cranford, how can you be so controlled? I could never pass up one of Mrs. Tewksbury's petits fours. They're renowned in Germantown," said Melanie, nibbling the glacé cherry off hers.

Buppy belched. *"Pardonnez-moi,"* she said, fanning with a vengeance. She leaned over to whisper to the princess, "Eleanor Dewhurst has her servants give a little performance at the end of her soirées. I must mention it to Julia for next time, because it's a waste just having their coloreds serve when they all sing. Not that Jonas doesn't play well. But these Colonials . . . one can't expect them to have an ear for concert standard."

X

Almost eight p.m. and it was still so hot, Ezekiel armed himself with smelling salts in case one of the Tewksburys' guests fainted, because Mister Tewksbury's first wife had always made him do that. But even Mrs. Orestes Adams, strapped into the tightest corset, held her own with the others in the conservatory. Meanwhile, out on the veranda, Alexander paced like a panther. The heat and a battalion of gnats didn't help his temper. It still throbbed over the Candy incident.

As restless as townsfolk roaming the streets in search of a breeze, Alexander saddled his gray for a ride to the square before the gaslighter started his rounds.

In his dinner jacket, he was galloping toward Main Street as Teenotchy trudged across Carpenter's Meadow from Miss Sullivan's, with his glasses in his overall pocket and his shoes in his hand. Coincidence tugged them to meet at a quarter past nine.

Teenotchy was sorry he hadn't accepted Miss Sullivan's invitation to camp in her yard. But no sorrier than Geronimo. "But if you come home with me," Teenotchy told him, "who's gonna keep an eye on Chopper?" adding, "My sister worries if I'm not back right after dark."

Alexander nearly caused an accident cutting past a Model "T" Ford when he spotted Teenotchy crossing Main Street at Coulter Street.

"No-account saddle tramp," a trolley-car conductor yelled when Alexander overtook it. Not that he heard. He was remembering his grandmother's words, when he'd returned home aged eight, having been quarantined with diphtheria. "I have the most splendid book to read to you, called *Uncle Tom's Cabin*. There are lots of wonderful friends inside just waiting for you to get settled in your bed so that they can meet you. I'll be up as soon as nurse has tucked you in."

Teenotchy recognized the horse kicking up dust and timidly acknowledged Alexander, who shouted above the evening traffic, "Where're you headed? I'll give you a ride."

With no cap to tip, shoes to scuff or glasses to fiddle, Teenotchy cowered on the busy street corner.

Alexander offered his hand for a boost. "Entelechy won't mind," he said of his horse. "She's used to Edison and I bet he weighs more than both of us combined."

Home was the last place Teenotchy wanted a lift to. He pictured old Miz Brandauer's snuggies on the line, or a row of Helga Kleber's stockings. Or, worse, Aunt Em guzzling bread pudding on the stoop.

He could never have guessed that in Alexander's daydreams since he'd seen him ride General Lee they'd already schoonered the high seas, trampled the Yorkshire Dales, won the Derby, cruised from Bangkok to Tobago, dined on blintzes in St. Petersburg and chop suey in Hong Kong, cavorting like truants. Not that Alexander'd believed it possible until that moment he looked into Teenotchy's eyes and said,

"You'll have to hold on tight. But what we really need is a bicycle built for two."

Teenotchy was longing to clean his cruddy feet, thinking about Atlanta's scorn for "countrified niggers barefoot on Main."

After enduring fourteen lonesome days on a ship and two weeks of the Tewksburys, Alexander wanted to believe he'd found a kindred spirit. "Fancy a drink?" he asked, stopping outside the Buttonwood. "There's a niceish room at the back."

Teenotchy had swept the Gambicinis' sidewalk on odd occasions. "Mister Alexander, sir . . . coloreds can't . . . aren't . . ."

"Ridiculous!" Alexander flared up, the Candy episode still irritating him. "When we get to England . . ." The slip exposed his powerful imagination playing leap-frog with Teenotchy's future. Not that Teenotchy noticed. "What I mean is," Alexander corrected himself, "if this were England . . ." But knowing it would've been the same, he didn't bother to finish. "Shall we sit on the bench opposite the Civil War Monument?"

As his horse clomped west on Main Street, Alexander felt the loneliness that burdened him most of his life slip away. But Teenotchy was scared to breathe. Walking barefoot on broken glass would have been less risky since he associated "Mister" Alexander with Jonas C. Tewksbury. "Watch ol' man Tewks," Edison had warned him. "I'd swear he's in the KKK."

One after another gaslights flickered on, highlighting Market Square. It was always mucky by Saturday night, but Teenotchy'd never known it smell so bad.

"Somebody's peed down the Gettysburg Address," announced Alexander, tying up his horse. The stench reminded Teenotchy how badly he had to go himself. Although with Dusty Simms's home training he could control his bladder till midnight at least.

Alexander caught a June bug. "Make a wish," he said, before making his own. He closed his eyes and prayed, "Hope Jacques likes him too," because his cousin's likes affected his own.

But Teenotchy's wish was to know what was going on, until the lightning bug flew off and he decided all he wanted was to get home alive.

Sensing his fear and embarrassment Alexander kicked off his own shoes, stuffed his silk socks in his pocket and sighed, "That's better." Teenotchy's mouth fell open. "Shoes are ludicrous in this heat, don't you think?" asked Alexander, wriggling his toes.

Teenotchy tried to smile in agreement, wondering what ludicrous meant. But since "speak when spoken to" had been drilled into him, he asked nothing and allowed himself to be interrogated. He genuinely believed he had nothing to tell and little to hide, having blanked the uglier incidents of his life. But he didn't know what to say when Alexander asked why his eyes were gray.

Swatting gnats and mosquitoes, Alexander said, "Didn't Thomas Jefferson have gray eyes? Maybe you're one of his lost descendants."

Teenotchy's burst of laughter was so spontaneous, Alexander laughed too, relieved to see him spark after a tense half hour.

Despite his worldliness, book learning and gracious manner, Alexander's breathless monologue about the Revolution was boring. After an hour enthusing about Benjamin Franklin's role he had Teenotchy off guard and yawning.

"You must be exhausted. Starting at the stables at five and then cleaning for those Quakers."

Teenotchy wondered how he knew and broke into a sweat thinking of stories he'd heard about nigger baiting after midnight. Edison'd said he'd had a friend taken to the southern woods and tracked by dogs in the dark for sport. Teenotchy wanted to escape.

Picking up this anxiety, Alexander said softly, "I just want to be friends," because it was 1913 and unthinkable to say, "Let's run away . . . I'll take care of you."

They were the last to leave the square, and Teenotchy's ears were ringing with tales of Valley Forge and Redcoats and the Battle of Germantown.

"I know an old lady who worked for somebody who fought the Redcoats," Teenotchy said. In the hazy gaslight, his eyes glowed and Alexander would have wanted to kiss them had he known men of honor did such things. But he had to be thankful for smaller mercies: a reason to meet again seemed a great blessing. "Will you introduce me?"

It was close to midnight when Alexander dropped Teenotchy at his dead end. "If next Saturday's no good for Miss Sullivan," Alexander whispered, "any day will do."

Riding back to Holybrook Manor, he could still hear Teenotchy saying, "Mind your head by your uncle's orchards. I noticed a few low branches when I was there this morning."

To Alexander, Lord Blake, that timid warning was as good as a love vow.

It was even hotter the next night, which made Atlanta irritable, although that was no excuse for her saying, "Teenotchy, you can't take that Indian to the Emancipation Parade. If you have to go, take Fanny Witherspoon. She's always been nice to you and she's shorter than Beulah even." Atlanta assumed her brother's height made him girl shy, and even he didn't know that hearing his mother raped had strangled his mating instincts.

Teenotchy never wanted to be kissed.

"Ever since Beulah's older brother got a chauffeuring job and you started working for that Tewksbury woman," he said, "you and her act like you're better than everybody."

"Teenotchy, nobody with sense would be caught dead lining up on Main to watch that pitiful marching band from the Holy See Church hold an Emancipation Day Parade.

They can't even afford instruments or uniforms. Making toot-toot sounds with only a trumpet and a kettle drum." She wound another strip of hair around her paper curler. "Emancipation this, emancipation that, emancipation the other . . ."

Teenotchy pronged her on the back of the head with a dried-up horse chestnut that had been shriveling all summer on the windowsill. "If the Women's Auxiliary was organizing it, you'd probably march down the street in a ball and chain just to please Mrs. Tewksbury."

"I'm not listening," said Atlanta, making a loud noise to drown out his voice. It was times like these he hated having a sister. "Anyway," she went on in a mothering tone, "where did you get to last night? I was worried to death."

"No you weren't. You were snoring when I went to bed." Like his knowledge of German, he'd decided to keep his talk with Alexander to himself.

Atlanta eyed his feet.

"Aw shut up," he said, leaping down the stairs three at a time to avoid a lecture. She was good at smothering his smallest initiatives.

Landing in the kitchen unexpectedly, he didn't give Aunt Em time to swallow the broken cookie she'd stuck in her mouth while she darned one of Helga Kleber's petticoats.

"You know what's happening, don't you?" he said. "Atlanta . . . curling her hair all the time, taking airs. She's gonna try to become a Catholic. You watch. . . . Trying to get her mitts on Fernando Whatcha-ma-call-it."

"*Her*-nando Lopez," Atlanta yelled from upstairs, having heard every word.

"Don't matter if she comes a Jew," Aunt Em said, intending her voice to carry upstairs. "She'll burn in Hell any which-way. And a dollar to a dime, you'll burn right beside her." It always made her angry when she got caught eating, so she took it out on him.

Teenotchy rarely rose to Aunt Em's bait, but he and

Atlanta both knew that to rattle her biscuit tin was the quickest way to rile her.

Aunt Em acted like she didn't hear him doing it.

"What's that I hear y'all talking about emancipation?" It was one of the biggest words she could say and picture and it made her feel their equal. "There's gonna be another one?"

"Seems like we could use it," said Teenotchy, "but I wouldn't hold your breath."

XI

Saturday, August 16, 1913

The following weekend Teenotchy was scrubbing the back wall of Mister Tewksbury's cowshed, wondering if he'd make it to the Klebers' on time. But Edison seemed to have more important issues on his mind.

"Course you ought to be racing Gen'ral," he said. And of course Teenotchy took his suggestion as a compliment. " 'Cause none of them other horses could make Gen'ral's time with you riding him. Not that ol' Tewksbury needs the dollars. And this fuss about that horse being four is foolish. He only has to go round the track five times. I saw you cut loose on him with my own eyes. And think about this here. . . . Say you could get over here every morning at five, even the mornings you're not meant to be here."

Edison fantasized aloud. To Teenotchy it sounded like pie in the sky talk as he dipped his scrub brush, attached to a long handle, in the bucket of water. "Say you could get

Gen'ral on the track for an hour while I held the stopwatch."
His dream aired on until the Tewksburys' tall iron gates
clanked like prison doors.

It was his assistant, whose honey-brown face was an assortment of sags and wrinkles.

"This is Horatio. He's not growing a beard, he just hasn't
shaved for a week," Edison said, introducing Teenotchy.

As old and worn as Horatio looked, the spirit atwinkle in
his jet eyes seemed too juvenile for the hand-rolled cigarette
dangling from his lips. Horatio's right suspender was low-
slung to accommodate the slight hump in his back.

Edison sensed his old friend was on the boil. "Oh-oh,
what's eating at your gut *this* morning?"

"If you had to set up half the night listening to my daddy
groanin' and moanin', you'd be a mad so-and-so too."

"Long as I've known you and Uncle Willy, he's been
keeping you up. So quit raising Cain. Griping won't make
his back better."

"Ain't nothing else to do," said Horatio. One eye closed
as a dovetail of cigarette smoke rose to greet it. "If it was
one of these here animals in as much pain and misery they'd
shoot it."

"Uncle Willy's past ninety," Edison explained to Teenotchy, who was splattering as much water on himself as on the
whitewashed wall.

"Cotton-pickin's what's got Daddy bent up."

"Why you wanna sing that ol' tune?"

"If it ain't sweet notes on my banjo, you ain't got stomach
for it."

Edison changed the subject. "We need four sacks of saw-
dust. Sign for it over to Naumann's."

Horatio eyed Teenotchy. "Can't he git it?"

"I asked you to."

"After thirty-seven years . . ." Horatio stubbed out his
roach.

"Nobody needs a history lesson, 'Ratio, at this hour."

Anger buoyed up Horatio's steps but dragged his spirit in the gravel.

"He stays mad," laughed Edison. "But I couldn't have made it working circus trains if Horatio and Uncle Willy hadn't kept a lookout for me. Get him playing his banjo, and he makes up for a month of all that fussing, he does. I try to tell him, poking his lip out is for rich folks."

"He's old, I guess," said Teenotchy.

"I was thirteen when I teamed up with him thirty-seven years ago. You wouldn't know it now to look at him, but Horatio Finlay was a bad son-of-a-gun riding bareback."

"Rodeo stuff too?"

"Shooooot," grinned Edison. "I've heard white fellas compliment him in *Texas*." He pronounced it like it was Hell. "Honest to God. Look, I'm raising my hand on my six children. . . . I've seen 'em *shake* 'Ratio's hand after seeing him riding a bull. No lie."

"Why'd he come to Germantown?"

"He heard Tewksbury wanted me to keep a' eye on these stables. So Horatio packed his duds and made Uncle Willy come too. We always have been just like kin. But where I got a wife working, Horatio's making it on what ol' Tewksbury gives him. And to tell the truth, if it wasn't for that bit of extra Artema gets cleaning for the butcher's wife, salary and odd cuts of meat . . . if it wasn't for that, I'd probably wake up mad every morning too, Uncle Willy or no Uncle Willy. But 'Ratio's problem is he refuses to take a wife."

"Girls are a pain," said Teenotchy.

"That's what my youngest boy says," laughed Edison. "He's nine. What's your excuse?"

Teenotchy didn't have one, so he was glad that Edison carried on. "My wife's got a cousin in Jersey, got a couple cute little ol' gals I'd bet you like. Good hair. Light-skinned like my wife. Matter of fact, Artema wrote to their mother last night asking 'em to come for the race on the sixth." Edison's excitement about a matchmake grew, but he saw no interest from Teenotchy, who never stopped scrubbing. "You'd like the littlest one. Fourteen I think she is. Thick braids . . ."

Teenotchy forced a smile and a nod, and thought about the ruckus Atlanta made when he admitted to her that he didn't fancy one girl in the whole of Germantown High School. Not that there were many their color to choose from.

He stood back to let Edison examine the wall.

"Throw a little Bon Ami on that corner," Edison said to exercise his authority. Teenotchy thought he was nearly as bad as Helga Kleber for insisting that things be done in a just-so way.

"What'd you want me to do next?" Teenotchy asked.

"You can see as good as me what's got to get done. So go on and do it. I'm heading over to the big house, and, I meant to tell you, Miz Julia's nephew said don't you slip off. He wants to see you."

Teenotchy tried not to look worried.

"What's that face for? You know what they're like," said Edison strolling away. "Act right and everything'll be hunkydory."

While Julia and Atlanta addressed invitations to the race, Mister Tewksbury stormed into his wife's study later that same morning. "Don't let that nephew of yours get ideas that this is his race. He'll have the place overrun with coons, and the only ones I want on my track are Edison and the stable hands."

Atlanta couldn't stop thinking about Mister Tewksbury as she marched home. She stuck pins in his eyeballs; pulled out his teeth with pliers; scalped his wife and made him watch; nailed him to the ground in the midday sun; burned his house to cinders; cut out his tongue. But nothing satisfied her as much as the thought of stabbing him.

She was still fuming when she bumped into Beulah, who was always full of big ideas.

"Atlanta, you can't let fifty dollars slip by you without trying for it. If one of my brothers could ride like yours . . ."

"Even if Teenotchy won it wouldn't be my money."

"Think of all the dimes we've had off him. And you know he'd never ask old man Kleber if he could borrow that horse to be in a race. So if you do, he's sure to let you have a few dollars." Beulah'd learned to connive as the only girl in a family of seven brothers. "Think of the material you could buy for a yellow dress. Think of Hernando's eyes popping out." The girls had been best friends since they were thirteen and, being spoken for herself, Beulah plotted to get Atlanta betrothed. "It's no good going to see the old man empty-handed, either. After missing work this morning, you'd better walk in with something sweet after church."

"What'll I wear?"

"Not that burgundy dress, that's for sure."

"It helped me get the Auxiliary job."

"You can't go begging favors dressed up like somebody who should be handing them out. You look like a Five Hundred in that." She could see Atlanta hadn't got the point. "Girl, look like a beggar . . . wear something nankty."

"Beulah, how'd you get so smart?" marveled Atlanta.

"My mother says make obstacles your stepping stones," laughed Beulah. "Now, let's go shake my peach tree," she said, pulling Atlanta toward her house. "Mister Kleber needs a cobbler."

In her kitchen, Beulah yawned, watching Atlanta roll a crust.

"What about Aunt Em? If I take this home, she'll eat it before I can get to bed," complained Atlanta.

"Well, don't leave it here for my brothers . . ." Beulah's best ideas reeled off the top of her head. "The back steps! Leave it there. Since I'm working tomorrow afternoon, you won't have to knock to collect it."

XII

Sunday, August 17, 1913

The next morning while the chiming Sunday church bells beckoned late parishioners, Atlanta squeezed herself between the wall and bed of the seven-by-seven square she called her room to pull out an old fruit crate. It was covered by a yellowed front page of the *Germantown Courier* and contained all she possessed of her mother.

A brown button-eyed sock-doll named Sukey had guarded Dusty Simms's few belongings, which Atlanta treated as pearls. She rubbed the doll against her chin. "I've got to borrow your bed, Sukey," Atlanta said. That year Teenotchy spent with the Klebers, the crudely made doll had been her sole comfort.

Before Dusty'd set off with Teenotchy that fitful September evening in '99, she'd made a mattress for Sukey from a red and white gingham dress. "Sukey'll rest good on that," Dusty had told her little daughter, folding the dress neatly at the bottom of the box. "Rock her till we get back."

119

Aware that she should've been getting ready for Sunday school as the church bells pealed on, Atlanta couldn't resist fondling her mother's other things: the red velvet pincushion was patchy and hardly the size of an apple, but when Atlanta was little it had seemed as big as a pumpkin; and the felt hat with the pigeon feather her mother'd told her was good enough for a queen. She'd also told her the stained blue ribbon rubbed before midnight made elves sing.

Stroking those few things, Atlanta clutched the checkered gingham dress and rocked herself back to sleep.

Coming in from the yard an hour later, Aunt Em stopped in disbelief when she saw Atlanta ironing that red and white dress.

"Lordy, where'd you find that old rag? Lemme have a see," she said, grabbing at it.

"What for?" Atlanta kept a tight grip, prepared for a struggle.

"I just wanna look at it!" Aunt Em huffed, not letting go.

"Oh, here then!" Atlanta said gracelessly. She had to avoid tearing it since she planned to wear it to ask Mister Kleber to lend Teenotchy Blossom.

Aunt Em held the dress to herself. She was triple its width, though it was practically the right length.

"I just pressed it," said Atlanta. "Don't let it drag the floor." The kitchen was always a lint bed from the laundering.

"You wearing this out in the streets?" Aunt Em asked, wide-eyed with amusement. "Used to be mine."

Atlanta snatched it back. "This was Sister's."

Not wanting to be questioned, Aunt Em shuffled back out to the yard with a few clothes pegs she picked up from the floor.

But Atlanta suspected the old woman lay in wait outside

to gibe her, so, leaving the house, she grabbed her shawl for a camouflage.

The eleven o'clock heat made her outfit all the more outlandish, the dress being inches above the ankle length fashionable.

Heading for Beulah's to collect Mister Kleber's cobbler, Atlanta didn't want to believe that the old gingham, cherished as her mother's, had belonged to the person she most despised.

She felt disinherited, but marched on with purpose.

That red and white dress also preyed on Aunt Em's mind as she plopped herself on the stoop. She distinctly remembered the first time she wore it. It was October 1895 and she had gone to visit her daughter, who'd had to take a job housekeeping for James Van Zandt.

At the time Emma, who'd been free nearly three decades, wore age like the overworked and underfed. She was thin and haggard, her gray hair tied in a gingham square which matched the dress she'd made to see Exodus.

Those three decades after the Civil War had been kinder to James. Having returned from battle with mind and limbs intact, he had married a wealthy war widow who'd died before his twenty-fifth birthday. She left him a substantial farm just a stone's throw outside Deauville, Mississippi, where "Lottie," renaming herself Emma and tacking on Van Zandt, struggled as a lone sharecropper with their timid daughter, Exodus.

But when an extended drought forced the two women to resort to heavy field work at a neighboring farm, Emma decided it was time to call in favors, remembering that James had always promised that when times got good he would make "Lottie" his house nigger and they would eat white turkey meat "all the durn day." Fixed on this memory, she eventually found the courage to don her best headrag and

climb the hill to James's. That place she'd come to idealize
as "the big house."

He hadn't even recognized her, or so he said when he
found her knocking at his back door begging for handouts.
Maybe he didn't want to remember what she'd been to him
as she stood there, looking three times his age, wringing her
hands as his eyes mocked her.

"You done got old and ugly, Mammy," he said, although
he had never called her mammy the whole time she'd been
his hostage. "But," he said, examining Exodus's breasts and
backside, "I can find some use for this wench."

Her mother's zealous protectiveness had made Exodus a
little backward. Slow to talk and slower to face the world,
and there at James's door, though all of twenty-eight, she
had the meek presence of a fifteen-year-old.

But she settled into her father's plantation, happy for
the work and ignorant of who he was to her, while her
mother pined on a little farm outside Deauville, aching for
her daughter's company and living for the rare visits to
James's place. Like that one she'd made that October of
'95, when she approached the steep hill to the Van Zandt
spread with her red gingham dress blowing in the morning
wind.

A little girl, swamped in a man's tattered Confederate
coat, was raking leaves, singing, "Wisht I was in the land of
cotton, look away, look away, Dixie," in a voice as blue as the
Mississippi sky that morning. It made Emma sad to see the
urchin barefoot on the cold dewy grass. Not that Emma was
wearing shoes herself.

"You know where I'll find Exodus?" she asked the child,
eleven at most.

"Don't know no Exodie," the girl answered. Her corn
rows badly needed recombing.

"This still the Van Zandt place?" Emma'd heard even
big farmers had lost their holdings through the drought.

"Yes'm. This Van Zan's, but ain't no Ex-what'ch-ma-name here 'bouts."

"She tall, gray eyes."

"Aw, you meaning Miz Dusty," hooted the girl, like a leg-pull wasn't wasted on her. "Her works up the big house."

Exodus had been there three years and Emma was happy to hear that she wasn't picking in the cotton fields.

Though she'd visited her twice early on, Emma had never been asked inside the house, and didn't expect it. It looked grand and she was proud that James, with a new young wife and two children, lived the high life. "We gonna eat white turkey meat every durn day," she could remember him telling her from year to year.

The little girl hadn't stopped raking and Emma said, "Lookahear. I'll get these leaves piled for ya if you run yonder and tell Exodus her mama's here."

She got a blank look.

"Dusty," she corrected, although Sister is what she'd called her daughter for years.

To free her skinny bow legs the girl grabbed her coat-tail and did a tumble and run down one side of the hillock and up the other.

Emma beamed, watching Exodus spring across the base of the hill. She was still a girl at thirty. But it was surprising how she'd changed in three years.

A curly-headed baby rode her hip.

"Mas'r James keepin' you busy?" her mother called. She still had mother love for James, having nurtured him from babyhood. It had never mattered while she raised him that his breath was rank, and she'd always excused his cruelty as male cussedness. Like the times he'd kick her from bed to make his breakfast.

Emma smiled at her daughter, noticing she'd filled out.

"His missus feeding you good, huh?" The big gray bow in Exodus's hair matched her eyes . . . and the baby's, which were a shade lighter.

"Ain't he handsome," Exodus said, seeing her mother staring at the baby. She grabbed the baby's hand. "Wave to your grandma, Teenotchy."

At that moment the girl in the big coat came running up.

"You said you was gonna make a great big pile," she groaned. "That just bitsy," she told Emma.

Emma was shaking as she passed her back the rake. But the little girl threw it down. "Miz Dusty, gimme a hold of the baby."

"Sure, Maybelle." With her hands free, Exodus tried to hug her mother.

"Sister, I told you not to fool with none of Mas'r James's niggers."

Dusty eyed Maybelle to indicate they shouldn't talk around her. But Emma was angry and persisted. "Don't sass. Standing there holding a raggedy wench." Such harsh words for her daughter didn't come easily.

"Teenotchy's a boy," laughed Maybelle, bouncing him on her hip. "Ain't ch'you, Teenotch?"

Emma's eyes welled.

"Mammy, don't worry," said Exodus. "Missus say I got him trained good. He ain't never crawlin' round her feet when she comes to the kitchen." She reached out to touch her mother.

"Get off," shrugged Emma. "You worse than poison ivy." Her mind was triggered to the Van Zandt homestead some thirty years earlier when James's mother accused, "You been fornicating with my boy, ain't you, Lottie? Now you got poison in you, black wench!" Lottie couldn't figure what sickness had her belly swollen and made her vomit through June and pee away August nights.

Emma was wrenched back to reality by Exodus's sob. "It

ain't right you to talk so in front of Maybelle," she whimpered. Like a child herself, she lost courage confronted by
her mother's sternness.

"Get your stuff, Exodus," Emma ordered.

"Why? I'm all right. We get lots to eat and Mister James
don't raise a hand to us."

Emma held out her nine fingers, each calloused. "I
been working like a mule to save for you to go north. To
live decent." Her anger became tears and she wiped her
eyes on the hem of her gingham dress. "For what? For you
to lay up."

"Aw, Mama, don't be like that."

The first time she as "Lottie" had an orgasm Emma felt
her own spirit for the first time. Her caw stirred the wild,
and as the moon sank jealously behind the barn, James'd
hollered, "Ya-hoooodhy. Where did we get to."

Tears streamed down Emma's cheeks back then, as they
did now when her daughter tried to explain. "I kept to myself
at first, but 'bout Christmas, Mister James said I wasn't acting
right and was gonna have to git."

From the day she'd been labeled cargo as a little African
captive, that child who was to be known as Emma and Lottie
may as well have been deaf and dumb and blind. Until James
laid her on her back and fingered her instinct. As much as
it hurt, his violent pumping thawed her soul after the first
time. But to think he'd done the same thing to their daughter
made the gray-haired Emma reel.

"Mister James ain't so bad," she heard Dusty say.

"Yes he is!" cut in Maybelle, clutching Teenotchy. "He
whips me all the time!"

"Only 'cause you mouth grown folks' business, Maybelle," blurted Dusty, like she was chiding a little sister.

Teenotchy started to cry, although he looked snug in
Maybelle's arms. "He ain't used to strangers, 'cause I keeps
him with me," Dusty cajoled.

"But he come to me nights when Miz Dusty's up the big

house," chimed Maybelle, telling more than Exodus would have.

"The big house to do what?" demanded her mother like she was talking to a daughter thirteen instead of thirty. As her temper rose, she remembered how James insisted that she sleep at the foot of his cot because he hated having her in his long johns while his face and hands grew cold to the biting northeasterly winds that howled through his room. Once he forgot and kissed her, but it made him so mad that he punched her in the face, yelling, "Nigger, don't put your mouth on me." But no sooner than her lips healed, he took to kissing her when it suited him.

Maybelle, unaware that the old woman was churning up memories only, realized from Emma's expression that she'd said too much. "Wanna know why I named him Teenotchy?" she asked Emma to change the subject, but Emma just stared off toward the big house. "I'm gonna teach him to cut a somerset when he gets two. But that ain't till Christmas," Maybelle continued.

"You swore to keep to yourself if I let you out," said Emma to Dusty.

"I can't work for the man and don't do what he wants."

It flashed through Emma's mind how James's mother used to complain to him, "I'm sorry I give you that slave, 'cause you don't want her to do nothing but ride you."

Wiping her eyes again with her gingham sleeve, Emma remembered that, big or little, James could no more get his fill of her than of the sweet potatoes she as Lottie mashed with thick cream, because he liked it. At sixteen he only needed to look at his hostage. The wide set of her coal-black eyes, her blackish brown lips gently parted so her square white teeth flashed like crystal in the sun . . .

James got hard seeing Lottie bent over a stone scrubbing his pants at the river. He got harder still when her hips swayed down the hill to fetch him a pail of water. And he got rock hard when she bathed him, wrapping her tongue around his name and any part of his body he felt needed to be licked or sucked.

But whereas he owned her from the Christmas he was eight, up to the day he left for war she possessed him. Not that he ever said "I love you" and nor did she expect it. But if there's a speck of love in passion, there was a pound of love between them. It wasn't only need which made them wrap their arms around each other, but neither of them had words to explain the love-hate bonding them that was fathoms deep.

"How're you feeling?" never crossed James's lips, because it never crossed his mind, and no matter how often he beat Lottie for ruining the cornbread, hot nights he expected her to creep to him, as eager as he was to go to that place that left them quivering and out of breath or laughing till their sides ached.

"Your mind ain't on nothing but fornication, and if I get back and find a yellow-faced nigger favoring my James, I'll take it downriver and drown it," Miz Emma would tell Lottie sometimes, using the same tone a mother might to scold a child who'd left a toy out in the rain. Although other times she was as likely just to hit her a few times with the broom handle.

This is what was running through Emma's head as she suddenly took a mind to yank Teenotchy from Maybelle, running toward the same river where James'd made her eat worms, spread her legs and serve him as it suited.

Exodus foresaw the looming tragedy. "Mama! What'cha gonna do?" she yelled, seeing her mother's gingham blowing in the wind and her baby boy being dragged toward that river.

"I ain't your mama and this ain't your bastard," wailed Emma, chased by her long-legged daughter, imagining her baby face-down in the Mississippi. It gave Exodus wings.

"Mama, you gone crazy!" she screamed, bold and out of character.

Maybelle, having known that baby's loving arms, also yelled to stir the cows at pasture. "Get her, Miz Dusty. Don't let her!" the scrawny urchin squealed.

To see Teenotchy dragged like a rag doll formed a moving-canvas image which Maybelle couldn't forget and would later describe again and again, embellishing upon the basic story to suit her gossipy streak.

"You can't keep your daddy's bastard," she heard Dusty's mother say.

"I'll keep him," yelled Maybelle, catching up to the women as Dusty hurled herself like a cannon at Emma's ankles so that mother, grandmother and child came down to earth in a heap.

"He got your daddy in him," sobbed Emma.

"No more than me," returned Dusty, rescuing her squalling baby from the pileup. Having never been told James Van Zandt was her father, she misunderstood.

Emma refused help. With her forehead banging the ground, she bellied a native wail from a continent forgotten. Though she'd lost the language, she knew the cry.

The little girl tugged Dusty's skirt. "She your mama sure?"

With Teenotchy outbawling his grandmother, Dusty didn't know who to console.

"Drown him. You done mixed with your own kin," was the last thing Maybelle overheard before Dusty shooed her off.

She adored the baby and would have followed Dusty like a lamb had she been allowed. So off she went reluctantly, unaware she'd never see her again.

Aunt Em, with these memories colliding, stood transfixed in the Germantown yard. She rubbed her stiff knobbly

hands, which stung from sudsing somebody's linen tablecloth in borax. "Wish I was in the lan' of cotton," she heard
herself humming as she moseyed into the kitchen for a
stale cracker.

She needed to eat to keep from thinking about the year
of nightmares that followed that episode when they walked
the eleven hundred miles to Philadelphia, stopped by
weather, poverty and Dusty discovering she'd stolen away
from the Van Zandt plantation with another baby inside her.

They were working on a poor farm in Mobile when she
told her mother the news, although the girlchild wasn't born
until they got to Atlanta. Homeless, jobless, they squatted in
a deserted shack that June of 1896 and did everything but
whore to keep from starving.

"Who should I say is their daddy?" Dusty asked her
mother.

"The first man that'll have you," said Emma, who prayed
her daughter would find a husband in Philadelphia. "And
we can't tell nobody I'm your mama 'cause ain't no telling
who'll poke in our business. Best call me Auntie." And Aunt
Em is what stuck.

Emma Van Zandt couldn't relate her violated past because the English she was forced to speak never became hers.
But silence eased none of the humiliation and horror that
fed her self-contempt and left her joyless. Though of course
she had small delights, like finding an extra clothes peg to
finish hanging a wash or discovering a half macaroon among
Tessie's crumby offerings.

After they'd settled in Philadelphia and her daughter
still refused to drown the children, as Aunt Em regularly
suggested, she gave up believing that the place she slept
would one day be more than a washhouse. She stopped noticing the detail on those Venetian handkerchiefs she ironed
for the Belgian family long before Atlanta was old enough
to be ashamed of the lint in Aunt Em's hair from shaking

other people's clothes out in the kitchen. And finally, as Dusty became more attached to the two children, Emma, once called Lottie, abandoned that hope that others call God.

And it didn't matter that Atlanta used her as an example of what not to become; Aunt Em was proud to be as strong as an ox, in spite of rheumatics in her left hip and the four remaining fingers on her left hand.

XIII

Turning into Main Street on her way to the Klebers' that Sunday morning, Atlanta glared at the ivy-covered house with tiny roses painted in the corners of its white shutters. That someone inside had put a bowl of pink geraniums by the front door and washed down the flagstone steps irritated her. "Hmph," she grunted, considering herself above the houseproud. Every year she grew more contemptuous of anybody who had what she wanted, and envy poisoned her as much as Aunt Em's mistreatment.

At twelve, with a wash bundle balanced on her head, Atlanta used to pass that same house imagining she lived in it, hung Belgian lace at the kitchen windows and had a jar of daisies on the table. But by seventeen she knew she'd only stand over a hot stove in that colonial kitchen as a servant. It wouldn't be the first time that reality strangled her American dreams.

In fact, passing the Fire Insurance Company, she automatically made a face at the bricks and mortar, because she knew Beulah was right: no matter how fast they typed or how nice their penmanship, they'd never work there.

Arriving at the Klebers' back door, Atlanta counted ten Mississippis to cool her temper before she knocked. Whereas Teenotchy'd assessed his broad grin provoked Helga Kleber most, Atlanta'd discovered that her speaking in an even, measured tone made the widow boil.

"Good morning, Mrs. Kleber," she said sweetly, like the Norwegian twins.

"My father-in-law is sleeping." Helga's hate matched hers. "And you're the last person he'll want to see. Especially on Sunday."

Not understanding why, secretly Atlanta held Mister Kleber responsible for her mother's death. For a week after Dusty's murder, the three-year-old believed her mother and Teenotchy were at "Mister Paul's," as that was Sister's excuse whenever she was late. With only Sukey's comfort, Atlanta sobbed herself into a fever once Aunt Em had hollered, "Teenotchy's staying with Mas'r Klabber, and your mammy ain't never coming back."

Traumatized by her daughter's murder and left with grandchildren she denied made Aunt Em meaner than a caged Alsatian. "And quit blubbering or you'll get a lickin'," she'd scolded the three-year-old girl.

Atlanta didn't express her pain until she was thirteen, when she finally wailed at Teenotchy, "Why didn't Mister Kleber take me in too!"

"Aw, Atlanta," he said. "Sister's been dead ten years. Let that mess rest."

But she couldn't.

She tested Mister Kleber, who feared Teenotchy'd probably told her about his twilight kisses with their mother. By letting Atlanta have her way and giving them a home, he prayed they'd never defame his pious name.

Balancing the peach cobbler baked at Beulah's in one hand, Atlanta smoothed her other down the gingham dress, which felt sticky from the sugar she starched it with.

The delicious waft of the cooked peaches made the widow try to sound nearly agreeable when she asked, "Who's that for?" But she'd already propelled Atlanta into rage.

While she pictured herself beheading Helga with a meat cleaver, she hid behind the Norwegian twins' gentlest smile and calmly replied, "I baked this for Mister Kleber. But I need to see him, so I'll give it to him myself."

"Wait in the yard." Helga knew Atlanta's signs before a flare. That calm voice was one. So Helga stalked off, saying something about, "Every panhandler from here to Philadelphia . . ." as Atlanta headed for the garden.

The faded squares of her gingham were ashamed to call themselves red beside Teenotchy's crimson begonias. "Mister Greenthumb," Atlanta laughed to herself, surprised that while grander gardens like the Tewksburys' withered from sunstroke, Teenotchy'd had Mister Kleber's three rambling acres thriving.

It was hard to stay angry in that beautiful garden. But the brutal and the brutalized had equal claim to her, since Nature honors both father and mother. James's arrogance, Lottie's innocence, Miz Emma's temper, Dusty's placidness. Like Teenotchy, Atlanta was their progeny.

But sure that Teenotchy's passion for gardening was influenced by Mister Kleber's, she couldn't abide it. "What do you want to hang around there for?" she'd deride. He put it down to her jealousy when she was younger but, as she grew taller than him, he suspected she was right about most things.

"You shouldn't bother with that old man's garden unless he pays you *something*." She could chastise him with as much bluster as Aunt Em.

"Atlanta, everybody's not money crazy like you," said Teenotchy, worried she'd do or say something to jeopardize his privilege of spending every spare minute there. He loved

that land surrounded by a choir of orioles. Gardening was
his obsession.

With a hoe in his hand he was content to be who he
was, and seeing the last evening light glow upon a flower
sanctified him. But he could explain this no more than Aunt
Em could explain her belly god or Atlanta could explain her
crush on Hernando or Alexander could explain his on
Teenotchy.

Because some passions are of the spirit and may be inherited like the color of one's eyes.

Church bells signaled the end of Sunday service at the
German Reform Church and Atlanta hoped she wasn't going
to have to wait half the afternoon for Mister Kleber. But no
sooner than the thought crossed her mind, she spotted him
at his bedroom window. "How long's that old crow been
watching me," she said to herself. "Probably thought he was
going to catch me stealing one of his stupid ol' flowers."

She smiled and waved.

She resented his righteousness, and benevolence, and
the way he talked to her, like she was a child when she'd had
no childhood. In fact, the only good thing she said about
Mister Kleber was that he never "tried" anything. Not like
the father of the children Beulah babysat for, who found any
excuse to pat Beulah's behind or brush against her breasts.

"Mister Kleber just beckoned me from his window," Atlanta announced to Mrs. Kleber on entering the back door.
She felt renewed by that one slight and threw her shoulders
back, rushing up the stairs, not expecting for a minute that
Mister Kleber would scold her for the missed Saturdays. He
never did.

Collecting herself outside his bedroom door, she made
one last face in the direction of the staircase, hoping that
Helga was snooping at the bottom.

"Atlanta," Mister Kleber called.

"Morning, Mister Paul, sir. Teenotchy said you weren't

faring well in this heat," she lied, "so I thought I'd bring you a Sunday treat."

In spite of the stream of light, she found his creamy bedroom depressing and was glad that it was Teenotchy's domain even when she turned up for work.

Few entered the bedroom without remarking on the big doll's house, but she always refused to acknowledge it. All the years she'd labored there she saw it as bait and refused to bite. Even at six she'd stopped being easy prey.

A mound of downy pillows supported Mister Kleber's back. "Sit thee down, child." He looked paler than she'd seen him but in no other way had he changed. "Would thee like some water?" He always offered what he wanted.

"No thank you, sir, but I'll get you a glass."

At the window, with a jug in her hand, he saw her as Dusty, although Atlanta's dark-brown hair was wavier, her brown skin milkier, her eyes less forgiving. In form and feature, he'd said she was the image of her mother. And with no recall of Dusty Simms, Mister Kleber's impressions became Atlanta's own.

Those fourteen years were yesterday to a man of seventy-three, old for his age because bed made him think and think again.

His guilt cut such a lasting impression, he could have carved Dusty's face quicker than his wife's. Though he never knew exactly what he'd been guilty of. It hadn't been his hands which had choked the life from her, and his dollar rewarded her kisses, but he felt her death had been an indictment on him and being bedridden his overdue arrest.

Like Teenotchy, he remembered Dusty's hands, calloused and strong like a man's though her fingers were as lean and shapely as her daughter's.

But his memory had photographed her face, which seldom smiled, and had he had the talent of a Bertram, the traveling artist who robbed her of her life, Mister Kleber could have painted her exactly.

"Why has thee missed work these past three weeks?" he asked Atlanta.

"I came to bring you that peach cobbler." She smiled, avoiding the question and pointing to the bowl she placed on the chest at the foot of his bed.

"Thy mother used to make that."

She had no time for his niceties and went straight to the point.

"Mister Kleber, there's going to be a race sponsored by the Women's Auxiliary in three weeks and Teenotchy's not entering."

"Betting is sinful."

She cocked her head. "But there's a fifty-dollar prize for the winner and twenty-five dollars for the runner-up, and my brother could use that money to start up a little business. A flower business or something like that." She saw no need to mention the material she was hoping to buy to make Hernando's eyes pop out.

"I sold the hackneys and palominos ages ago."

"But you still have Blossom."

Mister Kleber laughed until he coughed. "Blossom! That shows thee truly has some imagination."

She had Hernando in the forefront of her mind and didn't get the joke. "Mister Kleber, my brother takes that horse of yours out every few days . . ."

"I taught Teenotchy to ride," the old man added defensively.

For all her resoluteness, Atlanta was quick to feel rejection and quicker to cry. He could see her eyes welling. "Thy mother had a dress the same," he said to appease her.

"I told Aunt . . . I knew this was my mother's dress." Atlanta perked up, wiping the corners of her eyes. "But I thought you said she was tall, like me."

He eyed her ankles. "Perhaps it shrunk."

It annoyed her that he could make her smile so easily. "I hope I put enough sugar in your cobbler," she said, giving a slight curtsy, ready to leave. Fifty dollars or not, she wouldn't humble herself with him and was already conjuring up who else might lend Teenotchy a horse.

"Send Helga up, and tell Teenotchy to mix Epsom salts and cooked apple in Blossom's feed. There's not much time to bring her weight down. When's the race?" said the old man, both fearful and vexed that he was always forced to give in to this mere child.

XIV

Saturday, August 23, 1913

As usual, while the rest of Germantown slept, there was activity at the Holybrook Manor Stable, where the stable boss held his morning court.

Teenotchy didn't know where to look when Horatio said, "Poon tang ain't the answer to everything," referring to the female anatomy.

Edison laughed. A few hefty guffaws around sunup was his panacea for the insults he might encounter before sundown from Mister Tewksbury.

"Get a woman!" he told Horatio. "And forget about—"

"I want to remember," Horatio scowled. "Had'na been for my daddy bustin' his backside, cotton would'na been king of nothin' but a hill of boweevils."

"You trying to claim Uncle Willy made cotton king?" Edison laughed again.

Teenotchy declined the offer to strum Horatio's banjo, but buffed his harmonica to pass him while Horatio said, "I ain't claimin' it was just Daddy." He turned to Teenotchy. "Used to have me a mouth harp 'fore somebody give me that banjo. You know 'Blue Monday'?"

"You can't expect everybody to know them slavery-time songs," Edison said. "Tee's not but nineteen."

Horatio bent a few notes on the harmonica. "It's a old washerwoman song my grandmammy showed me. You still don't recognize it?"

"I told you he wouldn't know that slavery-time mess."

"Niggah, why you always talk like you got raised up out the Red Sea. Your mama was branded same as mine and I ain't 'shamed."

"That was fifty years ago."

"My left foot it was. Some of that mess is still going on. So don't shine on like you don't know nothing 'bout it."

"Your talk poisons a strong man's gullet."

Horatio pulled down his sock. "Looka here." He showed Teenotchy the dark-blue scars that marred his ankles.

Edison let out a storm of laughter. "Half the niggahs working round town got worse, so why're you complaining? You can walk."

"That's where Debs was going to do us better," said Horatio.

Refusing a toke of the cigarette, Teenotchy beamed. "Roosevelt should have won."

" 'Cause ya'll got the same name can be the onliest reason you wanted him, 'cause he didn't do nothing. Talkin' about a full dinner pail."

"That was McKinley," Edison said.

"Whoever it was didn't change a dangblammit thing."

"Well, least we got to vote this time."

Teenotchy loved sitting on the stump with them for their morning powwow before cocks crowed and horses were watered. A slight breeze freshened that early hour and a clear morning light glittered the gravel and the Tewksburys' lawn.

"If these women get the voting like they want," said Hor-

atio, "we'll end up with any ol' body, like that fella over to
the trade hall that offered a free can of Dutch Cleanser. . . .
Now tell me I'm lyin'."

"True or not, don't come round my place again talking
that mess like last time. Artema was gonna lay a skillet on
me after you left."

Horatio couldn't hold back a grin. "Well, I couldn't let
no woman get away with what she said 'bout Wilson."

"Why not, after you sopped her cornbread?"

"You let a white man sweet-talk her about New Free-
dom?" said Horatio, as though Edison had let Woodrow Wil-
son in the kitchen to speak to his wife. "Like I told her,"
Horatio went on, "that New Freedom's for Russians and
Groats and anything else flockin' in the thousands to Ellis
Island."

"You mean Scroats," Teenotchy said with authority, because Horatio agreed with Edison's suggestion that Teenotchy, with a high-school diploma, could correct them as and
when necessary.

"Groats. Scroats. Billy Goats!" Horatio complained. "I
don't care what their name is. New Freedom's for them." He
hit a banjo chord and sang, "We still ain't had a taste of that
old Freedom yet," asking between lines, "Got ch'you a girl,
Tee?"

"Not yet."

"Get ch'you one, but don't be no fool like Edison and
marry her, 'cause wives get to hitting a man with a frying
pan."

"Don't listen to that," Edison butted in. The stub he
smoked was so short it nipped his fingertips. "Nothing wrong
with Artema. Her and the kids are the best thing in my life."

"You musta threw your girl over," Horatio told Teenotchy, " 'cause with good hair and light eyes like you got, I
guess you got 'em lined up round the block."

Teenotchy's face sank with an embarrassed grin.

"Lord! Lookahere, Edison!" Horatio laughed. "Boy's blushing like a woman."

Just then all three heard the gravel crunching under sure footsteps. Their hearts beat a red alert and lesser mortals might have run, but being used to fear they stood their ground.

"What splendid music!" Alexander said as the three played out their stooge personas. They hung their heads. "Hello, Mister Alexander," they chorused, standing to tip their caps with a smile.

"I was just coming out for a ride on Entelechy."

Edison, Horatio and Teenotchy remained at attention. Once a hostage, Horatio decided industry was for cowards and loyalty and politeness to his captors was merely a means of survival.

He performed a bow and scrape. "Well, Mister Alexander, suh, I best be getting back to mixing mash, so these ponies of Mister Jonah's can have 'em a good nosh t'day." He stuck his banjo behind the door of an empty stall and jaunted off, while Edison, who'd seen white men be cruel and irascible, moved with greater speed. After nudging Teenotchy with a look, he said, "Yessir, Mister Alexander. We *all* best be getting back to work. C'mon, Tee."

To establish his allegiance, Teenotchy didn't return Alexander's smile. Alexander sensed him freeze and smiled again. "I'd like to have a word with Teenotchy."

But Edison's look warned, "Careful, Teenotchy. You don't know who you're messing with. It would be wise to get to steppin'." Not that Alexander could see more than Edison's smile, because Edison was a master of body language and passing information with his eyes. Though he was born free, these skills had passed to him from a mother born into captivity.

Teenotchy read him. But he read Alexander too and judged him safe, although he sensed it was wrong to tell the others. He didn't want to alienate himself, yet his talk with Alexander at Market Square the previous Saturday told him the Englishman wasn't trash.

As Edison walked off, leaving Teenotchy, he heard Alexander say, "I've a mind to go to Valley Forge later today, after I've had a ride and breakfast. Do you know the way?"

Wildwood, northeast of Germantown, was no way near Valley Forge but it was where Alexander had planned all week to take Teenotchy. Its forest was spongy with moss and acorns, and only here and there did the gigantic old trees let in sun. The scent of pine made Alexander think of Christmas. "Ruth must've put rocks in this picnic basket," he said, having insisted on carrying it while Teenotchy followed by his side, holding the blanket.

They stopped under an old sycamore. "This is perfect. And stop looking so worried, Teenotchy."

"Yes, sir." Unsure of what he was up for, he fidgeted with his glasses.

"Can you please drop the sirs and misters."

"Yes, sir."

Alexander shook his head. "How would it be if I kept tipping my hat?"

Teenotchy'd been silent the whole five-mile journey, listening to Alexander talk about things more personal than even Miss Sullivan would have. "But sir, I don't know how you want me to act," he admitted, while watching Alexander examine the endless supplies in the picnic basket.

"Why act? Just be."

Being was as alien to Teenotchy as Alexander's clipped accent. Even among those his own color he played a part after that year with the Klebers. Trained to please, only with Geronimo was he entirely himself.

"We can't be friends if you're acting." Alexander sighed

with frustration, looking at his watch. "Ten thirty and I'm ready for lunch. Are you?"

"Ten thirty, Saturday" formed a picture in Teenotchy's mind. He was meant to be in his apron polishing Mister Kleber's chest-a-robe with the old man propped up in bed, making furniture for the doll's house.

"Mister Alexander, sir," tumbled out before Teenotchy could catch it. "Mrs. Kleber . . . my job . . ."

"What happens when you miss work?" Alexander asked matter of factly, having intended to help Teenotchy skive when he asked to be driven to "Valley Forge."

Teenotchy shrugged. He'd missed only one Saturday when he'd had measles, aged eight. What added to his anxiety was that Atlanta might miss that morning too.

"Let the bastards scrub their own floors," said Alexander, pleased to hear his call for anarchy ripple through the trees. "I'll see to your wages."

"They'll put us in the streets if I lose my job," Teenotchy told him, having constantly heard such from Aunt Em.

"You're on this earth to do more than clean for the Klebers, I'm sure of it." Alexander sounded like Atlanta, and Teenotchy wondered if he also had her temper, although he seemed calmer and more controlled than Mister Kleber. "I didn't expect you to know about entelechy," he went on, the English accent pronounced.

Teenotchy eyed Alexander: was he harmless enough but crazy? "I've groomed your horse, but it was Horatio you asked to see to him while you had breakfast."

Taking the blanket, Alexander said, "I really must sit down. That bloody diphtheria I told you about leaves me short of breath."

Teenotchy could visualize Aunt Em evicted on the sidewalk with her collection of boiling tubs, kettles, biscuit tins, clothes props and pegs piled high beside Atlanta's cot. (There was hardly furniture, his bed being four tea chests shoved together and covered with a horse-hair mattress.)

Having heard a lot about Cleveland from Edison, Teenotchy thought he could go there if Mister Kleber threw them out.

Alexander's mind mulled over loftier thoughts. "Entelechy," he enunciated. "It's Aristotle's theory of actualizing one's potential." Teenotchy looked so blank, Alexander imagined he was hungry and added, "What I really want is some of Ruth's Boston cream pie, but she said it would spoil on the journey in this heat. The same with lemon meringue. So all we have is gingerbread. But there are cherries and peaches." He took a flask out of the basket. "And rye. Potent stuff this. I'd best explain entelechy before I take a sip."

Teenotchy loved cherries but was afraid to have any and declined the pigs' feet, knowing there was no way to eat it without sucking the bones. But Alexander made him take one sip of rye, which burned the back of his throat. He was still coughing when Alexander said, "I'll give you a book about Aristotle when we go to Miss Sullivan's."

While Alexander explained the theory of actualizing potential, Teenotchy hoped he could keep from reeling and was surprised he could speak when Alexander asked, "Now give me an example of entelechy."

Teenotchy thought about his garden and how two plants grew differently if one was nurtured in shade and one in light. But, unsure if that was entelechy, he relied on the example Alexander had given. "If you only use a automobile as a chair, it's OK, but you're not using its full potential until you sit *and* ride."

"I knew you were smart," clapped Alexander. "Now have a pig's trotter and relax. Or try the gingerbread. Ruth swears it cures winter colds. Not that I'll be here to test it." He smiled, giving the dark-brown slice a sniff.

"You'll have to come to Miss Sullivan's with me next Saturday," he told Teenotchy, who took it as an order. "She'll

never be candid about her past if I'm on my own." Alexander
gave no hint that Teenotchy's company was the real purpose
of the visit. "This Geronimo isn't dangerous, is he?"

Teenotchy couldn't believe Alexander would come.
"There's another man that can't hear." It wasn't easy to describe his misfit family and, while he refused to describe Geronimo as a simpleton, he suspected calling Chopper deaf
was equally disloyal.

Something rustled a nearby bush and he looked ready
to run.

"You're so jumpy, you make me jump," said Alexander.
But Teenotchy better understood the racial divide. Socializing was unacceptable to both sides and Teenotchy was nervous that anyone should spy them sitting on the same
blanket.

But otherwise he was a master listener, never inter-
rupting, eyes attentive. And though Alexander enjoyed the
audience, he said, "Conversing's easy once you get the hang
of it. You talk about what you know and ask questions about
what you don't. Like I could go on and on talking about
being eight. . . . Gingerbread?" he offered, taking a chunk
himself. "Everything changed that year, my grandfather says.
1901. First Aunt Henrietta drowned, then Victoria died while
I was quarantined with diphtheria."

"Who was Victoria?" Teenotchy was proud of his
question.

"The queen. I remember the nurse letting us out of our
cots to watch the funeral procession cross Waterloo." Alexander took a swig of rye. "I hated hospital and was always
waking from heavy sleeps forgetting why I was there and
wondering where everybody was. Thinking I'd never see my
granny again and hating the smell and the mean nurse."

Teenotchy slightly stirred from his soul sleep, but not
enough to make a difference as Alexander talked on, relating
a trauma in line with Teenotchy's own.

"Granny came down from Norfolk once a week, and although I can't remember my mother coming once, she talks as though she camped on the hospital forecourt. But I recall my grandmother standing with the others, tapping on the window at us prisoners on the other side. I'm not mad about gingerbread. Are you?"

Teenotchy ate nothing to be polite.

Alexander pushed a chicken leg into his hand. "When I did finally get home after months, I had to stay in bed or be pushed about in a perambulator. At this point, Teenotchy, you could ask why, just to keep the conversation going, and I'd say, 'Weak heart.' "

Ruth's fried chicken was so juicy, a bit dribbled down Teenotchy's chin, so Alexander passed a napkin. "I never tasted fried chicken until I came to America. Anyway, if I'm careful, my heart doesn't stop me doing much. I can play badminton and walk miles if I take my time. And I shouldn't ride too fast."

Slowly chewing his chicken, with the birds calling and the smell of pine enveloping them, Teenotchy's tension eased a bit.

"Eight was hellish, though, and nine worse," explained Alexander, sensing his monologue was having a good effect.

"Granny died the summer I was ten, and I hardly left my room for months after. I read bits of *Uncle Tom's Cabin,* which she liked, convinced it could bring her back."

Teenotchy remembered polishing the Klebers' Bavarian table at the same age and hoping that if he did a perfect job it would please his dead mother. As his memory was stirred, he listened as intently as he did to Miss Sullivan.

"Had it not been for my cousin Jacques," Alexander said, "there's no telling what would have happened to me. But he'd come from France and slept in the room next to mine. 'Doing what you're told is bad for your health,' he used to say, and make me get out of that bloody perambulator to walk if no one was around." Taking another swig of rye, Alexander burped. "He's your age. When's your birthday?"

"Christmas," Teenotchy admitted.

"How extraordinary! So's Jacques's!" Alexander was elated. "All the more reason for you two to get on. Although he's becoming a bit of a rogue and loves having everything his way. Not that I mind."

Whereas Teenotchy considered Alexander risky, Jacques sounded dangerous.

"You haven't gone to sleep, have you?" Alexander asked, ignorant that his two hours of kindness couldn't uproot Teenotchy's fear, though he finally accepted a handful of cherries, and remembered how plentiful fruit used to be when he lived at the Klebers'.

"Diphtheria and Granny's dying made me old before my time, so my cousin says."

Teenotchy didn't understand and Alexander could see it in his eyes. "Mind taking your specs off? Just for a bit," he asked. "I feel I can see you better without them and you've had a long enough look at me." But really he wanted to examine those two round gray clouds in the heatwave, carrying on as Teenotchy placed the wire frames upon the blanket.

Alexander popped a cherry in his mouth and spat out the pit. "I haven't one decent picture of my grandmother. There are portraits, but none of her old and fat, like I remember. She had a blubbery lap . . . adored bread pudding."

He was so happy for Teenotchy's laugh, hoping he'd struck a vein. "Granny often smelled of garlic, so whenever she read to me, I'd get great nosefuls and she used to say she could have knocked out a whole army with one good belch. But the family try to paint her as the grand duchess, which she was, but she hated jewels and totally opposed feathers, being on the board of the Anti-Plumage League. . . . Did I tell you she was a staunch abolitionist?"

Teenotchy enjoyed the ramble through Alexander's childhood more than the discourse about the Revolution and Aristotle, since Alexander was likely to test him on those.

"Speaking of grandparents, what do you think happened to Thomas Jefferson's Negro grandchildren?"

Teenotchy's silence left room for conjecture. "You did say earlier you didn't know why your eyes were gray," laughed Alexander. "And tracing your genealogy can't be any more difficult than rummaging around the Revolution." The rye made Alexander bold. "We could start with your mother," he said, unaware she was dead.

Teenotchy was drawn out by Alexander's interest. "I remember her hands," he began. He colored in his year with the Klebers in faint pastels and Alexander's curiosity did a square dance, although he knew better than to show it, because Teenotchy's timidness was as familiar as his own at fourteen, when his voice was breaking.

"Wouldn't you like to find out what happened?" he asked.

"No," Teenotchy's memory screamed, but his lips were saying, "Yes." His hand trembled as he reached to put his glasses back on.

"My uncle wants me to go hunting with him next Monday after the race, but I'd much rather see what I can turn up about your mother's murder," Alexander said, hoping to get a sign of approval from Teenotchy but receiving none.

XV

Saturday, August 30, 1913

That following Saturday, with images of their Wildwood picnic still fresh, Teenotchy couldn't believe that Alexander'd
purchased the whole of Mrs. Gambicini's strudel for tea at
Miss Sullivan's. Not that Mrs. Gambicini was happy about
depriving her regulars, but since Alexander agreed to pay
double, she couldn't resist charging him a dollar extra for
the baking pan.

"A whole dollar!" Teenotchy yelped, thinking of how
much better the money could've been spent. Not that he
wanted to deprive Miss Sullivan or Geronimo. But he *was*
rational.

So Alexander didn't tell him that was only for the pan,
which he held with both hands while Teenotchy peered on
tiptoe into Miss Sullivan's side window.

"She's in bed," he whispered, uncertain why his old
friend was sitting up wearing a black lace bonnet and dark-
blue shawl in spite of the heat. She looked like a relic of

more than one bygone era. "Maybe she's sick," he said, ready to leave.

"All the more reason for us to visit," Alexander told him.

While they whispered, Geronimo pulled a miniature American flag out of his pocket and stuck it in the middle of the strudel.

"Where'd you get that?" Teenotchy scolded.

"Dunno," grinned Geronimo, shaking his head so his hair flopped from side to side.

"Yes you do," said Teenotchy.

Alexander hoped it was all right to interfere. "Does it matter?"

"He probably found it scrounging around somebody's rubbish heap."

"Surely that's the point of scavenging," quipped Alexander.

"Suppose some old biddy catches him in her yard. Next they'll put him in jail for stealing." He regularly had to rescue Geronimo from attacks, whether it was Ned Cleary's little hooligans or Atlanta's remarks when the Indian would turn up unexpectedly at their back door; it wasn't natural to Teenotchy to play the hero. He longed for Geronimo to cut his hair and act right.

"Let's go in," said Alexander.

Teenotchy opened the door for him.

"After you," Alexander insisted, but Geronimo rushed ahead of both of them.

Alexander tried not to notice the smell of boiled beans.

"Did you say 'Afternoon' to Miss Sullivan?" Teenotchy asked, refusing to let Geronimo forget his manners. But instead of parroting Teenotchy, Geronimo grabbed Alexander's boater, popped it on his own head and settled in his corner with his circle of various rocks.

"I thought you were early," said Miss Sullivan as church bells struck four o'clock just minutes after they'd arrived.

Everything ever given her by past employers was displayed. The kiddie's chair missing a leg, the speckled enamel roasting pan with a hole that was missing a lid, the two pastoral prints in broken frames with cracked panes and a perfect oval mirror were arranged to their advantage on the rag rug she'd made herself. Of course, her best chair had been reserved for Alexander and she'd pushed her floral dress into the corner of it to hide the springs and the stuffing coming out.

Posed against the potbellied stove was the guitar with the broken neck. The other side of it was Teenotchy in her rocker. Four chipped teacups with no handles sat saucerless on the table, next to a box of cinnamon tea she'd been saving for years. Chopper was unpacking boxes at the general store, she said with great pride before Alexander insisted cups without handles were practical, "like the Chinese use."

"Which reminds me," she sighed, "is that Chinamen's on Bringhurst still about to put Aunt Em out of business?"

Everybody smiled, but after introductions and small talk, tea was poured and they fell into an uncomfortable silence.

A madam Miss Sullivan had cleaned for in Maryland had accepted callers in bed and, as Miss Sullivan thought her shoes too rundown to wear in company, she'd decided her narrow bed, covered with a stained tablecloth, was the best place to receive her English visitor.

She'd had Chopper scour the walls and, although Teenotchy had never seen the potbellied stove cleaner and more pristine, she wasn't satisfied with it.

Conversation started and stopped several times. But after Geronimo lapped up the last piece of strudel, Teenotchy finally convinced Miss Sullivan that they really wanted to hear her tales of Utah.

The mere mention got Geronimo rolling with laughter. He'd wrapped his black hair around his neck and had Miss Sullivan's corncob pipe in his mouth, although she insisted it wasn't to be lit "with company." "You-taw," he laughed and giggled, sometimes making such a ruckus he interrupted her story of the first Indian settlement she saw on the trail. She didn't mind and was proud he was as clean as the stove.

Alexander's eyes were wide when she said, "The wagon trains used to come past the Hochfield place at least three or four times a year. Some of 'em turned up with the arrows sticking out the wagons where they'd met up with a war party."

In her room he was living his fantasy of the cabin depicted by Harriet Beecher-Stowe's novel; Miss Sullivan could have been rattling off the weekly wholesale order at the general store and he would have been just as riveted.

It was almost inconceivable for a nineteenth-century woman not to like his old-fashioned charm, and in his presence Miss Sullivan, having never been in white social company, thought Heaven's gate was about to open for her.

They agreed they'd have another cup of tea and Teenotchy went to the well for water while Alexander knelt for fifteen minutes, examining every one of the plain rocks Geronimo showed him like they were gold nuggets. That's when Teenotchy knew for sure he was a friend.

"Ready to leave?" he asked Alexander when the church bells struck six.

"Let the boy stay," interrupted Miss Sullivan, sensing how content Alexander was. "Maybe he's hungry."

"No thank you," said Alexander, declining bean stew. "But Teenotchy says you have poetry . . ." He was hoping none of them would remember that he'd come to hear about Mister Hochfield fighting Redcoats. He wanted an excuse to return.

"You don't wanna see my old scribblings, Mister Alexander, sir," she said coyly, motioning Geronimo to fetch her writing tablet from under the bed.

"I'd be honored," he said as Geronimo brought out her hidden boots and sat them by Alexander's feet.

Teenotchy and Miss Sullivan pretended not to notice.

"Miss Naomi wants her writing tablet," said Alexander.

"You're gonna read for us," she told Teenotchy.

"Do I have to?" he asked, like somebody at Sunday school.

"I wouldn't mind reading," chimed in Alexander, suddenly worried about the time.

Miss Sullivan's faded handwriting was difficult to decipher and, skimming through the tissue pages, Alexander faltered at every line.

"Read 'em, Teenotchy. Teenotchy, read 'em. Read 'em, Teenotchy. Teenotchy, read 'em," Geronimo shouted from his corner. Alexander could see he was sitting on his hat.

Teenotchy accepted the notebook. "I think it's better if Alexander reads."

"Oh, I disagree. And you being familiar with her hand, you'll do it justice."

"My dear," exclaimed Miss Sullivan, "can't this child make a lot of nothing sound like something?"

Teenotchy cleared his throat and rose from his chair. He never read aloud while seated.

"I'll read our favorite," he said, smiling at Geronimo, who stood because Teenotchy did.

" 'Ode to Harry'!" shrieked Miss Sullivan, disbelieving Teenotchy. "You don't want to read that thing. Read the one about the daffodils."

" 'Ode to Harry' sounds rather risqué," teased Alexander.

"Harry. Harry. Harry. Harry!" agreed Geronimo.

Teenotchy didn't wait. It was on the first page. Clearing his throat twice, a stage-shy boy before an audience, he started.

Miss Sullivan motioned him to sit back down. "I know it by rote."

Alexander was glad. Her recitation allowed him to stare into her bony face. Frail with age, her oak-brown skin, drawn taut over high cheekbones, was grainier than her old leather shoes hidden under the bed. He loved her quiet expression and got drunk on her slow, Southern voice. It was as smooth as a sweet tawny port when she recited.

That May they raised the roof,
I took his life and gave him mine.
We didn't need no wedding
Nor preacher to reside.

I'll never wear a wedding band,
Nor never say "I do."
Why swear by what is Heaven-sent?
No need when a love is true.

One bullet pierced young Harry's heart,
One kiss made me his bride,
And I could feel, when our lips met,
Angels dancing by our side.

It's the prettiest dance from Heaven,
God calls it The Soul's Embrace.
It's what our guardian angels did
That day at the Hochfield place.

That May they raised the roof,
I took his life and gave him mine.
One shot rang through our valley
That made young Harry close his eyes.

I gave my lips as his guiding light
To show him the short road home.
He gave his kiss to say "It's all right,
You'll never be alone."

When love is a choir of angels,
Then a kiss is the soul's embrace
And love is blessed by the Lord of Lords,
And marriage is by his grace.

That May at the Hochfield place
I gave my life, 'cause I took his.
That kiss was my redemption
And his eternal bliss.

Geronimo, back in his corner surrounded by his rocks, was almost asleep.

"That was wonderful," said Alexander. "Let's hear it again."

"Again!" Miss Sullivan grinned with her hand to her mouth to hide her three missing teeth. "Why d'you want to hear that thing again? I've got one about daffo—"

"Who was Harry?"

"Nice young fella, was passing with the wagon train. I wasn't but fifteen, but the minute he laid eyes on me he said, 'Y'all go to California without me.' He couldn't read or write, but boy could he lasso. And Mister Hochfield figured he had run away from somewhere. Not that he cared, because he had a roof to raise and was glad to have an extra hand around. Two of the Hochfield gals were spoken for at the time. Not much older than me, and their mama had been keeping hope chests for 'em. But I always wanted to tell them Adam and Eve didn't have linens and they managed."

Miss Sullivan adjusted the tablecloth, which she was using as a bedcover, and mopped a trickle of perspiration.

"Anyway, Harry—he didn't have a last name—this was before the Big Surrender."

"The Big Surrender?" asked Alexander.

"When Lee surrendered to Grant. It was after that colored folks started using last names more. But Harry didn't have one, so we would have had to use Hochfield I guess, if we'd got hitched."

A fly buzzed around the room and the wild geese on the pond and the barking dogs that belonged to the next cabin could be heard with the noisy mix of blue jays and robins complaining about the ninety-six degrees outside.

Miss Sullivan straightened her lacy black bonnet and Alexander marveled that she was able to sit poised, dressed as she was. "Anyway," she carried on, "Harry knew as soon as he saw me that I was for him and he was for me. Part the reason being that I was the only colored girl I guess he'd seen for a while. He asked me to marry him right off and told Missus Hochfield we were going to have ten children, and he was going to spend the rest of his life with me. Sadly, that part of it came true the very next weekend, because he was up on the roof with the rest of them and fell."

Teenotchy could see that Alexander was going to say something sympathetic, so he interrupted, "She doesn't mind talking about it. It was so long ago."

"I begged Mister Hochfield to put the boy out his misery. But the old man told me that every time I looked at him after I'd be blaming him for taking what was mine. So he went in the house, got the rifle and handed it to me. Young and foolish as I was, I'd never shot nothing. Killed a lot of flies, but homemaking was all I was good at."

"And poetry," said Alexander.

She blushed. "Mister Hochfield said the same. Anyhow, back to Harry. See, in those days if somebody got hurt real bad, there wasn't much else to do but shoot 'em. But massa . . ." She cleared her throat, having maintained that she was born free. "Mister Hochfield said nobody had the right but me. The only thing Harry wanted apart from a bullet in the back was a kiss. Said he didn't need a prayer, 'cause he was so sure that he'd get to Heaven. I wasn't even bashful with all those folk watching us. I knelt down . . . couldn't speak, couldn't eat for a week after, so of course I fell ill. At that age, I hardly had more sense than Geronimo. While I was laid up, I wrote that poem."

Sitting in that dismal room, Alexander was living old dreams. His treacle and toffee characters were within arm's reach, and his boyhood compassion for the characters his grandmother introduced him to got confused with real life. Or was it the other way around? He saw Teenotchy, Miss Sullivan and even Geronimo being as perfect as the red cardinal he'd finally spotted at Holybrook Manor. He wanted to stay. And stay. And stay.

"Why don't you read something?" said Teenotchy.

"No," smiled Alexander. "I couldn't do the work justice."

"How about something from the Bible?" said Miss Sullivan. "It would do me so much good."

Teenotchy was relieved that she hadn't talked much of dying. He reached for the Bible and Miss Sullivan pretended not to notice the cobweb that stuck to his hand when he disturbed it. "Don't wipe it on your clothes," she started to say, but he had already, and she made the sign of the cross, wanting to ease the bad luck she was sure it would bring. "Page five fifty-five," she told Alexander.

" 'The Song of Solomon,' " Alexander read.

"It's a sonnet," said Miss Sullivan. "Do you know it?"

Alexander had no time for the Bible. "I'm busy with history books," he said, but began reading.

" 'O that you would kiss me with the kisses of your mouth.' Hmm," he read, thinking to himself, "it really isn't a sonnet."

He took his time, and hoped that Teenotchy was listening.

> *Upon my bed by night I sought him*
> *whom my soul loves; I sought him but*
> *found him not.*
> *I will rise now and go about the city*
> *in the streets, and in the broad*
> *ways I will seek him whom my soul*
> *loves.*
> *The watchmen found me as they went*
> *about the city.*

*"Have you seen him whom my soul
  loves?"*

*Scarcely had I passed them when I
found him whom my soul loves.
I held him and would not let him go
until I had brought him into my
mother's house, and into the
chamber of her that conceived me.*

"The souls," laughed Geronimo. "My country 'tis of thee."

Teenotchy yawned. "Don't start," he warned, horrified to notice that Alexander's hat was under the Indian's behind.

But it was Miss Sullivan who really ruined the romantic air that Alexander's clear tone had been building.

"Stop!" she yelled. They all thought she was talking to Geronimo. He looked sheepish. "Sorry, children. But I just realized why I'm not hearing right." She undid the bonnet, and swung her knobbly feet from the bed. "Teenotchy, let me have that rocker, son, 'cause this may be the last proper Bible reading I get, and I don't want to miss a word." Her white hair was flat to her head in a series of connecting plaits. For a second Alexander could see the young Naomi Sullivan.

"Ready?" he asked, beginning again.

*Make haste, my beloved, and be like
a gazelle, or a young stag upon the
mountains of spices.*

She rocked herself to sleep, and Alexander's voice finally lulled Geronimo before he and Teenotchy tipped out, the sun still bright.

Half an hour later, when he was alone on the road to Upper Germantown, heading for the Tewksburys', he set horse and buggy at a fast pace, sorry that he wasn't riding Entelechy.

"Teenotchy," he repeated, over and over. It became his mantra. "Teenotchy, Teenotchy." It clung to his lips like the sweetest honey.

XVI

Saturday, September 6, 1913

A full seven days later at Holybrook Manor, Alexander was still asleep while sun and moon hung about the predawn sky, with Horatio in full voice, strumming and banging his banjo.

> *Camptown races sing this song,*
> *Dooda, Dooda.*
> *Camptown race track five miles long.*
> *Oh, Dooda Day.*

"That ain't a drum, man," Edison called.

They were in racy spirits and Edison hadn't heard Horatio sing as loud since they'd moved from Kentucky. Though Mister Tewksbury's Germantown Derby was supposed to be for the locals, some of his Philadelphia cronies were due at seven with thoroughbreds.

"We got these stalls so clean," Horatio had said on arriving at four a.m., "horses'll be scared to shit."

Edison had camped in his gunnysack outside General Lee's stall and wasn't well rested, so when three knee-high girls in smocked dresses darted with a hide-and-seek squeal from a nearby hedge, Edison barked, "Martha Edwards! What're you scallywags doin' round here this time of morning?"

Edison's six-year-old granddaughter and her friends, Minnie and Flora, weren't used to him being grumpy.

"We come to see the race," Martha whined.

"Ain't for about six hours yet," laughed Horatio, with no reason to grouch. "You girls sure do look pretty."

"Tell your mama I'm gonna tan her hide," said Edison. He didn't know why his daughter-in-law was out at that hour in the morning.

"She's over there." Martha pointed toward the banquette, assembled for two days now, thanks to Alexander's organizational skills.

"Y'all get on back home," Edison whined, worse than Martha.

"Grandma said get here early to get down the front."

"I got too much to do to have you round my feet. And why haven't you got shoes on yours? You see Minnie or Flora barefeet?"

Minnie, tallest though youngest, was fearless at five. "Martha took her shoes and stockings off so she wouldn't get 'em dusty, Mister Edison."

"Sound like good thinking," said Horatio, who went back to his song. The girls reeled with giggling.

"Martha, you mocking your Uncle Horatio!" he teased, so they giggled louder. Children before dawn added to the festive atmosphere. But Edison wanted to get rid of them without tears.

"Lord, 'Ratio," he said, as the girls began a contest to see who could stand on one foot longest. "You think the whole town'll be here before we can get a cup of tea off 'Zekiel?"

"I don't fancy none," Horatio answered. "Daddy got my cornpone and cider first thing. But why don't you send these little ol' frisky gals over the big house to see what Ruthie got on offer?"

"What's the betting she already threatened 'Zekiel's life this morning?" said Edison.

"The woman never sleeps. Probably baked a dozen cakes last night."

"That's why she's always fussing with that poor man," Edison added.

"Poor man, my foot. Ain't he hanging with Marie Annette. That's what I heard. He's chasing skirt-tail every chance."

"Watch your mouth in front of Martha," whispered Edison. "You didn't hear that," he called to her, although she and Minnie and Flora were still preoccupied with their balancing contest.

"The one with the ruddy eyes is sure cute, ain't she?" remarked Horatio. He was feeling young and playful for the first time since they'd moved north. "What's your name, pumpkin?" he asked her.

"Minnie Lee Mondicourt."

"You out!" laughed Flora. "You out, Minnie!"

Responsible for making her lose, Horatio reached into his pocket to sift out some pennies. "Can you count?" he asked, passing her six, which could have bought him a nickel pouch of tobacco.

"I can read," hollered Flora. She'd lost interest in their game when she heard change jingling.

Martha was not to be outdone in front of her grandfather. "I could write my name before I was five."

To be fair, Horatio asked Minnie, "And what can you do?"

Before she could speak up, Flora said, "Momma says Minnie can clean good as her."

Minnie beamed. At five and three months, her vocation was set.

"Come round my place when you get bigger, 'cause my daddy don't get in the corners," said Horatio.

"Martha, I want y'all to skidaddle. There's too much to do for you to be underfoot." Her pout got a nickel reward and she and her friends were ready to run after Horatio reached in his pocket to find pennies for Flora.

"Now give your ol' grandaddy some sugar." Edison warmed to Martha. "And I bought you them shoes to wear, so don't save your shoes when you ought to save your feet. Dirt can't hurt good leather. But get to aching in your toe joints and you'll be crippled up like Uncle Willy."

They skittered across the track.

"What time you got Teenotchy comin'?" asked Horatio.

"My son Joseph's comin' in for him at five. 'Cause I want Tee to win this race and he needs to get some rest."

"That gardening he does over that Quaker's needs four *good* men," Horatio said.

"You know they won't give him the day off. Specially for a race."

Every morning that week, Teenotchy'd been up before five, putting Blossom through her paces, and although he couldn't sleep that Saturday, he was relieved not to have to work at the Tewksbury stable.

Nearly seven a.m. outside on the stoop, Geronimo sat as close as a shadow to Teenotchy, with both of them polishing opposite ends of Blossom's rein. Each time he inched away, the brave inched nearer. "Geronimo, move to where my arms won't touch you if I stretch them." Teenotchy swung his arms back and forth to indicate how much space he wanted. "I've got to be free to breathe. To move."

"Free to move," Geronimo parroted. "Free. Free to move," he repeated. Flapping his arms, he sounded ready to break into song, though he only ever sang the first line of the national anthem.

"Wait here. I'm going to get my harmonica," Teenotchy instructed, since Aunt Em refused to have Geronimo in her kitchen and was already at her post by the potbellied stove. Though it seemed unlikely he'd have time to play it between his morning at the Klebers' and noon at the racecourse, that mouth harp was his trusted friend.

As he leapt back downstairs, Tessie arrived in the kitchen. "I'm coming to see you ride this afternoon. Prayed for you to win," she smiled. "Though God don't hold much with horseracing, fifty dollars could change y'all's lives." Like Beulah, she saw his winning as communal..

An hour later, when Teenotchy appeared in his apron at Mister Kleber's bedroom door with a vase full of gladioli, neither of them made a fuss. But Mister Kleber'd always taught him it was sacrilege to cut flowers unless it was a special occasion. They were too long for the vase and he tried to arrange them to stand tall.

"Why are ye fearful, o ye of little faith?" said Mister Kleber almost too quietly to be heard. It was what he usually said when Teenotchy trembled noticeably.

Mister Kleber, his fingers twisted with arthritis from years of handling wet pigskin, used tweezers to stick a tiny table leg in place. "It's cooled down. But no rain." His bed was more of a jumble than usual and Teenotchy looked at the mess, not sure whether it was time to throw some of it away. "What's the date?" Mister Kleber asked, slapping at his hand when Teenotchy picked at small bits of thread littering the bed cover.

"Sixth of September," answered Teenotchy.

"Blossom'll be trembling worse than thee! Get thee gone."

Teenotchy adjusted his spectacles. "Go," Mister Kleber

ordered, waving his tweezers like a wand. "But wait! Does thee still fit well in that saddle?"

It was the only good thing about not growing. Shoes and saddles didn't need changing. "Yes, sir."

"Others will race with my saddles. None made with such care as yours."

Dusty Simms's death brought her children a protection she never could've given them in life, with Mister Kleber adopting a guardian's role. Maybe she was dancing in her grave.

"I don't approve of racing or betting," he said. "But each must choose what's right, and I hope no harm comes to thee." It was as close as he'd come to "Good luck." "Get thee gone," he waved.

Even at nineteen, Teenotchy never journeyed the dim upstairs passage without looking over his shoulder a few times. When he was five, it took twenty-seven giant steps to get him to the staircase. But the day of the Germantown Derby, he needed only nine.

As Teenotchy, riding Blossom, turned into his dead end, he wanted to hide, spotting a white rider with two horses. He had had a feeling all morning that somebody would tell him he couldn't enter the race, but approaching he could see it was Alexander in a linen suit and Panama. After weeks of sun the young Viscount looked like a Brazilian planter astride his black stallion. He held his gray, Entelechy, in rein. "Is that the Quaker's horse?" he laughed as Teenotchy and Blossom trotted toward him.

Mister Kleber claimed shyness is what made Blossom's ears droop around strangers. But he couldn't explain away the shape of her head and insisted her mane be kept long as a disguise, though Teenotchy was sure she had trouble seeing with it over her eyes. So he'd plaited it for the race, tying the end in bits of rag left over from a floral blouse Atlanta remade for the occasion.

Blossom nuzzled Entelechy. "She's friendly enough," said Alexander, "but you can't expect to win on her."

Mister Kleber'd bought her for her stamina and good nature. "The Nez Perce Indians outsmarted the whole of the cavalry on one of these," he'd told Teenotchy one day. "She's a bit splotchier than most Appaloosas," he'd apologized whenever anybody complained about her appearance. But Teenotchy thought the old man loved her all the more for her homeliness.

"You want to win, don't you?" Alexander said matter of factly.

Winning was the furthest thing from Teenotchy's mind, particularly after he'd come out early from the Klebers' to find somebody'd hurled a rock at Geronimo while he was waiting for Teenotchy under the parlor window. That had happened around ten and the biggest ordeal of the day was to come.

Alexander was more enthusiastic. "You could be the next Jem Robinson with your talent and Entelechy's speed."

Having never heard of the famed English jockey, Teenotchy smiled and nodded, as he did whenever Alexander mentioned anything he was ignorant of. He'd agreed to race because his sister had begged him, but she hadn't mentioned winning. Nor did she admit she wanted him to win so she could buy material and to spite Mister Tewksbury.

Teenotchy slouched. "Mister Alexander, sir, I can't ride your horse. You said yourself it was your uncle's rule."

"I've handled all the necessaries," grinned Alexander. He was like a kid in a pet shop paying for a puppy he'd been eyeing for weeks. He produced a sales document from his pocket. "Reregistered last Wednesday." He handed it to Teenotchy.

"The Big Surrender?" said Teenotchy, scanning the elaborately scrawled ownership papers. He didn't notice his name on it and tried to pass it back.

"My uncle will be absolutely livid when they announce

that name as winner." It was rare for Alexander to be so tickled, and Teenotchy laughed along with him until Alexander refused to accept the sales slip. "She's yours."

More than once Mister Tewksbury'd told Edison to keep a careful eye on his nephew's horses because they were worth more than Holybrook Manor. "That boy's got more money than sense," Mister Tewksbury enjoyed complaining.

Teenotchy patted Blossom and pretended he didn't notice Aunt Em peeking from the kitchen window. He'd enjoyed the joke with Alexander and was waiting for the punch line. But when Alexander repeated, straight-faced, "She's yours!" Teenotchy couldn't take it in. The title deeds to another planet would have been as beyond his realm. To own a world-class racehorse, two pairs of overalls and a harmonica?

Pushing back his glasses, he said thanks. But whereas it was impossible to comprehend all that the gift entailed, he could apply himself to practicals.

"What about Blossom?" he asked.

Most of the people on Main Street that Saturday were strangers drawn by the race and accompanying festivities. Cake stalls, tombolas, and not a stable free to take another horse. It was a big day for merchants. And horsethieves.

Blossom flapped her tail and whinnied. Did she understand she'd been outclassed, or was she as embarrassed as Teenotchy that he was in that dead end talking to a white boy? Like it was normal. Like Tessie and Aunt Em wouldn't ponder it for weeks to come. And how could he explain Alexander getting off his black stallion and bowing to him as he insisted on helping Teenotchy dismount to take Blossom's reins? Hopefully nobody was looking at that moment, Teenotchy thought, breaking out in a sweat.

"Your humble servant," Alexander said with his deep bow. Sometimes he enjoyed making Teenotchy uncomfortable. Not that it was behind the gift of Entelechy. That was from the heart. "Now, do mind that gray, Mister Simms. He's fast." His teasing eased the embarrassment of profound generosity, although not even his modesty could devalue a thoroughbred given as unassumingly as a daisy.

Across town the Tewksbury stable was rank with cigar smoke and tension as Mister Tewksbury checked the list of entrants.

Edison couldn't understand why Teenotchy was down riding The Big Surrender but knew better than to ask as his boss bellowed, "No horse named that on my track. Disqualify it and I don't care how."

"Gen'ral Lee ought to be racin'," Edison said meekly. "Can't be another horse for miles that got his speed."

"Boy," Mister Tewksbury accused, "you been tipping rum. Gen'ral would probably run in the wrong direction, and that thief who sold him to me needs to be pistol-whipped."

"Theodore Simms can ride him," Edison explained to a puff of cigar smoke in his face. "And you being from Kentuck ought to win a ribbon, sir. If not the blue, the red." Edison prodded on Teenotchy's behalf. "Folk'll be coming from Philly."

He didn't realize quite how much he irritated the old Confederate.

Mister Tewksbury only employed him, Ezekiel and the rest as an interim measure while waiting for the Emancipation laws to be nullified. He was positive they would be, permitting him to claim servants, their children and grandchildren as property.

Brashness camouflaged that Tewksbury ego, still choking on Lee's surrender. After a half century, he could still picture family slaves freely straggling the countryside around Jacksonville as he walked back home after the war. Some didn't bother to nod, let alone bow to Jonas, a skeleton of the gutsy eighteen-year-old who'd rushed off to support the South's call two years before.

It was January 18, 1866, when he finally made it to the back door of his family's plantation, to find his father's throat cut and all two hundred and fifty slaves gone, their sheds abandoned. Though he didn't break down until he found his mammy's empty. "I'd rather starve than pay you a penny," he told her when she drifted back a month later, asking for ten cents a week to work. He felt it a duty to teach her a principle she'd taught him: respect for property, her being his.

His prayers seemed answered when vigilantes asked him to join, anticipating a Confederate recall. Jonas endangered his life most nights in the late sixties in raids to scare off government agents who organized subsidies and information for freedmen.

Slavery had been his birthright and he lived to restore it. And fifty years of emancipation hadn't changed him.

"Boy," he scolded Edison, "I decide what my horses should and shouldn't do." He threw down his cigar on the clean stall floor.

Ezekiel had combed Jonas's hair into a middle parting but, with his skin bronzed by the sun, it was apparent his white mane was thinning. He'd considered wearing top hat and tails as the heatwave had broken, but Julia'd convinced him full dress was inappropriate for a local affair. Still, he wasn't sure the new linen suit was good enough and considered changing as he steamed out of the stable, demanding, "Get that horse out of the race."

Edison inspected the entrants' list but couldn't read, and with horsemen and crowds arriving, there was more than he had time to attend to at ten o'clock. His face was sterner than usual when Alexander arrived, asking him to find a post for Blossom. "Mister Alexander, this looks like Teenotchy's."

"He's riding . . ." Alexander didn't need to explain.

"Not The Big Surrender, sir," Edison finished. "Mister Tewksbury just left here saying no horse with that name would ride his track."

XVII

Alexander held out five ten-dollar bills. "Please. This is my fault and I know you need it," he said, having greeted Teenotchy with the news that The Big Surrender was disqualified. That his uncle so easily upset his plans for Teenotchy's win vexed him, as did not being able to think of a better solution than Teenotchy riding Blossom.

Teenotchy stroked her and wouldn't look at Alexander or the money. "Thanks," he said quietly. Horses, money and wild jubilation as Germantowners converged onto the Tewksbury estate—the combination made him sorry that he'd listened to Atlanta insisting he race.

"Don't thank me until you've taken it," said Alexander, waving the bills impatiently.

Seeing him be disagreeable for the first time, Teenotchy thought, "Just like ol' man Tewksbury."

"You can't squeeze out of this mess I've made by dismissing me as being like the rest." Alexander nearly reading his mind made him twitch. It wasn't the first time. "Why go to the starting line if you can't win?"

Blossom nudged Teenotchy. "She doesn't look much. But we're used to each other." Mister Kleber was the only other person who could see past Blossom's splotchy coat and coffin head and, having ridden her for years both bareback and in the saddle, Teenotchy knew her looks deceived.

"The fifty dollars is in my pocket when you want it. And I'm sorry." Apology wasn't as natural to him as generosity, and Alexander didn't sound convincing.

Seeing Atlanta crossing the field took Teenotchy's mind off the strain of the moment. "Here's my sister," he said.

"Good luck, anyway, if I don't see you again," said Alexander, using her arrival to exit.

Had it been a dress contest, Atlanta deserved something for originality. She'd made her pink floral blouse from an old dress of Beulah's and sewn pale-yellow bows around her dark skirt to match the ribbon on the straw hat, also compliments of Beulah.

"I told Mrs. Tewksbury you weren't riding a horse called The Big Surrender. Like I said, I put your name on the list myself, so I don't know where she got it from. But you know you can't tell 'em nothing when they think they're right. But I wonder where she got it from? The Big Surrender." Atlanta chatted on, more nervous than Teenotchy. "Anyway, I guess you have stuff to do, but I brought you something," she said, taking Sukey out of her borrowed string purse.

"Ol' Sukey." Teenotchy wanted to smile. Atlanta never let him touch it when they were little.

"Sister made it," she said. Sometimes his shyness softened her. "Maybe you can tie it to your saddle."

A giggling trio cut her off. "Tee, Tee, Teenotchy," hollered Martha from a hiding place.

Atlanta, suspecting it to be Geronimo, revved up to chastise. "Lord. Did you bring that Injun?"

Without Aunt Em to team against, theirs was never a lasting peace.

"Aw, shut up, Atlanta. Somebody gashed him in the head with a rock while he was waiting outside the Klebers' for me, so I took him back to Miss Sullivan's."

"You cleaned this morning!" That he'd worked was a perfect reason to rile her.

"Mister Teenotchy . . ." the little voices sang like they rehearsed.

"You can't clean and win," Atlanta sighed. She didn't know whether to be sad or mad.

Martha, Minnie and Flora didn't want to ask who Atlanta was, but they pondered it together, chiming, "Tee's got a girlfriend."

Blossom twitched and Teenotchy went looking for Martha, hiding with her friends behind the water trough, where strangers came and went as noon drew on.

"I better find Beulah and her brothers," Atlanta said. "Don't you go losing my doll," she called as he found the girls.

"Your bootlace is undone, Martha," Teenotchy said, discovering them huddled like three bunnies. Martha's red satin bow flapped over her ear, and pride made her draw back when he bent to do her lace. "C'mon now. You'll trip an' lose another front tooth."

"Tell him," said Minnie, rising for the occasion.

Martha passed the order to Flora, who could hardly be heard. "Martha's grandaddy give her a whole nickel and know what she's doin'?"

"Buying everybody sugar candy?" Teenotchy guessed to get a rise out of them.

"She's bettin' it all on you," exclaimed Minnie.

Martha chewed on the tip of her satin ribbon. "My grandaddy said do what I want." Not that she dared asked Edison for betting instructions. "How d'you bet, Mister Tee?"

"I doubt they'll take nickels. Why not just make a wish?

Then if you win I owe you a taffy *and* you'll still have your nickel."

Flora's bottom lip drooped faster than Minnie's as Martha stuck out her tongue at them.

"Y'all help her," said Teenotchy, wondering where he'd get taffy money if he lost. "Think up a cheer and say it ten times if any of you can count that high," he teased before their legs bounded across the field faster than Flora's were meant to carry her.

She fell and Teenotchy didn't know whether to run and help, but he could hear a voice clucking in the distance and looked toward the Tewksburys' south entrance, where scores milled in.

Overjoyed to find him before the race, Tessie waved frantically from the bakery wagon. "Hey, 'Notch! Hey!"

He was used to seeing her beside Mister Schaus, the Jewish baker, making morning deliveries, but with him dressed in black for his Sabbath and Tessie togged in white Sunday best, they looked an odd couple.

As the baker's wagon pulled up, Teenotchy was shocked to see Aunt Em propped in the back among Mister Schaus's assortment of bread baskets and a half dozen red-headed children. Her snores were as loud as their combined wriggles and hellos.

Tessie sprinted from the wagon. "She was huffing and puffing from the minute we passed the Fire Insurance Company. Hadn't of been for Mister Schaus, don't guess she'd've made it."

Teenotchy tried to look nonchalant and offered Blossom's feed bag to Mister Schaus's stout, hairy workhorse.

"Thought Aunt Em would come down with heatstroke," Tessie said, as freckled tots climbed over and around the old woman napping on a heap of straw. Her navy skirt and white apron were paper-stiff with starch and she looked incapable of an unkind word. So the others wouldn't hear, Tessie hedged closer to Teenotchy whispering, "Couldn't get her shoes on, but she said she wasn't coming barefoot up your work, so I borrowed boots off my brother."

Aunt Em looked like she could sleep years as megaphone and trumpet called riders to the starting line.

"There's a wagon park," Teenotchy told Mister Schaus, who looked anxious to move on.

"It's the Sabbath," he said disdainfully in a thick Hamburg accent.

"Reckon you can help me get her down?" asked Tessie, moving in her usual birdlike jerks.

"We'll help," yelped the ten-year-old Schaus twins.

"Gustav! Karl! Sit down," Mister Schaus ordered, telling Tessie, "I can drive you nearer."

"Wasn't that the last call?" she asked Teenotchy when trumpets sounded again, stirring activity across the flat meadow.

"I'm not racing," Teenotchy told her. But hearing him say it lifted a dead weight that fell heavily on Tessie's shoulders.

"Aunt Em walked the length of Main. No shoes. Young folks pushing like they was rushing to the Second Coming. And every step me worried it was her last. But no matter, she wouldn't stop though I begged her to."

Teenotchy wouldn't look her in the eye, so she addressed the rest to Mister Schaus. "Didn't she look like I do mornings when you make me go back home to bed? If it wasn't for some of your bread pudding . . ." Tessie released a sob. "She come too far. Old as she is . . . won't matter if you and that nag come last, but you got to ride."

Aunt Em's snores made it seem unlikely she'd come to, and though the Schaus twins shook her, she didn't.

"Bread pudding," Tessie instructed as she watched Teenotchy undo his saddle and remove his specs. "Gustav, let her whiff that . . . 'Notchy, what're you doing?"

"Mister Schaus, sir, I'll sweep the bakery free for you Monday if you'll keep hold of these for me till tomorrow."

"You riding bareback?" the eldest Schaus boy asked, hanging over the back of the wagon.

"Bareback!" the twins chorused as their father took the saddle.

"Lemme keep his glasses," Tessie said, grabbing them before Mister Schaus could. "He got 'em off the Quaker man he works for," she explained, knowing that Mister Schaus had a hard enough time keeping track of his own.

"Good luck!" the children yelled as Teenotchy galloped toward the starting line, with the sun on his back and Sukey stuffed down his bib front, while Aunt Em kept her eyes shut, faking snores and wondering how they believed she could sleep through three-year-old Rachel crawling over her.

Pretending to sleep was easier than saying good luck to Teenotchy, whose mother she'd raised. And father. And grandfather. Although these facts meant even less than his being of her. She'd beaten the devil out of him as best she could, having been prevented by Dusty from drowning him, and Aunt Em saw his size as the devil manifested, blind as she was to the part fear played in stunting his growth.

"I'm only going 'cause Miz Llewellyn's so mad that somebody pinned a sign on her elm inviting us'n." Not that Aunt Em could read what Alexander'd posted on Johnson, hoping it would be seen by domestics, and several did.

COLOREDS WELCOMED AT HOLYBROOK MANOR
BRING THE FAMILY TO THE DERBY, SEPTEMBER 6

When he reached the starting line, Teenotchy hesitated to peek at the town divided: pale skins seated, brown ones standing, and those within eyeline of employers being particularly subdued. Not that they had a lot to shout about since Teenotchy was the only one of them among the twenty-three riders.

The rider beside him yelled to another, "Horse called The Big Surrender got disqualified."

"Good thing for us," a second gibed. "Heard it was a pure Arab."

"Couldn't have been," contested the first. "Was a nigger riding it."

Mister Kleber's voice replayed in Teenotchy's ears, "None has a saddle made with such care." Bareback suddenly seemed a mistake. But as good as he knew Mister Kleber's handiwork was, Teenotchy believed horses hated saddles, no matter how well made. So, provided he could stay on, he hoped he'd given Blossom a small advantage, knowing if he fell he could be trampled to death, which seemed easier than losing with so many wanting him to win.

The motley crowd of horses and riders was no less nervous than he was, all of the jockeys checking and rechecking reins and stirrups. Teenotchy peered down his bib front to see that Sukey was safe with the talisman Miss Sullivan had given him when he'd returned Geronimo to her. "Just as well he hangs with me, as you can't keep an eye on him. Come twelve o'clock we'll be praying for you," she'd said.

But there on the track, at five minutes to, Teenotchy was thinking what Mister Tewksbury was: "How'd I get talked into this?"

Even Alexander forgot the purpose of the event as he spied Teenotchy through his binoculars. "Bareback," he said aloud, "is suicide."

"What did you say, Lord Blake?" Melanie Fullerton asked. Julia'd made sure Melanie was on Alexander's right. "Are you looking at my brother? He's got by far the best horse, I think."

A few of Germantown's top breeds belonged to Quakers, all of whom had gathered outside their Main Street meeting house for an Emancipation thanksgiving service timed to boycott the race.

Melanie'd had a touch of the runs that morning, and had she been less determined for Alexander to see her in her new white lace blouse and beige linen suit, she might have stayed at home. "It's twelve," she said impatiently. "Why haven't they started?"

"They may as well give your brother the blue and let us all lunch now," said Julia, impressed by Edgar Fullerton's elegant habit as much as by his thoroughbred bay.

Teenotchy in bib and braces was glad he hadn't bothered with a shirt. He was already sweating so when a filly jumped the gun, salty perspiration stung his eyes.

"Mister Tee, Mister Tee, Mister Tee-not-chee," Martha, Minnie and Flora squealed in a skipping-rope beat.

Edison's daughter-in-law was embarrassed. "Y'all stop that hollering. This ain't no farm."

They'd already infected an eight-year-old boy standing next to them and his older brother who joined in, tempting Atlanta two behind. But with Hernando at arm's length she resisted until the starter's pistol burst.

"And they're off!" hailed the voice in the megaphone, as horses and riders hurtled around the track.

All but Blossom.

Edgar Fullerton's bay was quarter-way around, with a palomino and two mustangs in pursuit, as Blossom, still at the starting post, raised her coffin-shaped head like a wolf poised for a night howl.

Poor Martha Edwards nearly swallowed her tongue yelling, "Run! You're supposed to run!"

"Of course a rider of Edgar's caliber shouldn't have been allowed to ride against local bumpkins, but his winnings are already promised to the Auxiliary," explained Colonel Fullerton, who stood on the other side of his granddaughter.

Blossom still hadn't budged.

Standing on an orange crate, Tessie described the sorry sight to Aunt Em, who'd consumed so much bread pudding she needed to lie down; although the excitement of every wife, lover, brother and son screaming as twenty-two horses soared around the track was almost contagious.

Stationed opposite the spectators, Edison and Horatio

refused to look at each other. To say, "I told you so," seemed heartless.

But a full minute into the race Blossom hadn't begun because Teenotchy had signaled her to wait for the dust to settle. He patted her mane, stroked her like a cat, making kissing sounds. "Here, Blossom. Thatagirl, Blossom," he said, like Mister Kleber used to to calm her, realizing that fear shortens the gait.

"The nigger hasn't moved," laughed Jonas as Alexander focused his binoculars on Teenotchy's figure frozen on the track.

"Don't give up the ghost. You can win," Alexander whispered, and phantoms shot like an arrow to pierce Teenotch's heart with his message, as his mother simultaneously pleaded from the grave, "Run, Teenotchy! Don't stop!"

He gave spur and the wild in Blossom catapulted to lead the herd.

"Hang tough, cowboy!" Horatio cried as Teenotchy vaulted by.

Martha, Minnie and Flora did a shake dance. But Alexander maintained a mental chant. "You can win. Don't give in. You can . . ."

The dark nation roared and Tessie raved, "The last will be first and the first last. Go, 'Notch. Ride 'em."

Teenotchy clung so that Blossom's heart beat for them both. Was it a centaur hoofing the turf, past a young filly, past the old thoroughbred ridden by Mister Naumann's nephew? Or a four-legged Nijinsky?

"I told you that little niggah could ride," Edison hollered.

In spite of spectators rollicking in track madness, Alexander kept mind and binoculars focused, positive Teenotchy could hear. "You can win. Don't give in . . ."

Melanie Fullerton needed the toilet. "How many more laps?" she asked her grandfather as Teenotchy edged into seventh place. She didn't like the idea of walking back to the house on her own and was glad her grandfather wouldn't have permitted it.

But only such a bowel call could have distracted anybody's attention from the pristine track as a bareback rider stole the show.

Atlanta's straw hat bobbed about and three little voices sparked a chant that soon smoldered and flamed as dark voices joined, "Mister Tee, Mister Tee, Mister Tee-not-chee. Mister Tee, Mister Tee, Mister Tee-not-chee."

Tessie rocked on her orange crate and yelled to Aunt Em, "Lord, s'pose he wins and we didn't bet nothing!"

"Horatio," Edison called to him, "don't you have no seizure. Not till we win, anyhow."

Seven minutes into the race and Edgar Fullerton was still leading in the third lap without challenge, the palomino having slipped into fourth. Those like Jonas, who preferred the sport to be competitive, mourned because none of the Philadelphians had arrived with thoroughbreds, as anticipated.

"With the way the niggers are shouting," bawled Jonas, "you'd think they expected something to happen."

His wife shut her pale-green parasol and looked over at her nephew. He was sweating more than anybody at the track. She prodded him, thinking if he fell ill her sister would never forgive her, but Alexander refused to have his concentration broken, believing he was as important to Teenotchy as Blossom's sure foot. "You can win," he repeated, refusing to mop the perspiration that suddenly became all his aunt could think about.

"Last lap," shouted Colonel Fullerton to his granddaughter. But her stomach rumbled so, she sat stiller than Mrs. Orestes Adams, whose Calvinist sensibilities taught it was vulgar to get excited. Wishing she could shut her ears to the din, the crowd's elation assured Mrs. Adams that racing was a vice. "Prostitution," she said to herself. "We'll have that here next." Mouthing the Lord's Prayer, as Teenotchy and

Blossom passed the palomino in fourth, she hoped she was
keeping temptation in check.

Nobody could have been more excited than Edison, who
bounced and screamed with as much passion as Martha, who
was ready to stampede onto the track. And poor Tessie
jumped so on the orange crate she fell through, cut her leg
and missed Teenotchy nose into second place. But the pan-
demonium of brown supporters surrounding her made it
clear that Edgar had a challenger.

"Is bareback allowed?" asked Colonel Fullerton as his
grandson saw a coffin-headed horse pass.

Edison was sorry that he'd told his son Joseph to take
charge of the finishing tape and felt like he did when Jack
Johnson knocked out Jim Jeffries. "I can go back to believing
in miracles!" he squealed, running like a twelve-year-old,
tailed by Horatio despite the fact that several also-rans were
still making their way to the finishing line.

Maids and butlers, washerwomen and catering staff, day
girls, street sweepers and yardmen—all ran. Three teachers,
a doctor and some ministers among them. Along with Atlanta
and Aunt Em, Beulah and Tessie, Martha, Minnie and Flora.
Theirs was a wall of "Teenotchys," screamed as they rushed
to the barrier that kept them from the track. Scores of brown
children were hopping.

"He won, Mama?" asked Martha, who'd witnessed what
she might not see again in her lifetime. "He beat them white
men?"

For Teenotchy it had seemed a day and a night and the
dream had ended too soon. He wouldn't let Edison guide
him to the winner's circle and refused to believe he'd won,
as did Jonas and the Cranford brothers.

"Bareback's unacceptable," Alexander heard Melanie
repeat.

"It hardly matters," said Julia. "It's not Epsom, Jonas,
and it's Alexander's fifty dollars."

"Principle," returned her husband. "We have principles in this country, my dear."

Edison and Horatio looked at each other and Teenotchy smiled. "Winning's all in the mind," Edison said, as his granddaughter and the children who saw Teenotchy break the tape began, "Mister Tee, Mister Tee, Mister Tee-not-chee."

"I'm so proud, I'm busting," laughed Tessie, trying not to notice the trickle of blood on her gashed leg. "Wish I could see Atlanta," she told Aunt Em, who couldn't take it in. Winning was beyond comprehension, and she stood at the fenced barrier behind a little child as Horatio placed the blue ribbon around Blossom's neck.

Mister Tewksbury took so long congratulating Edgar Fullerton for coming in second that the crowd had begun to disperse before Alexander presented Teenotchy with fifty dollars. They couldn't look each other in the eye and Alexander could just manage, "Congratulations. See you at the stables at six p.m. You've got a horse to collect, we mustn't forget." Teenotchy didn't look at the money and wanted to explain that the lump in his bib and braces was his sister's doll.

"Hey, 'Notchy!" Tessie waved from the fence. "He's talking to a white boy," she explained to Aunt Em.

"We ought to head back 'fore the crowd," said Aunt Em.

Tessie wasn't surprised that the old woman wasn't elated, and excused those who'd slaved too long for joylessness. "He come first. No saddle," she said, to make sure Aunt Em understood.

"Least it's downhill home," Aunt Em mumbled.

"We got to get through these vittles 'fore we start back," said Tessie.

Aunt Em had a picture in her mind of James aged twelve riding bareback on a mustang. There had been a lot that had raced through her mind while the crowd jostled her. Memories and a sense of loss overtook her as Teenotchy overtook Edgar. But it wasn't something she could explain.

Maybe if Emma Van Zandt had been a philosopher instead of a washerwoman, she would've wanted to rant at that
moment about how being shut up and shut out had dehu-
manized her. Or had she been born a poet she could've
mouthed daring verses about being raped, buggered, violated
by a surrogate son with clubbed fists and stinking breath.
Maybe, had she the words, she could've spewed some ditty
about her fear of choking on his come and birthing his gray-
eyed bastard. So Tessie could fathom her joylessness that
Teenotchy was able to ride like James.

Instead she wore her dumbness less comfortably than
Chopper, who was born to it. And Teenotchy's winning
changed nothing. Having been taught only doing words—
sweep, iron, boil, fry, hoe, crawl—she could find herself only
in the sweet oblivion of a macaroon when she could get one.

She was still that child kidnapped from the continent
where the sun blazed orange, though her spirit was more
mutilated than her four-fingered hand. Fear and anger and
shame diseased every corpuscle. Even there at the track she
expected a penalty for winning, because she'd been trained
to lose.

From that day back in October '95 at James's farm, she
believed Teenotchy was sin personified. Hers. Dusty's.
Though not James's, because forgiving him had of course
become second nature to keep from killing him. But it didn't
surprise her Teenotchy rode like it was in his blood.

At the Tewksburys' after-race buffet lunch Alexander
avoided the Fullertons making a performance of being good
losers, although Edgar joked less loudly than his grandfather
about their two-thousand-dollar thoroughbred being over-
taken by a "nag." And Melanie, when she wasn't rushing for
the toilet, teased that the Women's Auxiliary couldn't hope
to get the winnings off the "little nigger."

Twice Julia rounded on Alexander to ask if he'd noticed

how pretty Melanie looked. Though the girl was decidedly peaky and kept breaking out in sweats, Julia was at her most relaxed, having remembered to tell Ezekiel to give Candy the afternoon off.

Settling at a table with the Cranfords, Alexander was enjoying Ruth's sweet-cured ham until he'd swallowed too many of Mrs. Orestes Adams's asides.

"That piccaninny dressed as Lincoln was adorable," she remarked about a child at the race. "Did you see him? With cotton glued to his chin for a beard?"

"Surprising Jonas allowed him on the property," her cousin William sniffed.

Cornelius was equally dismayed. "There can't be more than fifty of their families in Germantown. But they're here in droves."

Mrs. Adams smiled less than usual, because she'd arrived hoping to find two eligible Philadelphia widowers who hadn't appeared. "My day girl brought her entire family."

The brothers had argued about bringing *her*, with Cornelius insisting that, as she'd dined with them when the event was decided, she'd expect their invitation. Etiquette being important to their breeding, William conceded, but not without saying, "Isn't racing against her religion?"

She had to waive that point as her September social calendar was thin. But Julia was more sorry than the Cranfords about their bringing their cousin when she said, "Mister Tewksbury shows true Christian toleration allowing our colored population to participate. Especially since the Women's Auxiliary canceled their picnic." Having bathed Jonas's wounds in salt, she reached for the sugar shaker and daintily sprinkled some on her shortcake.

In the wooded area beyond the Tewksburys', Edison settled his family, after taking the order from Ezekiel that Mister Tewksbury wanted none of their color on the grounds. And

though his wife, Artema, too was happy for an excuse for a
family outing, her cousin wasn't pleased they had to sit
among the brambles.

"Have something to eat, Maybelle," Artema told her,
"and stop fussing. You're just mad you missed the race."

Maybelle Collins wasn't actually a blood relation, but
working side by side in a Memphis hotel after the turn of
the century, she and Artema, both orphaned, claimed kinship. All they'd had in common back then was work, and a
passion for gossip, and that hadn't changed, although Artema's marrying Edison, widowed with four children, in Kentucky meant that she'd become a grandmother before her
time.

She envied Maybelle, with only two girls to worry about,
and wondered how her cousin afforded to dress them in lace
outfits. But Maybelle considered bringing her daughters to
Germantown a social means to their finding mates and marrying well, as she'd done at their age.

"All this land and sun," Maybelle complained, "and Edison got y'all way back here in the woods with bugs biting us
up and crawling over the food."

"Looks like you've had a fair share of sun, Cousin Maybelle," sniped one of Artema's stepdaughters, annoyed that
the woman hadn't stopped moaning since she'd arrived.

"I wanted to see the race," pouted Maybelle's fourteen-
year-old, whose prettiness was overcast by misery. "Mama,
what was the point, coming all this way and missing it?"

Martha agreed. "It was so gooood!" she yelled. "I was
up the front," she began, determined to relive the moment.
"Mister Tee, Mister Tee, Mister Tee-not-chee," she sang. She
posed, frozen, to describe the scene. "First Blossom just stood
there. Like she wasn't goin' nowhere. Then, whooosh."

"You and your mouth, Martha Edwards," her grandmother scolded. "Set and eat."

"I'm not hungry, and Mister Teenotch' said he'd buy me
a taffy if he won."

Maybelle's Mississippi childhood harbored some regrettable images. "Teenotchy?" She thought about a drama
played out in her youth.

"The kid that won the race," Artema told her, racial
pride basking her in a grin. "Reminded me of the rodeo
show where I first met Edison." Her two long braids were
wrapped around her head, German fashion, and though her
dark-brown face was unlined, mothering had stolen her
youth. She was a thirty-five-year-old grandmother who'd
taken on Edison's children as their own two, though his eldest was thirty. They all called her Mama.

Enviably, Maybelle looked in her prime and hadn't been
overworked since she married a farmer from Memphis, who
resettled in New Jersey when she was twenty in 1903.
Though James Van Zandt's farm was a fresh enough memory. She throbbed with excitement at the thought of finding
Dusty Simms. "Teenotchy?" she repeated. "What's he look
like?"

"Little bitty thing," said Artema, who didn't see him
through the soft focus that beguiled her granddaughter.

Martha was as moony as a sixteen-year-old in love. "He's
got gray eyes. Good hair," she giggled, her red hair-ribbon
still flapping at her ear, as it had been all afternoon.

"Didn't grandma tell you to sit and eat?" her mother
chided, pulling at the bow of her pinafore until she tumbled
upon the picnic blanket.

Maybelle was ready for another reunion, having concluded that the twenty-odd of Edison's clan parked there in
the woods didn't know what a good time was. "Tee-not-*chee,*
or Tee-*not*-chy?" she wanted clarified, adding, "Gray eyes.
Mother name o' Dusty?"

Having shared no family, there was a lot about Maybelle
that was new to Artema. "Girl, 'member I told you I used to
work down a farm in Mississippi?" she asked Edison's wife.

Her daughters, who'd never heard much about their
mother's impoverished past before their father rescued her,

listened with greater interest than Artema, occupied with distributing the food she'd spent a week planning and two days preparing.

"There was a girl used to work there," Maybelle continued. "Tall. Grayish eyes. Miz Dusty." She smiled, reminiscing. "Real soft-spoken and kept a lookout for me 'cause I didn't have kin. Way before I met you," she explained to Artema, who'd adopted her in Memphis in a similar way.

"Martha! If I tell you to set again, you'll get the belt," Artema interrupted.

"Miz Dusty had the cutest little ol' baby I used to mind for her. Real good hair and curly eyelashes."

"I wanna find Mister Teenotchy," begged Martha, pulling her mother's arm.

"C'mon, baby," offered Maybelle. "I'd like to find him myself. I made up that name. Can't be two with gray eyes."

Artema, knowing her cousin to be one for tales and gossip, assumed that, like everybody else after the race, Maybelle was looking for a connection with the winner. But she waved her grandchild off. "Where you think he'll be, Martha? Don't you and Maybelle forget where we're sitting."

"Nigger park," laughed Maybelle, referring to the woods as she and Martha strode off.

Teenotchy was still shaking hands with well-wishers and was glad for the blankets Horatio passed to him, although a drink of water would have been more appreciated. But he could see Edison and all the extra stable hands were busy.

"Hey, little fella," said a tall blond man, slightly balding. "Bet you don't recognize me. My daddy used to own a store hereabouts when I was a boy."

Teenotchy shook his hand but the man was as much a stranger as other well-wishers who'd greeted him with, "Remember me?" that Teenotchy couldn't recall. But this gentleman was more specific.

"I was one of those Boy Scouts who found you in the woods that time. Remember? You came up to our camp. Boy, did you look a sorry sight." Teenotchy was glad the man's wife kept tugging at his elbow, beckoning him. Otherwise he might have talked on. Instead he said, "My wife and I run a hardware store in Philly. If you get over there, drop by." He waved and was gone.

"Nice to see you," Teenotchy said to him, starting to tremble as Edison walked up.

"Who was that?" asked the stable boss, not waiting for an answer. "Everybody sure loves a winner."

Teenotchy wanted to be somewhere familiar and was relieved when Edison told him to get home and put on some dry clothes. "You're shaking like a leaf," Edison laughed.

"D'you know where I'll find Martha before I go?" Teenotchy asked.

"The town councilman's waiting to shake your hand and you looking for Martha." Edison shook his head. "She's off in them woods eating. Like you should be. Didn't your people come?"

Teenotchy thought he could see Edison's granddaughter among townsfolk milling by the pump and craned his head. "I promised her a taffy," he said, avoiding Edison's question. "But maybe, if it's OK with you, I'd like to get Blossom back."

"I give you the morning. But I can't give you the whole afternoon," Edison suddenly complained, because a gray-haired man had interrupted to say he was a friend of Mister Tewksbury's and expected better service. "Be back at three," he ordered, realizing that he was snapping at Teenotchy unnecessarily.

"If you see Martha, tell her I owe her a taffy," Teenotchy said. But Edison wasn't listening.

The grounds of Holybrook Manor were strewn with bits of paper and apple cores, as it was the season. And making his

way toward Main Street, Teenotchy wondered how late in
the night he'd be there cleaning up. Not that he minded the
idea. In fact it appealed. He was used to a broom in his
hand. Or a rake.

Had he been asked to make a wish, he would have
wished to be kneeling in his patch with the warm lunchtime
sun on his back. But Blossom nudged him and he pulled a
rag off one of her braids. "You look a sight," he laughed.
"But I don't think Mister Paul would get the joke, so I best
undo this mess," and he re-covered her with both blankets.
"You as tired as I am?" Teenotchy asked her as he bent to
unlace his boots. Her tail swatted him a few times, which he
took as a hint she wanted her flanks rubbed before they
walked the mile and a half to Mister Kleber's.

"When I was little," Teenotchy told her, giving her fore-
legs a quick massage, "Mister Paul said the main thing to
learn off horses was they treat everybody the same that takes
care of them. Liars, murderers, cheats, preachers, Helga
Kleber even . . ."

"Hey boy!" called an old guy on a mule. "Well done."
Man and mule were creeping so slow Teenotchy hoped they
didn't have far to go. "I knew a nigger smaller than you once
and told him to join the circus but he wouldn't." Teenotchy
waved back.

"And I used to think," Teenotchy continued to Blossom,
"that was good, 'cause, like Mister Paul says, we're all children
of God. But I'm starting to wonder, see, if it's not kind of
bad . . . being nice to any ol' body that'll feed you. I can't say
why it's not right. But I've been thinking about it for a long
time . . ."

"Teenotchy!" shouted a couple of kids in a junk wagon,
so he looked up and waved again. Being recognized made
him feel uncomfortable and he decided to move on. He felt
better with the boundaries he'd grown used to. Strange white
faces hailing him in Upper Germantown in broad daylight

could lead to no good, he suspected, being one whose invisibility had become a shield.

The earth beneath his feet had been an old Indian trail before settlers renamed it Main Street. With a mild yellow sun glow highlighting the trees, it looked a paradise and Teenotchy thought the Indians had been smart to live outdoors and not coop themselves up in houses. Not that he wasn't glad to spot the Klebers' stalwart red bricks.

"Blue velvets in summer," he whispered to Blossom as they passed the parlor windows. Winning opened his eyes and loosened his thoughts. Sharpened his criticism. Rather than petrified, he felt good.

"Afternoon, Mrs. Kleber," he said, spotting Helga as he led Blossom to her stall in the barn.

She saw the blue ribbon around the horse's neck. "That blanket's not ours. Take it back." She refused to acknowledge more.

"I've come to do the parlor," he said, kneeling to put his boots on. "Mister Kleber let me off early."

"He's napping. Don't wake him, and take that blanket back as soon as you're finished."

With fifty dollars in his overalls pocket, Teenotchy followed Mrs. Kleber to the kitchen to collect the arm sheaths she insisted he work in. The centaur was dead. So was the roar of dark voices chanting, "Mister Tee-not-chee."

The white porcelain doorknob, smooth, familiar, admitted him to the parlor. Home. To be himself.

He prayed Mrs. Kleber wouldn't come make him open the drapes. It was easier to resurrect his mother's voice and hands in the dim light. Beams snuck in from all sides of the window. He stood statue-still, to feel like Dusty Simms's little boy again.

Who could act right *and* shake the town councilor's hand?

Picking up the jar of furniture polish, Teenotchy's knees slightly buckled. It was the tension of forgetting his place. To win was to shine the brass lantern to Mrs. Kleber's specification.

The tick-tock-tick-tock-tick-tock of the grandfather clock almost drowned out the agonized moo of a cow two meadows away as Teenotchy unscrewed the jar of yellow beeswax polish to free that voice meant to save him, yelling, "Run, Teenotchy! Don't stop!" But he heard nothing.

Had he done something different, he wondered, replacing the lid to try opening it again.

Nothing. That smell filled the room, but still there was nothing but the tick-tock-tick-tock . . .

"Sister?" he said under his breath, snatching off the bleached arm sheath. But she said nothing to his third, fourth and fifth attempts, and suddenly he heard Mrs. Kleber's footsteps clicking a nasty counterpoint to the clock's tick.

His heart was in his throat when she opened the door. "Take that blinket back," she demanded, wanting him out of the house before her father-in-law woke at three.

Teenotchy shut the lid on the polish for the fifth time, surprised she didn't take issue with the white sheaths on the Bavarian table. "It's a *blan*ket, you stupid ol' crow," he hummed to himself as she waited for him to go. Hands on her hips, tapping her foot, she thought she'd got the best of him until he flashed her his toothiest grin.

He was glad to be back among the bustle on Main Street until he remembered he'd left Sukey behind. But he couldn't face going back or walking the mile and a half to Holybrook Manor and smiled as he saw the trolley coming, since he could afford to ride.

"Niggers," said the conductor, shaking his head at Teenotchy. "Coon, you can't ride this trolley with a ten-dollar bill." Teenotchy didn't understand. "Get off and get change," ordered the conductor with more venom than a rattler trapped in his second skin.

Teenotchy listened to the iron wheels screech away into the distance as he followed its glistening silver track, head down, hoping that nobody would call his name.

He kicked a stone along the cobbled street and tried to stay out of everybody's way. Ten dollars. What was the point if it was too much for the trolley car, he was thinking, looking at his scruffy brown boots. He tugged at his bib strap and thought how lucky he was that he hadn't had to explain to Mister Kleber he'd won riding bareback.

The clock of the German Reform Church had only struck two as he arrived back at the Tewksbury stable and by five Edison had been called boy once too often. He took it out on Horatio, who'd said, "I want to go up Ellis Island and line up for the free handout with them Polacks and Italians."

"What have they got to do with you, nigger?" Edison demanded, as Ezekiel arrived to say Alexander wanted a buggy and pair.

"Main'll be a mess," Horatio said, batting at a pesky fly. "Automobiles, folks on foot, crutches, God knows what. Seem like the whole town come out."

"Tell it to him," said Ezekiel, who was in a testier mood than Edison, having dealt with the Tewksburys' guests since the buffet, and was relieved that the Tewksburys had an invitation to dine out. "I'm glad to be rid of 'im. And he's expecting Teenotchy to drive."

"You win, you drive!" laughed Edison, who'd found something funny for the first time since the race. "Losers sweep," he told Horatio, who didn't get the joke.

"I don't mind sweeping," Teenotchy said.

"No, you won't," Ezekiel told him. "Mister Alexander said he didn't care what he was riding in. But he didn't want nobody else driving."

*   *   *

The sun pelted down and Alexander, with his Panama cocked forward to protect his nose, talked about the Declaration of Independence all through the forty-minute journey.

"You must be feeling like I do when my uncle groans on about the States War," he said to Teenotchy at the reins as they passed Pastorius's monument. But, whether he lectured about Benjamin Franklin, enthused about Jacques or sat silent, he was composed and Teenotchy found his presence soothing. "Atlanta tells me you garden when you're not working at Holybrook," Alexander went on. He knew as much about Teenotchy as Teenotchy knew about himself thanks to Atlanta and Edison. "She says you've got a green thumb." Adding a "please" to sound less commanding, Alexander asked to be taken to Mister Kleber's garden.

As the brougham headed east toward Main Street, Teenotchy was thinking about the way the bleached sky bled into a peach horizon. But it was Alexander who said, "Haven't the sunsets been extraordinary these past few days? I hope Miss Sullivan's seen them."

At first it perplexed Teenotchy that Alexander seemed to read his mind, share his thoughts, but it made him comfortable to hear his own feelings expressed. "That's funny. I was thinking that same thing," he admitted quietly.

In spite of Mister Kleber's sign, Teenotchy expected Helga Kleber to dress him down if she caught him showing somebody around. So he drew up at the Klebers' west gate, the one furthest from the house. "Only a little tiny piece is mine," he said, thinking his sister had given Alexander a false impression.

Despite Teenotchy's best efforts, the heat was defeating his gardening skills. But Alexander accepted no apology. "Garden!" he hooted, after a quick walk to the pond and back past the meadow. "It's a park. How do you find time for anything else?"

"It looked way better last summer," Teenotchy apologized again, before Alexander, examining the begonias, heard him say suddenly, "Hey! Look at you. I thought we'd lost you." He was talking to a yellow rose and couldn't cover the fact.

"I talk to myself all the time when I go over ledgers that make no sense," Alexander said to excuse him.

"Things were better last year," Teenotchy repeated, relieved that Alexander wanted to drift off on his own to see Mister Kleber's oaks, though he couldn't resist sitting on one of Hans's benches.

"It's perfect," he said when Teenotchy finally came to find him. "Sit."

The way the light fell through the leaves cast a spell that made it feel right to share what he'd been thinking. "I'm returning to England in a few weeks," said Alexander, "and I want you to join me."

To Melanie Fullerton, this would have sounded like a perfect overture but to Teenotchy, still saving to take the trolley to Philadelphia, beyond Germantown was Hell. His dream was to stay out of the poorhouse, his bliss was a flower. He looked worried.

"My grandfather owns the finest studs and the gardens are . . ."

Whenever Teenotchy was overwhelmed, he turned a blind eye and a deaf ear. For a boy who felt lucky to own two pairs of overalls and a ten-by-thirty-foot allotment, England was the moon, and he was trying to recall if they still had slavery there as Alexander was explaining, "You could either have the gatekeeper's cottage or the smallholding until I inherit."

Fingering his harmonica, Teenotchy sensed a strangeness in the moment and wanted to play a tune that could blow it all away. "Aunt Em's expecting me to fix her a new clothesprop," he interrupted.

But having carried his cross thus far, Alexander was

ready to be crucified. His hat was on the bench between them
and he looked younger without it, his face copper from the
weeks of blazing sun. He mopped his brow and refused to
stop. "Would you hate me if I said I love you?"

Trees. Flowers. Blossom. The saddle Mister Kleber'd
made him. His harmonica. His mother's hands. These Teenotchy loved. But it was beyond his comprehension that men
could love men. Kissing stuff?

Alexander's hand reaching to caress his cheek was more
answer than Teenotchy Simms could stand. He broke and
ran. But he couldn't shake shame. It chased him. Along the
columns of oaks.

Past the pond. And the swans.

Across Carpenter's Meadow. Trampling buttercups underfoot.

Grief-stricken, he collapsed in Fisher's Hollow, sweating
and breathless.

Didn't men swing for less?

To be given a plot of land, a horse valued beyond his
comprehension, he could almost accept, thanking from a hollow place. But love he knew as one of Miss Sullivan's words
and she'd made them drink it. Love. Even Chopper, though
he showed no thank-you in his eyes.

For some reason Teenotchy thought about the Christmas of '99, when he got his hairbrush from Mister Kleber,
believing it exceeded what the boogeyman's child deserved, but Mister Kleber'd made him take it. "You need
it," he'd said, though the child couldn't understand how
need altered the fact that he deserved nothing. Unable to
formulate the question, Teenotchy got no answer, and accepted the brush in silence, sensing thank-you wasn't
enough.

The hollow was noisy with hungry birds at that time
of evening and he sat on a rotten stump and dried his
tears, refusing to acknowledge that he liked the color of
Alexander's eyes, could picture the two tiny moles on his

right cheek and the way his lips curled when he wasn't smiling.

Slumping home an hour later, Teenotchy tried to forget, "Would you hate me if I said I love you?" But through the night it danced like a nursery rhyme in his ears.

XVIII

Sunday, September 7, 1913

"Cleveland," derided Beulah, sitting at her kitchen table with Atlanta. "Why's Teenotchy want to move to Cleveland? What he needs is a girl, that's what. School over *and* no friends. . . . What he needs is a girl to help him spend some of that money. Some girls like short boys, and if I'd just won fifty whole dollars . . ." The bone in Beulah's corset was cutting into her thigh as usual, but she forced herself to sit upright anyway.

Atlanta'd been there for fifteen minutes and had hardly managed to get a word in after confiding that Teenotchy'd announced that morning he was giving her two dollars, five for housekeeping to Aunt Em and using the rest to resettle in Cleveland.

"Two little stingy, mingy dollars," said Beulah. "If that's all he's giving you, I'm sorry I told you to rush around getting him into the race. That's hardly enough for the dress material I told you about."

Although Beulah'd claimed she was thinking about Atlanta making something to attract Hernando, in fact she was thinking about what her mother had said: Atlanta's maroon dress looked nice enough but was starting to whiff of borax from "hanging in that washerwoman's place."

Not that Beulah minded. But she knew other people talked and was relieved Atlanta hadn't arrived in it that morning. Actually the girls were having one of their bad days, which they suffered periodically, not seeing eye to eye.

When Atlanta knocked at nine o'clock to walk to church with Beulah and her family, it was obvious something was troubling her as she stood at Beulah's kitchen door, biting her fingernails. So Beulah'd asked her in, with the promise they'd follow the family on after she changed her hair.

"Again?" Beulah's mother'd asked, eyeing Atlanta's black boots and wondering why Beulah hadn't taken up with a better class of girl, while she, husband and sons marched proudly out the door in their Sunday suits and hats.

Their dim kitchen was crowded with a long table and eleven wooden chairs; the odd matching ones were accidental. Two of Beulah's older brothers were carpenters' apprentices and brought their expertise to their mother's kitchen, where she had them build neat shelves and two handsome corner cabinets. Even the table was their handiwork, and Atlanta loved the kitchen so, she often helped Beulah scrub it for the joy of seeing it sparkle. It'd been Atlanta's idea to cover the caps of the preserve jars in gingham fabric, like she'd seen Helga Kleber do, and it was Atlanta who had made the pretty calendar on the wall.

Sitting catty-corner to Beulah at the long table, the two looked like tawdry brown rosebuds: Atlanta in the outfit she'd worn to the race and Beulah in a dark-blue affair which she'd stitched on an aunt's sewing machine. But not as clever as Atlanta at dressmaking, she'd botched the darts at the waist, and the sleeves were noticeably different.

Nevertheless, the Cranford brothers would have been

tantalized by the two girls' European and African blends:
James Van Zandt's Dutchness smoothed the kink in Atlanta's
hair, swept under her straw hat with crinkly waves slightly
frizzing at her creamy temples.

She was glad that Beulah'd decided their discussion was
serious enough to warrant bringing out two squares of pea-
nut brittle, hidden since they'd cooked a batch two weeks
earlier. And although it distressed Atlanta to admit her
brother was planning to move in two weeks, she felt sophisticated mulling it over in her good clothes in that kitchen. But
the far-reaching repercussions hadn't struck her. Sometimes
being seventeen short-changed her perspective.

"You think my brother's not all there?" Atlanta asked,
pointing to her head.

Beulah tried to look as if she were giving it thought,
when in fact she had concluded with her mother that Teenotchy had to be a halfwit to hang around with "that Injun," as
she always referred to Geronimo. "He does spend all his time
in that ol' garden, and remember you telling me how he talks
to the ants and things? Well, that can't be right, can it?"
Beulah asked. "And with a lot of people, winning can go
straight to their heads. Like that time my brother won the
school spelling bee . . ." She couldn't finish the sentence, she
and Atlanta began giggling so, remembering how high Beulah's little brother Red'd held his head for weeks.

"Nose stuck up straight in the air," hooted Atlanta, with
her hand to her mouth, because she didn't think it polite to
laugh outright with Beulah acting her hoitiest.

Beulah stuck a minute sliver of nut brittle in her mouth.
"Crazy people say one thing one minute and do another
the next. Maybe next thing Teenotchy'll try to say he never
promised you the two dollars." The idea of his winning had
been far more acceptable than his being a winner, which she
imagined set him above her brothers. That rankled.

"You think I better run back home and get it?" asked
Atlanta, who knew jealousy to be Beulah's weak point and

suspected her friend was already considering how many congratulations Atlanta might get after church from anybody who knew she was Teenotchy's sister.

Atlanta refused the tiny piece of brittle Beulah offered from her mouth as a truce. Straightening her hat, she suddenly hated to have to say what was really on her mind when she'd arrived, suspecting that Beulah would secretly gloat. But who else did she have to tell? She cleared her throat, not at all surprised when Beulah said, "With Teenotchy gone, you think Aunt Em'll make you deliver the laundry he usually takes for her?" Only a razor could have cut deeper.

"Beulah, here's what I have to tell you," began Atlanta, sorry that she wasn't sharing the rest of her news with the Beulah of yesterday, all hope, all smiles because Teenotchy was "her best friend's brother." Atlanta eyed her across the table and wondered why Beulah had been born to have, whereas she'd been born to have not.

"I've decided to quit school and take a position in Philadelphia," she said, looking at her hands, sorry she'd bitten the nails she'd been careful to keep out of Aunt Em's boiling pans.

Both girls knew "a position" was the genteel way to describe domestic service, and Beulah nearly choked on her nut brittle, which went down unexpectedly with the shock of Atlanta's pronouncement.

"Housework!" Beulah gasped, sorry that she'd been acting a bit stuck-up when she realized what was on Atlanta's mind. Her eyes welled. "Atlanta Simms, you're the smartest colored girl at school. You can't do housework. What'll people say?" She rose to unpin Atlanta's straw hat, because church would have to wait. "We have to talk. Seems like it's you that's gone crazy."

Beulah's mother'd only allowed her to become best friends with "that poor child from the washerwoman's place" because Atlanta was so clever at school.

"I can't let you do it," said Beulah, stunned that Atlanta,

light-skinned and already engaged by the Auxiliary part-time,
would even consider anything lower than baby-sitting. A picture of Atlanta on her hands and knees, bandanna tied back
to front around her head, came up in Beulah's mind. "This
is all Teenotchy's doing," she said.

Atlanta tried to sound cheerful and nearly did, she was
so happy that Beulah looked truly upset. "Housework's not
all that bad and maybe in a year I can save . . ."

"Save!" Beulah shook her head, removing her own hat
and laying it on the table next to Atlanta's, which looked
paltry, even with the new ribbon. They were supposed to
be the "new colored girl," educated, well bred, housework
being OK for their mothers and grandmothers. Hadn't they
dreamed and schemed for more, with Atlanta already prov-
ing that she could hold down a secretary's job?

Didn't the hand-me-down gloves which she was carrying,
compliments of Mrs. Tewksbury, prove that Atlanta was
doing exceptional work?

Beulah wiped back a tear. "Maybe my daddy'll let you
come in with us. My mother was just saying this morning
that Robert, Jr.'s getting too big to still be sleeping in my
bed with his long-legged self."

Atlanta referred to Aunt Em when she said, "You know
the ol' hag won't rest till she has me doing laundry. And I'd
rather be dead than clean for the Klebers another Saturday."

The thought of being separated made them a team
again, so Beulah confided, "Marlene, that's married to my
oldest brother? She 'fell.' That's the reason my brother had
to marry her. So if you 'fell' whoever's baby it was would
have to marry you."

Atlanta didn't think having a baby was a good solution
and had heard terrible stories about how you got pregnant
anyway.

Since the first day she'd started school, she'd wanted to
be a schoolteacher and wear dark dresses and sweep her hair
back in a bun like Helga Kleber's to look serious. And this

dream was squashed only by Hernando Lopez's arrival in
Germantown. She bit her bottom lip to hold back a full-
blown gush of tears. "C'mon, girl," she said, rising from the
table, "you'll get into trouble if you miss church. And you
know your mother doesn't like me all that much anyway."

Beulah never denied the fact but said, "My daddy says
you're a real lady. He always says that."

It felt good walking arm in arm to church with the daylight bursting upon them as they scuttled along Main Street.
Atlanta was sorry she'd refused that piece of nut brittle
straight from Beulah's mouth earlier and said so. The secu-
rity of having a best friend made her troubles suddenly seem
light.

While she and Beulah were having their discussion, Artema
and Maybelle sat mulling over Dusty Simms until Edison,
who'd been trying to sleep, overheard Maybelle's chin-
wag.

"I don't know anything about Teenotchy's sister," he
heard Maybelle say, "but I swear to God, may He strike me
dead if I'm lying, about how Miz Dusty's mother was gonna
drown Teenotchy."

"You say it was her daddy's?" asked Artema, having
swung to gossiping heights with her "cousin" while Edison
dozed in the next room.

It wasn't Maybelle's mind for detail which had allowed
her to stretch the drama she'd observed in 1895 into a saga.
It was her penchant for exaggeration. Twenty minutes into
the tale, she had James Van Zandt begging "Miz Dusty" not
to leave him, " 'Cause you know how them ol' white men get
to carryin' on when they get a taste for the dark meat," was
how she'd put it. "Not that Miz Dusty was all that dark com-
plected . . ."

Edison's stern face appearing in the doorway between
the kitchen and the only bedroom would have been enough
to silence a minister in the full flow of a Pentecostal sermon.

Having half heard Maybelle's accusation about Teenotchy's family, with even mother and grandmother drawn into her tale, Edison decided his wife had listened to too much. He leaned against the doorway and pulled at the springy gray hairs of his goatee. "Maybelle, you got a mouth like a garbage can," he said.

Teenotchy was his new hero, practically his protégé, and he'd heard enough envious tongues slashing "the kid" after the race to make Edison wonder what made a winner so easy to despise. Having spent the better years of his working life at the track, he was used to hearing people accuse every jockey that nabbed the blue ribbon of cheating to win. But in Teenotchy's case, Edison concluded it was a case of pure envy goading the small-minded.

He looked over at the pile of blankets where Maybelle and her girls, who'd gone out, had camped the night before, saying, "If you had any sense, Maybelle, you'd of been rushing to get one of them little mealymouthed girls of yours to meet 'the kid.' But you so busy dropping maggots on my kitchen floor from that garbage can of yours."

Artema wasn't used to him fussing and, like Martha the day before, his crankiness caught her unprepared. She rose to put the iron skillet on the stove and flashed Maybelle a look to say, "Don't pay him no mind, but please don't get him going."

She'd "said" this by subtly raising an eyebrow after a slight pursing of her lips, followed by a nose twitch, hands on her hips. The two women, having spent so much time together in the days when they worked in the Memphis hotel, could practically hold a conversation without uttering a word. Maybelle answered Artema with teeth-sucking which was meant to say, "He's your husband. And I'm not scared of him."

Edison flashed his glare from one to the other. "Don't sass me, woman," he said to his wife. "And Maybelle, if you have to badmouth, don't let me catch you doing it in my kitchen."

"She knows the boy's people . . ." Artema began in a voice as quiet as Edison would have liked her to use while he'd been trying to sleep.

He folded his arms after giving his cheeks a brisk wake-up rub, unaware that the tale of "Miz Dusty" was one Maybelle had embellished from the moment the incident occurred back in 1895 to the point she went to work at a neighboring farm two years later.

That she'd included James Van Zandt in the scenario and had Dusty Simms dressed in a beautiful gown, restaging her more as an adored concubine than a sexually abused housemaid, made her story unbelievable.

" 'Notchy's name is Simms and I ain't heard a word about a Vander Zandt," Edison said to the sound of cold hominy grits frying in the skillet beside a piece of beef (Artema's job at the butcher's house meant he usually got meat).

"Not no Vander Zandt . . . Van Zandt is what Maybelle said." His wife knew it was a point he might let her get away with and hoped that she could get his food on the table quickly enough to shut him and Maybelle up.

"Vander Zandt!" he shouted to establish that he intended being his most bullish. So the women were silent, knowing him to strike if his mood was aggravated by a poor night's sleep.

Edison Edwards rarely struck his woman and never after midmorning, it being Artema who was more prone to lash at him before eleven, especially on Sundays when they were alone, since a few slaps and name-callings had at times suited as foreplay to a cosy embrace, Artema'd discovered.

But she hated getting hit if there was anyone but the two of them in the house, and she had her eye on the butcher's knife, an old but serious one passed on by the butcher's wife.

Maybelle saw how to alter the rhythm of what she con-
strued as a very tense situation. She said, "Where's this child
live anyway? I got my clothes on and I'm meaning to go on
over and see his mama. Her and me were just like that."
Maybelle's two fingers were plied together and held in the
air for anybody interested to see.

"His mama's dead. Died when he was a little kid. And
this grandmother I hear you talkin' into the ground . . . he
hasn't got no granny. It's just him, his sister and a aunt,"
explained Edison as Maybelle got up from the table to allow
him to sit down to the plate Artema laid there—an unsubtle
hint that Maybelle should rise and remember to act like she
was in Edison's house.

Artema asked her, "You want me to put on my hat and
walk on over there with you? I don't know where they live,
but this ol' ornery man of mine knows and I guess he'll tell
us to get us out the way. I know Germantown real good
and—"

Edison liked to eat with his fingers when it was just the
two of them, but with Maybelle in the kitchen he cut into his
hominy grit patty with the spoon Artema'd laid on the plate.

He said, "Y'all leave them alone. That boy's probably
sleeping like I want to be. Ol' man Tewks give us all the day
off. So don't you go over there bothering them people. And
Maybelle, you keep your lies to yourself," he said, dowsing
his meat with pepper. A few spoonfuls of grits had already
sweetened his temper. "Why don't you two go on over to
Joseph's and take what's left of that food from yesterday? If
there's any."

Artema gave Maybelle a wink, saying cheerfully to her
husband, "Mister Edwards, that's cooked like you like?" She
smoothed her apron before she took it off, checking with
both hands that the braid she'd freshly combed that morning
was pinned in place before she took down a basket and
loaded in the few leftovers from the picnic. Maybelle, folding
blankets beside her, was thinking that Artema was too nice-

looking to have settled for a man so much older with no money *and* a bad manner. But she waited until they were on their way to Joseph's before she said so.

It was an indirect jibe since she knew how devoted her "cousin" was to Edison, always claiming he was a good provider, though she worked because they needed her salary. Maybelle said, "You're better than . . . I would no more put up with that old man of mine talking to me like yours does to you." She didn't know where to take the statement but she was determined to have it open the discussion.

She and Artema walked shoulder to shoulder, with Maybelle insisting that she carry the basket of food, as she was the guest.

Artema's plain green dress, buttoned down the front, had a small grease stain on it which she hadn't noticed until they were in the street. She pretended to have her mind more on that than on Maybelle's charge against Edison, who Artema swore was a perfect husband. "This needs a wash," she sighed, "and speaking of wash, I bet somebody over on one of these streets can point us to the washerwoman's where Teenotchy stays. It seems a shame, you knowing him when he was little and not getting to lay eyes on him while you here. You want to try? Can't harm. But we'll have to tell Teenotchy not to mention we dropped by, 'cause if it got back to Edison, I'd have Hell to pay."

Teenotchy'd been out of the house for half an hour before they turned up at his door, finding only Aunt Em in the yard, sipping some buttermilk Tessie got from Mister Schaus.

The walk to Upper Germantown and back the previous day had worn Aunt Em out and she was nearly too tired to appreciate the five dollars Teenotchy'd handed her before he left for the Klebers', claiming he had garden duties since he didn't want Atlanta to know he was actually rushing there to collect Sukey.

Standing in her shoes with the heels and toes cut out, a red cotton bandanna tied around her head, Aunt Em was unrecognizable as Miz Dusty's mama in the gingham dress who had been one hundred pounds thinner, as Maybelle vaguely recalled.

She smiled at Aunt Em and spoke from the sidewalk, while Artema stood a way off, which seemed polite, them being uninvited.

"I'm looking for a Teenotchy," said Maybelle, who had equally changed from the scrawny kid that Aunt Em may have remembered raking leaves at the Van Zandt place that first time she'd set eyes upon her daughter's baby.

That Maybelle was so well dressed made Aunt Em curious. "Who's calling for him?" she asked, fully aware of the good-quality cotton of Maybelle's store-bought skirt and lacy trimmed blouse. Brown shoes polished. Straw hat brand new. It was rare for Aunt Em to see a brown face in Germantown which was completely unfamiliar and, although she didn't know Artema, she'd noticed her before on Main Street.

Maybelle was eager to be friendly. "I used to know him and his mama, 'cause we both stayed at a place down Mississippi. And his mama was like a sister to—"

"His mama's dead. Been dead years," said Aunt Em, without giving Maybelle another look. As fast as her legs could move, they shifted the old woman into the house. She made a point of banging the door, her heart beating so that it was a miracle she didn't collapse. Her body riddled with fear, she used the back of her four-fingered hand to mop the sweat on her brow, rocking with fury when she realized Maybelle had followed her to the steps.

"Is Teenotchy in is the thing?" called Maybelle to the door which had been shut before she could get to it. "I just wanna say 'hi' is all, 'cause he was way too little to remember me. But I was the one named him."

"He gone to Cleveland," lied Aunt Em, thankful that the notion of his leaving was fresh enough in her mind for her to have it on the tip of her tongue. Her full body weight blocked the door as though she expected Maybelle would try to force her way in.

"Cleveland?" Maybelle called back, raising her shoulders as a sign to Artema that she didn't know what else to say. "Tell him Maybelle from the Van Zandt place come by looking for him if you write, OK?" She lifted her skirt to make her way along the gritty yard, not realizing she was seeing it on a good day, since Aunt Em had no wash hanging.

Maybelle turned to look back at the house, telling Artema, "Gone to Cleveland. That child's gone to Cleveland. Just my luck. Seems like it wasn't meant for me to see him, huh? Me missing the race and then him going off before I can get to him. But Edison didn't say nothing about him going to Cleveland, did he? Making us waste our good time coming all the way to this godforsaken place."

"Maybelle, don't you start. It was you nearly had me ready to cut my husband this morning and he's the one told us not to come over here. So don't you get in his face about Teenotchy being gone. But it's surprising, like you say . . ." said Artema as they headed up the road, her allowing Maybelle to take the basket again.

Aunt Em didn't dare peer from the window and fifteen minutes passed like three days. Her heart thumping, she panted. Angry. Scared. Why wouldn't the past erase?

Aunt Em got on all fours, as though she imagined Maybelle might still be outside and able to see her movements from the street. Crawling across the linty floor, her dark skirt raised to free her fat, wobbly knees, she inched her way to the rickety stairs, never stopping to brush the dust collecting on her hands.

She hadn't counted the years since she'd chanced to walk upstairs to the squares they called rooms, which were nothing but tiny haylofts, ceilings low, windows barely large enough to call them windows. Aunt Em inched up the creaking wooden staircase, certain that if she moved faster than a brown slug, her two hundred pounds of flesh would come collapsing through Mister Kleber's handiwork.

Only twelve steep steps to conquer and, when she'd made it to Atlanta's room, Aunt Em was surprised to see complete order, dried flowers neatly arranged on the windowsill, five books stacked like a pillar in the corner by the head of Atlanta's bed, covered in a sheet, yellow with age.

It took Aunt Em no time to find the gingham dress and, tucking it under her arm, she inched her way backward down the steps into the kitchen, to open the potbellied stove.

Would burning the dress stink the place out? Was the woman still outside? Aunt Em longed for the outhouse, her insides grumbling her fears. But she knew better than to go into the yard before using scissors to destroy the evidence that Emma "Lottie" Van Zandt had once existed.

Guided by the gingham squares, she cut, while the voices rang in her head. "Nigger, did you clean this floor?" she could hear James's mother ranting. "Spread your legs, Lottie. C'mon, now you can get 'em wider than that," complained James, again and again.

But Aunt Em let nothing stop her cutting. Cutting through the past. Cutting up Sukey's bed just as Teenotchy, across town, arrived in the Klebers' yard to see his sister's sock doll on the pile of rubbish which Mrs. Kleber burned religiously on Monday mornings.

"Oh Lord," sighed Teenotchy, rescuing Atlanta's old comforter. "Just in time. And there was me thinking that maybe I'd leave you here until tomorrow." He brushed Sukey off and straightened up her black-button eye, which hung looser than its mate. "Witch," Teenotchy hurled toward the back door, which was shut.

He felt too downtrodden to garden all of a sudden, and wished he was already in Cleveland, the home town Edison had such fond memories of till he joined a circus passing through.

Stuffing Sukey in a side pocket, Teenotchy ambled along Main Street, sorry that someone he didn't know called his name.

"Hey, Teenotchy," waved a kid on a bicycle.

Teenotchy felt obliged to smile and wave back, hardly lifting his arm.

Every muscle in him still ached from the sting of Alexander's professed love, which felt like a painful jab the night before but, by morning, was an itch, dangerous to scratch. And unforgettable because . . . just because . . .

Teenotchy caught his reflection in a shop window. He was aware of being head and shoulders shorter than a reflection passing his in the glass. To stand taller seemed pointless, another inch making no difference to somebody who felt like an ant. He was wondering how anybody with good sense could love a midget, when he heard a deep foreign voice calling him from behind. "Teenotchy! Teenotchy! It's good what you do, *amigo*. You great. Yes. You great."

Teenotchy snatched off his glasses the same instant Hernando Lopez's long arm grabbed his shoulder, the Cuban pounding him on the back with such a thud that, had Teenotchy not known better, he might have imagined he was being attacked.

Some six feet three inches towered above him as Hernando's English, heavy with Spanish inflection, spoke. Teenotchy strained to understand him. "You do so good. Me and my friend we say like the others Mister Tee-not-chee." Overcome with enthusiasm, he gave Teenotchy a bear hug that lifted him off his feet.

The cruelest nightmare wouldn't have had Teenotchy, squirming to be released, in the arms of a young man who could have been mistaken as a Masai warrior in suit and tie on Main Street. Atlanta had a good eye—Hernando was black beauty.

"Hey, nigger. Put me down," yelled Teenotchy, not one

to let that word pass his lips in jest. "What d'you go and
do that for?" Teenotchy demanded, when he could feel the
sidewalk beneath his feet again.

Hernando Lopez's slanted eyes looked down upon him.
A lot of other things Teenotchy might have said would have
gone over the Cuban's head, but he'd been off the boat long
enough to know "nigger." He dusted off the dirty smudge
Teenotchy's overalls had left on his clean white shirt and
didn't bother to say goodbye, stalking off, to leave Teenotchy
feeling smaller still as the German Reform Church bells
chimed ten.

He considered going to Miss Sullivan's but decided to
leave that long walk for later. Her chatter only entertained
when he was in the mood for it. He felt lonely but wanted
quiet. To play his harmonica, which he felt for, making sure
he had it on him before he headed east for Horatio's.

An ancient raisin-faced man, his white beard and mustache
biblically long, answered Teenotchy's "Hello, anybody
home?" at the open ground-floor window of a house on Ash-
mead Street. Teenotchy didn't have to think twice. "Uncle
Willy," he was saying to himself as he asked, " 'Scuse me, sir,
is Horatio, I mean Mister Horatio, is this . . . ?"

Uncle Willy stared hard through cataracts, which gave
his eyes an eerie blue-gray tint. His head bobbed slightly
on thin shoulders. Bent, he received Teenotchy in the same
confounded way his son had done when Horatio and Teenotchy were introduced at the Holybrook Stables.

The wizened old man had his son's double bassy voice
when he turned his head to call over his shoulder, "Sonny!
Hey, Sonny!" They had only two rooms, but he was used to
shouting across fields and the habit died hard. "Sonny. You
hear me?"

Teenotchy nervously fingered his harmonica while Uncle
Willy let rip a second time. "Sonny! There's a young 'un here
callin' on you."

Horatio's reply sounded groggy but just feet away. Tee-notchy heard him say, "That woman. Tell her—"

"I didn't say nothing 'bout no woman. I said a young 'un." Uncle Willy turned to Teenotchy. "I don't know why that boy wants to sleep with rags in his ears," complained the old man, whose two-minute stand in the doorway was too long. He started to brace himself on the doorknob like he expected to fall.

"Sir, tell him Teenotchy came by," Teenotchy finished with a disappointed sigh.

The cataracts did a two-step and Uncle Willy laughed, his bony fingers reaching out to touch Teenotchy's shoulder. "Sonny told me how you won 'em," he said. "Sonny!" he called, straight into Teenotchy's face, "Sonny. Get out that bed. . . . It's that Teenotch."

Teenotchy felt he'd come to the right place as Uncle Willy steered him into a room with a stove, table, stool, two chairs and a canvas army cot piled with newspapers tied in neat bunches.

The small coal-burning fireplace with mantelpiece made it unexpectedly homely, as did four framed photographs gracing it.

Teenotchy was also surprised to see cards laid out on the table on a Sunday, but he managed to keep his eyes off them as Uncle Willy told him to sit on the stool.

"You're Mister Willy?" Teenotchy asked, curious why the old man had newspapers arranged on one chair so there was a large gap in the middle.

"Uncle Willy," the old man moaned, situating himself on that very chair. "Uncle Willy to you," he grinned, four front teeth missing to leave him with fangs. "Sonny told me how you and him did. Yessir. Said you rode like you was king of the ro-de-o." Grimacing, he eased his backside fully on the newspapers and leaned in on his elbows to examine the cards arranged in nine lines. "You ever play solitaire?" he asked, tidying the rows which were as neat as the room, although the corners were noticeably dusty. Turning over a nine of spades, he let rip, "Sonny!!!" before explaining with a smile, "That boy loves the bed. Always did. But he sleep more than ever since we come north. Shoulda stayed in Kentuck if you ask—"

"Nobody asked you!" shouted Horatio. The walls were paper thin. It was as if he was sitting at his father's elbow while Uncle Willy studied his cards, telling Teenotchy, "I can't win. Missing the queen o' hearts and jack o' clubs. Sonny said he didn't touch 'em." Uncle Willy winked, dropping his voice. "But when he cleans, he does like he wants. Throwing out."

He was as bony as his fingers, which slowly moved the cards, mumbling, his face the same mahogany as the table. "Gotcha! Gotcha! Gotcha!" he smirked, pulling a card from what was left in his hand and turning several over. Staying fully focused on the cards, he spoke to Teenotchy. "Sonny'll raise hisself in a minute, but I'm got him ruint. Sleeps every chance. Won't cook. He'll warsh out a shirt now and then, but won't iron. But you can't eat a shirt. Ironed or not. But he's a good boy, most the time."

Teenotchy tried to figure out the game, unable to see the point in playing cards alone.

Uncle Willy stretched his hand across the table and stroked Teenotchy's, and they both jumped when Horatio, in the doorway, said, "Daddy, get your hands off that boy. He ain't studyin' you."

Smiling at Horatio, who was barefoot and shirtless, his chest sagging like the cigarette from his lips, Teenotchy said, "Uncle Willy's OK."

The old man patted his hand. "This boy's nice-looking. Good muscles. Good hair. Teeth good. Ol' Mas'r woulda sure liked him, huh, Sonny? Woulda sure like to give him a what-for."

"Daddy," said Horatio, smoke tailing him from the doorway to the window, where he gave a hawk and spit, "don't start that talk. And take your hands off him. Move your chair back, boy," Horatio ordered Teenotchy, "and don't let him put his hands on you. He ain't right in his mind."

Seeing him drag his feet across the room, Teenotchy realized that what seemed different was that Horatio had no hat on, though his hair was creased from it sitting on his head in the same way day after day.

"You want me to fix you something?" his father asked, half rising like he expected the answer to be yes.

Footsteps walked back and forth across the floor above.

"Sow," Uncle Willy said, looking at the ceiling. "Next thing she'll start beating that boy again."

"He needs it," Horatio told the old man. "So mind your business and she'll might mind hers." He grabbed the other chair and turned it around, ready to sit down. "Winner!" he suddenly belched. "Winner! Sitting in my place. . . . What you doing here, boy?" he asked Teenotchy, offering his cigarette, which Teenotchy, as always, refused.

Horatio said, "You got to start smoking. Nobody likes it the first few draws but you get used to it. Go 'head, have a puff."

"Gotcha! Gotcha! Gotcha!" yelled Uncle Willy, clapping his hands, gleefully, though Horatio shook his head sorrowfully.

"Daddy, throw them old cards out."

Teenotchy couldn't help but notice that father and son resembled each other not at all, though their voices were practically the same. He liked being there in the company of men with a lingering smell of cider and dust, must and tobacco and smoke. The three of them doing nothing, hardly speaking for nearly two hours, when sounds in the apartment above rose from shuffled feet to muffled voices.

Horatio's eyes were open but he was asleep and, although he didn't make an effort to converse, Teenotchy sensed that rising was his form of socializing.

It was Uncle Willy who kept offering cider, but they were content to drink nothing, eat nothing, be nothing.

Needing neither words nor music until Teenotchy finally asked if he could look at the pictures on the mantel.

Horatio rose to bring them to the table, but it was Uncle Willy who explained. "Sonny used to ride good as you. But he didn't never get to win no ribbons like you done. Niggers wasn't 'lowed to win nothing back then. But they say times is changing." The old man hadn't looked up, hardly moving a card, going through what was left of the deck in his hand.

Teenotchy was used to a statement like that getting Horatio going, but he placed the pictures on the table and said nothing, his presence at home calm and easy like an owl that had found its perch and was content to observe.

Uncle Willy suddenly scrambled the cards on the table. "Lost again," he said, as if he expected that one day he could win in spite of the deck. He stacked them, cut them, cut them and cut them again. Shuffling was beyond him. "Stand the pictures up," he told Horatio. "The boy don't want to see them laid out like that." He prodded Teenotchy's bicep. "Ol Mas'r woulda never let you out to work the field," he said. "He'd of kept you at the foot of his bed. Like me and—"

"Daddy, shut up and get your hands off this boy," Horatio ordered. Teenotchy couldn't understand why it riled Horatio so and smiled anyway into the old man's blue-gray eyes.

Horatio'd renamed his father's piles "backache," but minor senility was gradually waking the old man's memory of his early slave days and he'd reminisce about being Ol' Mas'r's "boy." Horatio, finding that cider dampened his father's recall, kept him doused in it. For his father's sake, if not his own.

"This is Daddy," said Horatio, pointing to a well-built man in a white turban sitting on an elephant.

Teenotchy couldn't believe it. "Wow!" he smiled at Uncle Willy. "Wow!" His toothiest grin was Teenotchy's best, his most relaxed, and he held the picture practically to his nose to get a better glimpse of Uncle Willy in his youth.

"Fifty he was," said Horatio, standing up to take his tobacco pouch out of his pocket.

"Free," said Uncle Willy, his hand resting upon Teenotchy's again, until his son leaned across the table and slapped
him across the head.

Teenotchy laughed.

"Don't encourage him," said Horatio, rolling another cigarette, "or I'll put you out. You don't know what he's like,
and I don't want him to get started, 'cause he gets to talking
and'll say any ol' crazy thing. But don't believe nothing he
tells you. 'Cause it's all lies. All lies."

Teenotchy smiled and the woman above shifted from
one side of the room to the other. He wanted to ask why
Uncle Willy was sitting on an elephant, but thought it rude
to ask people questions in their own house. He assumed that
all the photos were from their circus days, apart from one
of Horatio on a horse.

"I still got those spurs," said Horatio. "You wanna see
'em? Real McCoy. But I got too big for the boots, so I give
'em away."

When he was in the back room fetching them, Uncle
Willy reached over to stroke Teenotchy's hand again. "Cute.
You wouldna had a bit of trouble in the war."

"The war?" asked Teenotchy.

Horatio called from the other room. "Daddy, don't start
with that slavery-time stuff this morning."

But his father went on, "Civil War. Had me a rifle and
a good time."

Horatio returned with elaborate silver spurs, decorated
with turquoise, and his banjo, and while Teenotchy examined
Horatio's rodeo souvenir, it was good to hear him strumming
some jangly chords.

No sooner than he opened his mouth to sing, there were
three knocks from above.

"Aw shuddup, woman!" hollered Uncle Willy, his face

even bonier-looking raised as it was to the ceiling. He shook a balled fist at the invisible enemy, concluding, "That ol' hussy's just mad 'cause my boy done finished with her, see . . . but Sonny shouldna been messing with a ol' liver-lipped wench like that no way. Smells bad. Looks worse."

Horatio stopped singing and leaned his banjo against the army cot behind him. "I don't know who's worse. Her upstairs or him," he said, pointing to his father. "She walks the floor all night, and he moans worse than an old sow. From about one in the morning till four. Now how's a man s'posed to sleep?" he growled, like a dog that was agitated but couldn't be bothered to bark.

"We shoulda stayed in Kentuck, that's what. I never did like Northerners. Weak. Lazy. Ain't none of 'em know what a day's work is. You should go on down Kentuck and get—"

Horatio interrupted. "And get yourself killed that's what. He don't know nothing."

Teenotchy wanted to ask about Cleveland. About where a boy could go and start a new life. But he figured if he asked the question, they might guess he had moving on his mind and he was too shy to admit he was planning a big change.

XIX

Julia tapped lightly at Alexander's door to tell him she and Jonas were setting off for church. Worship was unusual for Mister Tewksbury, but she'd convinced him he owed an appearance to the three deacons who'd supported the derby.

He was pacing up and down on the veranda for her as Alexander answered her familiar knock. Julia was surprised to find her nephew in his dressing gown at eight forty-five, since he normally read until midnight and rose promptly at seven, a habit left over from boarding school.

She wouldn't accept his excuse that a sleepless night was responsible for the dark circles under his eyes and said, "You look wan." Remembering how he'd sweated at the race and noting that his eyes lacked luster for the first time in weeks, she added, "Why don't you admit you're not feeling well and stay in bed today?"

He often used flattery to steer her away from talk about

his health but it was difficult on Sundays, because she dressed for church as though color and flair were anathema to true faith. Julia's gray dress made her look as somber as he felt, but he tried his grandfather's standby, "You look radiant. Enjoy the service."

"Radiant!" she quipped, aware it was how her father complimented women when he didn't know what else to say. "If you call this sad little dress Miss Schnickel made for me radiant then you really aren't well."

She was relieved to get a laugh from him, even if it seemed a bit forced, and wondered if she should have followed her sister's instructions to hold back any letters from Jacques and forward them to England.

Julia knew too well how distressing it was as a new arrival in America to wait for letters which never came, so her guilt pangs were weighty when readdressing Jacques's four letters to Irene.

But his consuming interest in Teenotchy allowed Alexander to make light of receiving no letters. He didn't expect his mother to write, or his grandfather. Now it seemed Jacques had joined the rest.

Julia spied the open tome on Alexander's bed. "Reading when you ought to be sleeping, I expect, is half the problem. I'll have breakfast sent up."

His attempted smile was worth the effort he put into it. "Tea would be nice, but I've no appetite."

Guilt made Julia flare more than his resistance to food. She snapped, "You must eat, Alexander!" while her mind was cast back to Tuesday, when she'd last intercepted one of Jacques's letters from the mailbox.

As she stood tight-lipped in Alexander's doorway, he wondered at how Julia was almost as severe as Mrs. Orestes Adams on Sundays. He said, "It is possible to be radiant in gray." But he was thinking about Teenotchy's eyes as she waved to him from the stairs. "And Aunt Julia, please don't trouble Ruth to send breakfast. I'd hate to see her hard work go to waste."

So when his tray arrived with a silver basket of Ruth's hot rolls, he imagined her toiling in the kitchen. Of all the Tewksbury staff, he'd grown fondest of her, although he'd trusted her least when he'd first arrived since she smiled less than the others. But he'd come to believe that when her sienna eyes twinkled, when she smiled, when she laughed, she was genuine.

Seeing the yellow rose she'd arranged upon his tray gave him the feeling it was a sign: it was a yellow rose Teenotchy'd spoken to in the garden. He told the servant leaving the tray, "Please tell Ruth to come up. I must talk to her."

Perhaps she was the sage who could clear up his befuddlement, just as his grandmother used to whenever as a boy he felt overwhelmed by life.

His innocent order wreaked havoc in the kitchen. The cook only made it above the second floor for the spring and January clean. Being summoned by the Viscount on the third floor unsettled her, and Ezekiel was nowhere in sight to come to the rescue.

Washing flour off her hands, she smudged some on her cheek, rushing to don a frilly cap and fresh apron from the staff's linen cupboard. "Marie Annette," Ruth tutted, critical of the way the apron had been ironed. "I don't know why Ezekiel won't fire her," she said, making her way so quickly up the stairs that she was on the second-floor landing before she remembered she wasn't wearing her gloves.

She stopped to rub the blackish blue M molded into the back of her hand. "Lord, why you want to do me like this? Cake in the oven and let me get all the way up these stairs just to have to go back down . . ."

Ruth looked down the stairwell and decided to risk appearing at Alexander's door gloveless. She stuck her left hand behind her when she knocked, out of breath, praying that there was nothing wrong with the rolls she'd sent up.

She considered Alexander, like his aunt, "calm-natured," and was glad he wasn't scowling when he opened the door, though she didn't know what to think when he asked her to sit.

"Sit down? You *mean* sit down, Mister Alexander?" she asked twice, sure that he said one thing and meant something else, since she'd discovered his English didn't match hers. Like the time he'd asked for biscuits and she'd fixed a tray to discover that he'd wanted some cookies.

Alexander was sitting in the high-backed reading chair and motioned that she should sit in its mate opposite.

Ruth hadn't been in the room since Mrs. Tewksbury'd had it redecorated in preparation for Alexander's arrival. The pheasants-in-flight design, on the wallpaper suited the new dark-brown velvet drapes, she thought—the old flowery pattern on the walls before having been more girlish.

But what most appealed was seeing the fake Louis XIV clock on the mantelpiece, which reminded her of the real ones she used to clean in the big house where she was born in captivity in Virginia. There she'd been a ladies' maid from the age of ten and had worn pretty dresses and had toilet duty, which she preferred to cooking.

Not that she minded the Tewksburys only having twelve staff. But thirty-five is what she'd grown used to from childhood and she missed the community and intrigues of greater numbers.

Alexander loved it that she always smelled of butter and to have her sitting in his room brought immediate comfort.

Ruth sat on her left hand and waited nervously for Alexander to finish saying, "I'm sorry that I've brought you away from the kitchen. But I needed to talk to you."

She smoothed her royal-blue uniform and perched her spectacularly broad hips on the edge of the chair. What could she have been guilty of, she wondered, eyeing the rolls,

which looked the perfect shape. Their aroma filled the room.
But she was ready to be wrong. "Sorry about the rolls, Mister
Alexander."

He tightened the silk rope belt around his waist. "Your
baking is perfect. In fact, it's your expertise which makes me
certain that you're the person who'll be able to tell me what
love is."

Relieved that her reputation for excellent service wasn't
about to be tarnished, she almost smiled. "Lemme go find
'Zekiel," she offered, about to rise from the edge of the velvet
chair, several shades browner than she was.

"No," said Alexander. "I want you to tell me. My grandmother always said colored women have a way with words.
You would've adored my grandmother. She was an abolitionist, you know . . ." It was the thing he was proudest of in life.

His compliment hung like the drapes. Heavy. But Ruth
accepted he meant well, so she mustered a smile, and turned
his question upside down, wanting to expound as impres-
sively as she believed her husband would have upon one of
the great mysteries of life.

The long silence, punctuated by the clock ticking, reminded them both that her answer was slow in coming. He
thought tea could help and rose to pour her a cup. "Tea
always helps me to think better," he said, asking if she took
milk and sugar.

To see him standing, cup and saucer in hand, took her
so off guard she said, "Child, you not s'pose to give me your
tea." She preferred white people who knew their place and
put it down to his foreignness that he would stroll into the
kitchen to say "good morning" or "good afternoon" and then
stand around as though he'd come to chat. "You can't give
tea to me. I'm working, see?"

"My nanny always took tea with me," he said, pressing
the cup in her hand. "But you'll need both hands to hold
this." He wondered why she sat on one, behaving as if he'd
passed her the Elgin Marbles. "A nice cup of tea might help

you answer this very important question," he encouraged. "What is love?"

Attempting to balance the cup and saucer in her right hand emptied Ruth's mind of all the powerful biblical notions of love she'd been conjuring up, as Ezekiel probably would have, with a fancy word here and there. "I don't know. Love's a mess," she blurted, thinking that vagueness might make Alexander dismiss her. "Nothing but a mess." Ruth shook her head as though she knew too well.

"A mess," he repeated, sure she was on to something and relieved when she put the cup and saucer down, since it was impossible for her to drink with one hand. It made him query for a fleeting moment how people with one hand did deal with a cup and saucer—another instance when his mind wandered. He'd been finding it hard to concentrate.

Ruth tried to qualify her anxious answer with some valid examples but was sure she hadn't chosen the right ones. She flushed, saying, "I knew a girl once, worked right here in this house. Ezekiel finally had to let her go, because she came to work with a black eye more times than I like to recall. That's why my husband give her her notice. How could he keep her, see, she couldn't serve looking like that, see," said Ruth, breaking out in a minor sweat, because she was sure that she'd said the wrong thing. But she pushed on anyway, since Alexander was staring so intently. "Her husband used to beat her, see, but she refused to leave him, because she said he only did it because he loved her till it made him act crazy. So Friday payday, he'd come home and give her every penny he earned 'cept for one dollar and then he'd beat her up so nobody else would want her, see."

"Hmmmm," said Alexander, his mind racing, since he was trying to find at which place he'd missed the point. He tied his robe a little tighter and studied his slippers as Ruth eyed the fake Louis XIV clock, and swore she could see a fine layer of dust on the mantel. "Mister Alexander, who dusts your room?" she asked, suspecting it was one of the girls they'd hired after they came to Germantown, because she noticed the Northern girls didn't take pride in their work.

Alexander was sure she could relieve his anguish and clarify why he could so love someone who didn't love him. He rubbed his tired eyes and wondered if his aunt was right: perhaps he was coming down with something. "Do you know any other love stories?"

Ruth thought a bit, hoping to come up with whatever it was that he was searching for, and he gave her a hint when he explained that he'd like to hear of any of the more extraordinary stories she knew.

He was longing to brush the smudge of flour from her cheek, but had come to accept that, whereas there were certain servants at home that he could touch, such familiarity was unacceptable in the Tewksbury household.

"I knew a man, nice-looking. Light-skinned. Nice hair."

"Nice hair?" interrupted Alexander.

"A good grade. Like mine and Ezekiel's. Growing hair. Not as good . . ." She didn't bother to go on, because she could tell from his dense expression that he wouldn't understand. "Anyway," she continued, "this fella married a real dark-skinned girl, because he said she had . . ." Ruth stopped mid-sentence, thinking she'd lost her mind, about to tell Mrs. Tewksbury's nephew about O'Dell C. Smith, who had married Mary Scrubs because she had big legs.

Ruth's heart was pounding, and she looked at the cup of tea which she'd placed on the small table beside her. Of course, it would remain untouched.

Alexander stood up. "Tell me about your mother and father," he asked, as though he thought her family tree would be as delineated as his own. "Did they love each other differently?" He wanted to say differently than white people, but couldn't think of the best approach.

"I didn't have a father, see? So I can't . . ."

Alexander looked into her sienna eyes and she, nearly fifty years his senior, looked away. "What you mean, Ruth, is you didn't know your father. But of course you had one."

Wasn't her reddish hair and reddish skin a giveaway? "Did your mother have red hair too?" he asked.

"No, sir." Ruth didn't know what this had to do with love and was sure if she didn't get down to the kitchen within five minutes, she would face disaster. Dared she tell this child she had a cake about to burn? Suddenly he picked up a book thicker than the Bible.

"Where were you born?" asked Alexander.

"Virginia."

He shook his head. "Good God! Virginia, red hair," said Alexander, flicking to the index of the book. "What do you know of your father? You see, it's possible that you could be a descendant of Thomas Jefferson." He was too exhausted to explain himself, but in his own mind he was tracking from love to her questionable parentage. Ruth, though, couldn't follow the link in this vague connection, and she suddenly concluded that she was in the presence of a madman and hoped he hadn't called her to his room to do her harm.

"You know about Thomas Jefferson, don't you?" he asked.

"He was our president," beamed Ruth, so pleased that she knew this that she wondered if she'd jumped to conclusions. "And he was the one wrote the Declaration of Independence. Ezekiel knows everything about him." She smiled. "Lemme get you Ezekiel," she offered again, thinking that if she screamed at nine thirty on a Sunday it was possible that nobody would hear her on the third floor, since cleaning started at seven and worked its way downstairs.

"He had a Negro woman. Did you know this?" Alexander asked, walking over to show her the excerpt he'd marked in the book which described Sally Jennings. "And it's possible that you might be one of his descendants."

"Yes," said Ruth. "Yes. Maybe you're right. But I bet it's

my husband related to him," she went on, easing herself up
from the chair, not even bothering to hide her branded hand,
as she prayed silently to herself, "Lord, just do me this one
thing. Just let me get out of this room and I swear I'll never
miss church another Sunday."

"Mister Alexander, how about I see to the cake I got in
the oven and then come on back?"

"Yes, of course," smiled Alexander, whose mind had
drifted from love to Jefferson to images of Teenotchy nosing
past Edgar Fullerton's bay. "Yes, of course, Ruth. We
wouldn't want anything to happen to your cake."

She looked at him, surrounded by the flying pheasants
on the wallpaper, books stacked by the side of his chair, a
few on the bed, and decided that Mister Tewksbury was
probably right. Too much reading caused dementia. She
even thought that too much Bible reading was bad for the
health, and could never accept the fact that it was being far-
sighted which had put her off reading before she was school
age.

Alexander looked into her eyes and was sure he could
see some resemblance to Thomas Jefferson, because he
wanted to. It would have made his time in America all the
more valuable had he been able to return to England having
interviewed one of Jefferson's slave descendants. But he appreciated that Ruth's cake was more important and allowed
her to leave with a curtsy that was half bow.

"Your being from Virginia, Ruth, it would be of great
assistance to my studies if you could put your mind to what
servants you may have come across who were born in the
Monticello vicinity . . ."

"Yes, sir," Ruth murmured, closing his door behind her.
She took her time going downstairs, thinking about what
she'd overheard Julia Tewksbury telling Mister Tewksbury
when there was first talk of Alexander's arrival.

It was something about the boy's father picking up with
a bad lot when he was studying in China and him having an

opium habit that nobody knew about until he'd married Julia's sister.

This was one of the things Ruth liked best about her job. People used to say all sorts of things in front of her, which she took as a sign of their trust, being oblivious to the fact that her employers merely considered her invisible—Mrs. Julia Tewksbury included, for all her English niceties.

Ruth didn't mind working for this second Mrs. Tewksbury, although she'd heard before Mister Tewksbury married the young Julia that, though her father had come from something, her mother was nothing but trash, an army nurse girl he'd taken up with when he was an officer in the Crimea. These titbits of gossip, discussed by Mister Tewksbury's guests when he was out of hearing distance, gave Ruth and Ezekiel the secure feeling that whatever happened, they knew more about Mister Tewksbury than the old man did about himself, and in time the fact that this knowledge included his wife and her family was a great comfort.

"Thomas Jefferson," Ruth laughed to herself, still making her way down the grand staircase, designed as a carbon copy of one from a Yorkshire manor house. "Maybe that child really is crazy. How's a colored woman supposed to be some relation to a president? That don't make good sense. Me and Thomas Jefferson!"

Her giggles rang through the house before she caught herself, adjusting her cap and putting on her more stolid face for the sake of propriety—and being a lady's maid from Virginia, she assumed she was better schooled in propriety than even Julia Tewksbury, or any Queen of England for that matter, if there was one.

XX

Saturday, September 13, 1913

With his mind on Cleveland and a plot to get there, Teenotchy felt as weightless as he had in the race and rode Blossom nearly as hard to Pear Tree Lodge, anxious to show Miss Sullivan the bundle he was carrying. It contained two shirts, a belt and suspenders donated by Mister Kleber after Teenotchy told him Geronimo would apply for the job sweeping the meeting house.

"As long as nobody expects him to do more than that," Teenotchy warned Mister Kleber. "Though I can probably teach him to put the chairs back." He was surprised that he'd taught the brave to sweep Miss Sullivan's, albeit that she complained about them wearing out her broom.

When she'd heard there was a job which normally went to a needy schoolboy, she'd asked Teenotchy to speak to Mister Kleber, saying, "It could earn Geronimo a nickel or two with you leaving."

Even before Teenotchy'd told Miss Sullivan of his immi-

nent departure, they'd occasionally discussed Geronimo getting an errand job. But they knew it was just talk to while
away an afternoon since he got lost on all but Main Street.

Clutching the bundle and reins, Teenotchy galloped
across the south side of Carpenter's Meadow, pleased both
shirts had a full set of buttons, though the collars and cuffs
were frayed from years of being boraxed by Aunt Em, who
rarely singed shirts but was sometimes accused of boiling the
life out of them.

Teenotchy was also carrying some peaches, compliments
of Mister Kleber, for Miss Sullivan. Mister Kleber'd told him,
"There's no mold on them, but they were already soft when
Deacon Frye gave them to Helga. But Miss Sullivan may
enjoy them. Probably got no teeth at her age." He always
thought anybody a few years older than he was was ancient.

That Saturday's afternoon light was soft. It was the second time in an hour that a fine mist fell, making different
sections of town smell of vanilla or roses or orange blossom.
Teenotchy was giddy from it as he reached the overgrown
path to the lodge.

Spotting Geronimo sprawled in the tall grass made him
feel even more part of Germantown life, and the thought of
leaving gave him a sharp stab of pain. He sighed to himself,
"Lord, what's Geronimo up to now?" It was like having to
play mother hen to an unruly chick. "Hey, pardner, don't
lay in the rain," he hailed from the opposite side of the dense
overgrowth, where they picked the sweetest wild strawberries
growing beside dandelions the size of carnations.

Teenotchy expected the usual excited greeting and could
only vaguely make out the odd angle of Geronimo's head
and outstretched arms. It wouldn't be the first time he'd
fallen and not bothered to get up. But he was soaking up
the drizzle.

"Hot or not," called Teenotchy, "you'll catch a death
laying in the rain." He slowed Blossom to a halt and removed
his specs, but while he was wiping them on his overalls he

saw better. The hairs rose on his arms and suddenly he was covered in gooseflesh. "Oh no, no, no. Oh no," he cried out, aware that Geronimo's eyes were dead. Teenotchy couldn't stop for death. "Giddy up!" he ordered with a yank of Blossom's mane and a back kick to her ribs. But he never treated her roughly and her feelings were too wounded to respond. She dawdled. But however fast she could've carried him from the ugly scene, the fact remained. Geronimo's forehead was washed with dark caked blood.

Misty rain settled like a thick morning dew on the hedges around the lodge and turned the brownish grass to spiky crystals. It looked more peaceful than usual as Teenotchy dismounted, quietly so Miss Sullivan wouldn't hear him.

He wanted to erase the sight of Geronimo in the tall grass but biting into a bit of soggy peach summoned no courage. He spat it out, hurling the rest with all his might. "Did he deserve it?" Teenotchy asked, his eyes raised pleadingly to the sky as if the rain was to blame. Was it mist collecting on his black lashes or tears?

The sweet perfume of wet grass and a raucous performance of birdsong made mock of his heavy heart. But he stood his ground, refusing to go for the shovel, using the excuse that if he budged, Blossom might whinny and Miss Sullivan would come out.

When the German Reform Church bells bonged four, all Teenotchy wanted to hear was Geronimo imitating them or screeching like two crows. But only the birds answered, catcalling to each other as Teenotchy threw down his small bundle from Mister Kleber to plop himself upon it and remove his boots.

Like that would solve something. He pulled up a handful of grass and stuck a blade in his mouth. A breeze blew a cock's crow through the trees. "Coward. Coward," the leaves seemed to whisper back, and he pretended not to hear. Dead flowers were one thing. Dead trees he could bear. But somehow even a dead sparrow brought a soul tremble that was

too fearsome. So Teenotchy tried not to think about Geronimo, stiff like a dead cat Mister Kleber'd found at the bottom
of the garden that year Teenotchy lived there.

Duty told him to go back and check. But he was paralyzed, terror banging like a frantic drummer in his ears, re-
verberating into a headache. "Somebody help," Teenotchy
begged, getting up to let instinct and Blossom lead him past
the path where Geronimo lay, his face half turned to the sky,
fine rain soaking his long braided hair.

When Teenotchy knocked at the back door of Holybrook
Manor, Ezekiel was outraged to find him winded and snort-
ing like it had been he and not Blossom who'd galloped
across town.

"Alexander!" derided the butler. "Nigger, don't you
come to this door talking about no Alexander. It's Mister
Alexander. And don't you forget it. Got the nerve to come
to this door barefoot as a sharecropper."

Hearing the commotion, Ruth rushed to peek over her
husband's shoulder. She tried to shush him but frowned like
he did at the mud between Teenotchy's toes.

Ezekiel the lion raged, "You that boy won the race . . .
and graduated high school? Your sister was raised right . . ."
He interrupted himself to push his wife's hand off his shoulder. "Woman, mind your business. I talk as loud as I have
to," he scolded in a tone meant to demean her more than
Teenotchy, who could hardly swallow. Ezekiel ranted on.
"This is Germantown. Not Alabama. And some of us are
trying to do better!"

Had Alexander, three floors up, not been drawn to his
bedroom window, he wouldn't have spied Blossom's distinc-
tive coat. Unaware Teenotchy'd come for him, he grabbed a
hat and bounded downstairs, anxious for it to appear coinci-
dental that he happened to be in the garden walking past
the back door. Heart in his mouth, hat in his hand, he felt

hopeless, having not set eyes on Teenotchy since that evening of the derby.

Both were disinclined to look the other in the eye, but it nearly took Ezekiel's breath away when he overheard Alexander say, "I'm glad you knew to come for me," after Teenotchy'd related something in a stammered whisper, touching only upon basics.

Neither boy was aware that two other servants were crowding behind Ezekiel and Ruth, who hovered at the pantry window. Ruth had her hand to her mouth, witnessing Teenotchy's dirty feet climb into the passenger side of Mister Tewksbury's favorite phaeton. In the driver's seat sat Alexander, his handmade linen suit almost touching Teenotchy's damp overalls when he cracked the whip to drive the manor's most elegant pair.

Ezekiel shook his head, smoothing back the crinkly waves at his temples—high-glossed from a daily dollop of petroleum jelly. The others waited for his pronouncement, his prophecy, as elder and seer among a dozen staff.

He said, "Walls got ears and windows got eyes. And what ol' man Jonas will make of a little sawed-off nigger seating on his leather seat . . ." The contemplation was too dire to go on.

Alexander Blake had to take care with speed on horseback for his health's sake, but only a Model "T" could have made his steady time driving the pair to Main Street, though Saturday evening traffic soon altered his pace. Automobiles, trolleys, horses and carts all vied for right of way until they came to a standstill near Mister Drieser's general store.

But there was no point shouting above the clamor, so Alexander sat as silently as Teenotchy, both of them suffering from butterflies in their stomachs for different reasons.

Teenotchy fought off a terrifying feeling that seeing Geronimo was a thing he'd experienced before. But having blanked that dawn he'd found his mother, her bare backside as exposed to him as her crumpled skirt, her body scarred and spiritless, he put the feeling down to a dream forgotten and was ashamed that he'd panicked.

Alexander's gentle manner was Teenotchy's balm. His stillness and his voice soothed from the moment they settled in the carriage at the manor and Teenotchy heard Alexander say, "Not to worry. It'll be all right. But you'll have to show me the way."

To sit so close to his obsession relieved Alexander, who'd spent the entire week unsure if Teenotchy would expose him. Almost braced for humiliation, fantasizing his courage in the courtroom, replaying the tortured scenes he'd studied of Oscar Wilde's trials. Alexander was ready to be crucified, like his cousin Jacques had been the summer before when Alexander rebuffed his advance. "You mustn't say you love me in that way. In any event, we've family ties," Alexander had snapped at Jacques, feeling all the more foolish for not having noticed his cousin's lack of interest in girls.

Long before traffic ground to a halt on Main Street, shoppers stared at the handsome green carriage: Horatio regularly polished the brass and woodwork so they looked better than new, and Alexander smiled and waved at the child crossing in front of them, who yelled, "Lookit, Mama. Is the circus coming?"

Teenotchy sat upon his hands to stop them shaking and Alexander strained to keep from coughing, because it drew attention to his damaged lungs. They were on display, and it may not have been the phaeton which made people stare and point . . . because side by side, the two boys were an exotic pair, different from the folk on Main Street. More delicate. More beautiful. Quite rare.

By the time they reached the turning for Pear Tree Lodge, Teenotchy had to grit his teeth to keep them from chattering. So Alexander got no immediate response when he said, "Why didn't you check Geronimo's pulse? It could be he's unconscious, not dead."

"Least it stopped drizzling," was as much as Teenotchy would say when the phaeton slowed to a halt at the lane.

Alexander leapt down from his seat and grabbed the tartan blanket that his uncle liked to sit on when he was a passenger. Teenotchy took his time, practically measuring each step, praying he'd been mistaken until he heard Alexander say, "It's been a while. Rigor mortis usually . . ."

That was as much as Teenotchy heard as he ran back toward the road, instinct forcing him to do what common sense never would. He sat on the stony, wet path, bent over like he was grappling with a stomach cramp and reached for his harmonica. Something to hold. Something to rub. His head upon his knees, he doubled up and eyed the poison berries dangling from a hedge. If he swallowed a handful, he wondered, would dying be fast?

Alexander as usual was preoccupied with facts and came upon him, spouting, "We must go for the police after we tell Miss Sullivan. He's got the most terrible gash."

"Shuddup. Just shuddup!" shouted Teenotchy. "I don't want to hear it."

Such spontaneity made Alexander want to clap and cry, elated Teenotchy'd spoken with force, but remembering how he'd felt himself when aged ten he saw his grandmother in an open casket, he lowered his voice. "Sorry. I'll go along and tell Miss Sullivan." But he still couldn't resist peeking again at the body as he headed for the lodge, aware he'd never seen a murder victim yet not in the least squeamish about the blood.

Alexander removed his hat the moment he spotted Miss Sullivan in her rocker on the narrow porch of her cabin. The air was humid after the short rain and he wondered how she endured it in her black bonnet and shawl. She looked much tinier than he'd remembered.

Before he could speak she waved, saying, "Poor Injun child. Stoned right there. A foot from my land that was gonna be his land. Poor thing. Four white boys. I heard somebody running and looked out. Not that I could say what they looked like." She rose. "You take my rocker, son. Chopper's round the back. Fixing a grave. You come looking for Teenotchy?" The boots she wore had hardly any black dye left in them. "He been and gone. Came and went." She smiled.

Red, white and blue anemones which Teenotchy'd potted in a barrel for her eightieth Fourth of July still had some blooms and the air could only have been sweeter with honeysuckle flowering.

Alexander had expected her distress to mirror Teenotchy's, because he didn't know she'd spent the past decade courting death. Her atonement was a happiness, and she pointed to her open window. "More flies inside than out," she said. "But that was a nice bit of rain. We could use some more. But I love how it shines everything up." It was true. Her yard almost glistened.

"Please sit, Miss Sullivan," Alexander insisted. Teenotchy came into the yard in time to hear him say, "I'd like to pay for Geronimo to have a funeral. And a suit of clothes."

Teenotchy found voice. "I betcha I can tell you which ones did it," he said, putting his glasses on, taking them off, a tinge of revenge in his tone that got Miss Sullivan back on her feet.

She said, "God did it and don't you forget it." With Alexander's help she sat again, but she wasn't finished.

"You're heading for Cleveland. Me praying every minute that I'll get to Heaven. Who was gonna mind out for Geronimo? Chopper goes and comes—"

Ignorant of Teenotchy's plans, Alexander interrupted. "Cleveland?" he said, wishing that he could place it on his mental map of America.

The lump rose fast, blocking Teenotchy's throat, but Miss Sullivan would have probably answered for him anyway.

"I'm glad he's going," she said. "Go west, I tell 'em. Yes. Go west. But first, Teenotchy, you ought to head round back and give Chopper a spell with the shovel. He's been digging Geronimo a grave by himself."

"I'd like to pay for a casket and a stone," Alexander repeated. "And he should be buried in a decent suit of clothes. He deserves a . . ." The dead marble-cold silence told him to be quiet.

Miss Sullivan eyed Teenotchy's face. Teenotchy eyed Miss Sullivan's. And although Alexander couldn't decode the exchange between them, he could hear their jeering banter above the wild geese calling from the pond.

Teenotchy fiddled with his harmonica, tight-lipped and angry as though Alexander had thrown the brick that felled Geronimo, tribeless Indian who didn't smell of perfume but was no longer stale either, like he was that first day under Miss Sullivan's roof.

She tried to resurrect her bright spirit, saying, "Soon as I saw that bundle of shirts, I knew they were some of your doing. Laying there beside your boots when I came out after you rode off." She started to rock ever so slightly and told Teenotchy, "Fetch my fan off the table, son."

The minute he was inside, she confided to Alexander in a whisper, "Sure I'd love to go on up to town to the cemetery and bury the boy in a coffin. Just to show the big shots an Injun's life's worth something. But . . ." She stopped as Teenotchy came out, handing her her fan, and addressed him. "Go 'head now, son, and do like I say. Give Chopper a hand. And don't let Miz Naomi catch you crying neither, 'cause we got nothing to cry about."

Teenotchy hardly lifted his feet or his head, stepping off the porch to make his way to the back of the house. Alexander didn't know what to say but thought he shouldn't follow, trying to let them do things in their way.

Miss Sullivan fanned off the flies. "Teenotchy," she sighed. "That poor child is so soft-hearted, I worry about

him way more than I ever did Geronimo. Ernest Hochfield
was just like him. Fretted over dead snails and worried when
you killed a fly. But see, we could have this whole thing
topsy-turvy. Celebrating birth, mourning death. From all I've
seen, we ought to cry when we come into this world and
laugh when we go out," she sighed.

Alexander smiled at her, but it entered his thoughts that
Geronimo may have been a burden that she was glad to be
rid of. Though he considered it an evil thought, he couldn't
brush it off and was relieved when a tall, muscular figure
lumbered from the west side of the wooden cabin to capture
his attention.

Alexander's "good afternoon" got no response. Not a
nod or wave. Not a smile or acknowledging glance.

"That's our Chopper," said Miss Sullivan with the enthusiasm of somebody pointing to a relative in a parade, although Chopper looked nearer remorseful, and his heavy,
plodding gait was a death march. He passed within feet of
them but gave no pause, though Miss Sullivan chatted on
about him. "Guess he took his shirt off. He sweats easy."

Barrel-chested, Chopper was covered in reddish blond
hair, chest, back and arms, although the pale crop on his
head was neither. It was nearly blond and in sharp contrast
to his dark beard and mustache.

As Alexander wondered at the strange way he'd brushed
his hair to hide his bald patch, Miss Sullivan studied Alexander's eyes, waiting for him to ask what others had. Was Chopper white?

She fanned and rocked. And smiled sweetly, waiting.

But the man's pale eyes and skin hadn't crossed Alexander's mind. Having surveyed Chopper's hair, he immediately
thought about Cleveland.

Miss Sullivan gave him one, two, three once-overs. The
expensive white shoes. The pocket watch. The immaculate
boater. They all suited his self-assurance and brought nothing to remind her of the Hochfield clan. She suddenly won-

dered what he was doing there, standing in her yard. "Betcha he's after my land," she concluded to herself, the same as she'd done after his first visit, annoyed she'd let herself be so easily fooled by his gracious manner.

Her fan kept time with her rocking, which kept time with a noisy bird, and her smile glowed as innocently as that late-afternoon light when Chopper returned with his giant steps.

But they were heavier still, with the dead weight of Geronimo tossed like a slaughtered lamb over his shoulder, legs bobbing up and down. Alexander's bowed head resisted the image of a cheap life and he asked himself again what he'd asked her, "Why can't he have a proper funeral? I'm not suggesting we build a mausoleum. But a casket and stone. He was a human being."

"Mister Alexander, sir, if a stone'll make you feel better, get him one. But right now, we best join them 'round back." She didn't know what to make of him when he rushed to steady the rocker, helping her up. "Your people raised you real nice," she admitted as he carefully assisted her from the porch, her pace less spry than her demeanor.

But she refused his arm as she walked slowly through the wet grass, stumbling slightly on the invisible.

Teenotchy was half Chopper's breadth and hardly reached his shoulder, standing next to him beside the hillock of dark-brown earth that marked their toil. The little afternoon drizzle hadn't begun to soften the earth, dried to cracking after the August heatwave. They both sweated, Teenotchy mopping his forehead with the back of his forearm and Alexander seeing him as an African prince snatched from court, his skin a dark even tint from the scorch of a long summer. No sign of his dimple. Absent the toothy grin. Eyes lowered to hide their gray sadness, he seemed elfin, and to Alexander he was a perfect sparrow, loved all the more for its twittering fright.

Having never been to a funeral, not even his mother's, Teenotchy looked worried, and Alexander longed to give him some word of comfort, except he needed comforting himself when Chopper suddenly rumbled a loud, gargled hum. It took a minute for Alexander to blurt, "Good grief! That's 'God Save the King.' You said he was deaf."

Teenotchy kept his head bowed, and Miss Sullivan answered, "Dumb. Nobody said deaf. Just dumb."

Chopper's resonant "aaaaahhhhh" made Alexander's skin crawl. He was ready to run, unsure how his morning's fears about a sensational trial that would land him in prison for a passion of the heart had dissolved into that bizarre moment. Geronimo's stiff limbs hadn't even been reset, his body simply lowered into the fresh hole.

Miss Sullivan found none of it out of the ordinary. Life on the plains taught her that death was no allegory and that getting the body in the ground quickly kept it from swelling or smelling. She was more of a mind to explain Chopper's condition. "He's got good pitch. Won't say when or why somebody cut out his tongue but he signed his name on my deeds just as good as me." Lifting her long skirt, she shifted herself to Chopper's left and warbled the lyrics:

My country 'tis of thee   Sweet land of liberty   Of thee I

sing   Land where my fathers died Land of the Pilgrims' pride

From every   mountain   side   Let   FREEDOM ring

She held her head high, singing it the second time, and the only thing Alexander could think about was being eight when his grandmother'd sat by his bed reading how Uncle Tom, lying in a barn badly beaten, wanted to forgive. Alexander recalled sobbing when he asked, "Aren't the soldiers coming to help him, Granny?" because earlier she'd explained that war had ended slavery.

"Sometimes tears are the only soldiers," she'd replied, dabbing his eyes with her elaborate Venetian handkerchief. But he'd turned from her, embarrassed that he was being mollycoddled.

"Tears can't save anybody!" he'd wailed back, wanting her to know he couldn't be so easily fooled . . .

Alexander stood alone on the opposite side of the grave from Teenotchy, Chopper and Miss Sullivan. "Bean stew'll dry those tears," she said to him, even though he thought nobody'd noticed him wiping the corners of his eyes.

What really hurt him was that she saw him as the enemy when his being was devoted to rescuing them.

The frail figure pulled her shawl tighter around her shoulders, glad she'd taken time to redo her hair and dress after she'd found Geronimo's body. "You think there was something to him just singing the first line?" she asked. "He saw lots the rest of us missed."

Teenotchy caught her thought and rushed round to the cabin, returning with a small bucket brimming with Geroni-

mo's rock collection. He strained to carry it and Chopper
stepped away from the graveside to give him a hand.

"You were his favorite," Miss Sullivan said to Teenotchy.
"You go on and pick first."

Among the various fist-size rocks, the rarest was slate
gray, with the overall roundness of a cannonball. Teenotchy
bent at the far end of the grave and rolled it down the wall
of fresh earth, disturbing it slightly so a clump fell with it at
the Indian's feet.

Although the group's goodbye made him less queasy, he
was afraid to look at Geronimo's face and had managed to
avoid it. He noted the flattest stone was the one Alexander
chose to place in the grave and expected Miss Sullivan would
want to pick the dazzling one, which is why he'd left it.

She gathered it with both hands from the bucket and
said, "I could always see what he saw in this one."

As if the pail of remaining stones was featherlight, Chopper lifted it with one hand, using the other to help him sprin-
kle them around the body.

"Careful!" warned Teenotchy, his second utterance since
he and Alexander'd arrived.

So relieved was Miss Sullivan, she cleared her throat,
suggesting he was best to lead the Lord's Prayer.

Remembering how he and Geronimo would sit for hours
at the edge of the pond, or walk miles with no word between
them, Teenotchy wanted to sound firm. But his voice was
thin and uneven when he said, "Geronimo liked silence."

The tall mute passed him the shovel, as a show of
confidence.

Miss Sullivan, sensing she was outnumbered, said, "Geronimo never paid attention when Teenotchy read the Bible,
but I expect he might get to Heaven without being Christian.
Y'all are probably right," she added. "I remember ol' Mister
Hochfield saying that some Injuns put feathers and beads,
moccasins and bones, and I don't know what all in their

graves. For the journey." Teenotchy was reaching in his over-all pocket as she spoke, pausing only as she said, "I used to hear how some buried the whole tribe in one grave."

His trusted harmonica felt smooth and familiar, each little square hole rippling against his forefinger. He was sure Geronimo needed it, and without a second thought, he tossed it into the grave.

It made a slight thud before Miss Sullivan could utter a word. Then Teenotchy began shoveling mound upon mound of hard, dark-brown earth.

The others were still, though the air was ringing with normal Saturday evening dog barks and bird twitterings. And Miss Sullivan motioned Chopper to take the shovel from him.

Satisfied that Alexander'd shown heart, she allowed him to give her his arm, but she was the strong one, guiding him back to the cabin.

He declined bean stew but patiently stood, hat in hand, while she sat back in her rocker and got through a bowl. "I'm hard to feed after five," she said, taking the smallest spoonfuls.

Alexander waited for her to finish before he asked if Cleveland was very far.

She knew it was in Ohio. She knew it wasn't near New York. And she knew Teenotchy had no family there, adding, "The best he had, you just seen him bury."

Alexander felt uncomfortable when she laughed, and played with the brim of his hat, feeling as unsure of her as she'd been of him. But he was glad to hear her speak of Teenotchy.

"Trying to raise Geronimo, Teenotchy raised himself. I've known him since he wasn't but a little fella. Eight or nine. Always by himself. That Quakerman's nothing but a slave driver, hiding behind his Bible. You know, Mister Alexander, I don't say all I see, but I see what I see. I'm brung up that way. Talking and talking about nothing keeps them all fooled. Laughing and talking keeps my mind off what's too wicked to change."

Alexander didn't understand her. But he knew he mustn't interrupt, hoping that she'd come full circle to the question of Cleveland. "Teenotchy," he said, to nudge her in the right direction.

"Patient and gentle. Watching for that poor halfwitted child. Did he tell you about the time he whipped a couple of Ned Cleary's gang?" She was making it up. Her little fantasy was meant to rectify Teenotchy's pacifism, which she had little tolerance for as the sentiment grew out of Mister Kleber's Quaker faith.

Alexander sensed as much. "He hit someone?" he asked her anyway, to steer her slowly back to what she knew of Cleveland and Teenotchy's plan to go.

Miss Sullivan said, "He knocked down two at once but he never likes to brag on himself. So don't tell him I told you."

Alexander watched her undo her bonnet. Those hands darker than her face. Pinkish palms smooth by comparison to the rest, which was as wrinkled as a poppy. No ring. Spinsterhood was her testimony that her vow to Harry had endured.

Trying to steer the conversation, Alexander asked, "Had he mentioned moving to Cleveland before the race?"

Miss Sullivan put her bonnet in her lap and he tried not to stare at the maze of tiny braids which covered her head. Then, as if Alexander'd disappeared, she began to muse to herself, so used to solo conversations even when Geronimo and Chopper had been in the room. Examining her long fingernails, she said, "It wasn't all that hot last Saturday that I couldn't have walked Geronimo over to that race. Me so selfish. Not that he realized what we missed, him calling Teenotchy all through the afternoon across yonder field. Like to drove me to chop his neck off."

She dabbed one eye with the corner of her shawl.

Alexander was sure she wouldn't want him to see her cry, so he bowed to leave. "Please tell Teenotchy I'll deliver Blossom tomorrow."

As his long legs glided him toward his uncle's phaeton, an antiquated rhyme spun in his head.

Ten little, nine little, eight little Indians.
Seven little, six little, five little Indians.
Four little, three little, two little Indians.
One little Indian boy.

It was still going round and round at supper when he told his aunt and uncle that he was forced to cut his visit to America short, a decision arrived at while returning from Miss Sullivan's.

"Leaving on Monday!" Julia said incredulously.

Her husband hoisted his glass of rye high to toast the departure. "Leaving on Monday." Jonas didn't even try to conceal a broad grin, and Julia couldn't decide if her husband meant to be charming or offensive. But in case it was the latter she stabbed him with a docile look when he suggested that they might celebrate.

She'd never known Jonas to behave as crudely as he had while Alexander had been with them and hated her nephew for provoking him. She glowered at Alexander, saying of him to herself, "He's more self-righteous than Mother was."

As long as Jonas kept his KKK wizard's cloak in a locked chest in the attic and didn't expect her to join the Confederate Wives for a New America Committee, which met every second Thursday in Philadelphia, she was quite happy with her lot and wanted Alexander to carry home tales of her glamorous life.

Julia flushed, thinking of what Irene would make of the Women's Auxiliary, and thought it wise that her nephew be made to stay until she could organize a few more soirées with some young people.

But when Ezekiel asked if she would like coffee served in the conservatory as William Cranford had arrived, her heart sank. She felt defeated.

"William Cranford!" Alexander brightened. "Just the man I want to see," Julia was shocked to hear him say as they rose to join the banker in the conservatory.

XXI

Sunday, September 14, 1913

The next day being holy, the streets were quieter than usual, and whereas other Germantowners were inclined to lower their voices on Sundays, Aunt Em's practically rattled the kitchen window when she shouted up to Teenotchy in bed, "Dat white knight is outside, waiting on you."

Alexander, astride his black stallion, held Blossom's rein. He heard her better than Teenotchy, cramped on his horsechair mattress and boxes, deep in sleep.

But when Aunt Em didn't hear his feet hit the floorboards, she used the broom handle to bang on the ceiling. "Boy!" she hollered, "I can't be foolin' wit' you. Get up!" Then she shuffled to the window for her third peek, nervous that Alexander was growing impatient and might knock again.

He was also being eyed by one of the pregnant neighborhood alley cats, hardly more than a kitten herself. She licked her paws, sitting on a garbage heap in the cul-de-sac, and seemed as curious as Aunt Em about why he was wearing a crumpled suit.

Alexander'd slept in it, having tortured himself through the wee hours pacing, packing and composing the letter in his pocket. It was dawn when he finally collapsed, fully dressed, across his bed.

Teenotchy, as always grouchy first thing, tripped down the last stair, ready for an argument. Stretches and yawns never improved his temper. He scowled. "I told you he *wasn't* a knight. But you'd rather listen to the old biddies' gossip." He stretched again. "And anyway, what'd you have to shout his business to the world for?"

"I never tell nothin'," she scowled back, "and whoever said so's a lie."

"You just screamed it to the whole of Germantown," said Teenotchy, whose morning mood only lasted until he was awake enough for his fears to arrest him. But he was testier than usual, realizing Alexander was outside. "Where's that tooth powder I saw you fixing up the other day?"

"Boy, I think you gone loony. Don't make me knock you side-a-ways," was her answer. "You get on over to them Klabbers wit' that nag 'fore they put our be-hinds in the street. Dat white boy say you s'posed to take it back."

"That white boy" was straining to hear every word and mistook her saying "be-hinds" for "bee-hives" but Alexander couldn't believe they kept the hive indoors.

Teenotchy sat on the creaking wooden chair to put his socks on, asking, "Did Atlanta go to church already?" As if it mattered. From the light he judged it to be just after eight. "Why didn't you wake me?" he demanded.

"I ain't your mama!" Aunt Em snapped, counting out the handkerchiefs she was planning to drop in the pot as soon as it boiled on the stove.

Since Teenotchy'd given up checking to see if any hairs grew overnight on his face, he rarely looked in the hand mirror in the morning. Atlanta often hid it anyway. He'd got used to brushing his teeth in the yard by the old pump. But with Alexander outside, he eyed Aunt Em's pot for water and rummaged through the only kitchen drawer, where she usually kept some tooth powder in an old tobacco tin.

Teenotchy sifted through the chaos of broken clothes pegs, old bits of soap, scraps of paper, cord, nails, matches, candlewick and everything else Aunt Em was scared to throw out.

"The hair grease!" he said, raising the jar. "I was looking for it all last week."

She paid him no mind, but the moment she turned her back, Teenotchy dunked his toothbrush into her pot of water.

He was embarrassed that Alexander was waiting but also knew Aunt Em would be secretly impressed, so he asked if she had any buttermilk, just to waste another couple minutes before going in the yard. But he may as well have asked for her last macaroon.

"Buttermilk," she scoffed. "Just 'cause you give me five dollars, don't think you drinking buttermilk every day. Last Sunday was last Sunday."

Blossom whinnied the first hello the moment Teenotchy appeared at the back door, tipping his cap.

"I told you that's not necessary," said Alexander.

Teenotchy felt as awkward as he had at their very first meeting, aware that the incident at Miss Sullivan's and his going for Alexander's help had established a bond between them that an uncomfortable night's sleep hadn't loosened. He dug the heel of his boot into the ground, hardly looking up, though Blossom expected a more gracious welcome, even if Alexander did not.

She whinnied again, but Teenotchy still didn't look up and went to fiddle with his harmonica, before remembering where it was.

Alexander tried to rescue him with a kind thought.

"Reuben's at the corner with Entelechy, Teenotchy. In spite of your returning her, I thought you might enjoy a ride." It was not part of his plan at that point to tell Teenotchy it would have to be his last.

From the moment Alexander committed himself to leaving, sure Teenotchy was heading for Cleveland to avoid him, Alexander was determined to leave first. And providence helped him every step of the way, beginning with William Cranford's arrival after dinner.

It was being unexpectedly able to complete a bank transaction on a Saturday evening which assured Alexander that returning immediately to England had Fate's blessing. Once convinced he was doing the right thing, he moved swiftly, letting his money remove such obstacles as unavailable seats on trains and his uncle's refusal to drive him to Pennsylvannia Station first thing Monday morning.

Julia was astounded to have Alexander knock at her bedroom door before she turned out her light that Saturday night to announce that his return cruise was completely organized.

How to say goodbye to Teenotchy was his last chore.

Hence his early Sunday morning arrival at the dead end, with the veiled excuse of delivering Blossom.

But seeing Teenotchy shift from foot to foot, Alexander lost confidence in his adventurous plan for a last ride and morning picnic. It had seemed less outlandish when he was alone at dawn.

From the window, Aunt Em gaped at the two of them hardly exchanging a word at first. But her mouth and eyes were no wider opened than Tessie's, snooping next door, watching Alexander get off his horse and shake Teenotchy's hand.

Crumpled suit or no crumpled suit, Alexander's black stallion spoke money, and Tessie knew its rider was somebody important.

"Oh-oh!" she gasped from behind her green curtain, as

she misread Alexander's fatigue. "He don't look too happy." She rushed to sit at her small kitchen table, in case what she saw as trouble might spread.

She was already dressed for church, though the service at the Children of Bethel didn't start until ten. "I knew no good would come from that racing," she told herself, sitting too straight-backed to relax on her wooden chair.

Tessie'd enjoyed the previous week, being able to brag to Mister Schaus's customers that she lived directly next door to "their" little dark-town hero. But she didn't expect Teenotchy's head to swell to the point he'd go forgetting his place, since she always remembered hers.

She was wondering what on earth could have provoked that early visit from a white boy and sat with her heart pounding, more for herself than for Teenotchy, as she envisioned the neighborhood surrounded by a KKK posse that would burst through her door first, as her house looked a bit nicer than his.

But when nothing happened after five minutes of sitting with her hands clasped before her in prayer, she got up to look out of the window again. To discover Teenotchy laughing. And on Sunday no less. Bold as daylight. Laughing and talking to a white boy. No hand covering his mouth. Cap still on his head. She criticized, "Umm, umm, ummm. That don't look right. Wonder where's Aunt Em. I know she taught him better than that."

With her four-fingered hand gripping a couple of clothes pegs, Aunt Em was thinking the same thing. But "acting the nigger" was how she'd have described Teenotchy's relaxed manner.

And Teenotchy did seem uncharacteristically at ease while Alexander chatted. Until his notion of a morning picnic was mentioned. Teenotchy was flabbergasted and, in light of the incident on Mister Kleber's bench, it was kind of frightening.

"I've got behind with Mister Kleber's garden," he stuttered. "Way behind," he added, which wasn't altogether a lie. More an exaggeration.

Alexander tried to wear a perky grin, pretending he wasn't exhausted and finding a quick escape from any rebuttal. "I'm not up on pruning, but I'm sure I can weed as well as anyone else." He knew how precious every moment was, with a car and chauffeur from Philadelphia coming in less than twenty-four hours to drive him to Pennsylvania Station, where he would catch his train for New York. And the port.

He would have willingly joined Teenotchy in cleaning public latrines had that been on the stable boy's chore list.

"Your suit . . ." was all Teenotchy could utter, and he felt the two women's eyes like four full moons on the back of his neck.

They would have given anything to be the pregnant alley cat that moved closer to hear all. She might have agreed with Alexander, had she been able to talk, when he said, "My suit's not looking much, I know. But I didn't think you'd mind." Then he waved to beckon Reuben, adding, "I know a bit about exotic plants, because of my grandfather's greenhouse. But I can't pretend I'm one for gardening."

Tessie and Aunt Em spied the brown-skinned Reuben, as handsomely turned out as any of the Tewksburys' staff, ride up to receive instructions before riding off again.

Teenotchy couldn't believe his ears when Alexander'd ordered Reuben, "Have Ruth prepare a hamper. Nothing elaborate. And I'll be waiting at Schoolhouse Lane and Main Street to collect it at midday."

By the time he and Teenotchy cantered off, Tessie was in a stink. Like Teenotchy'd offended her personally. "All that bread pudding I give 'em," she said, "and that boy won fifty dollars and all I got from him was a headscarf. A headscarf," she repeated, looking at where she had laid it on her dresser, because earlier in the week she'd thought it such a fine gift. "But he'll learn. . . . You wait. Airs get you nowhere."

*   *   *

Teenotchy stood beside the circular rosebed in Mister Kleber's garden, watching in disbelief as Alexander took off his jacket, undid his bow tie and rolled up his trouserlegs to expose his thin ankles.

All astutter, Teenotchy said, "Maybe you better prune a couple roses. It doesn't seem right you getting down on your knees."

Alexander responded as if his own mother was warning him off. "My knees are perfectly good. I know dandelions and various forms of bindweed, assuming these things look the same from continent to continent. But don't hesitate to stop me if I'm yanking a flower by mistake."

Teenotchy was imagining Helga Kleber's face upon discovering Alexander, slightly rumpled but in conspicuously expensive handmade shirt and trousers, on his knees weeding. It made Teenotchy sweat, but he also broke out into a toothy grin, and that in itself made Alexander sure he'd decided to do the right thing. So he smiled too, until Teenotchy picked his jacket from the ground.

"Don't touch that!" Alexander scolded, and Teenotchy's expression clouded like a six-year-old's who'd broken his auntie's best teacup. "I didn't mean to shout," Alexander apologized. "And it's kind of you to bother, but I've something important in the pocket."

He was worried about the letter that he'd rewritten eleven times, his wastepaper basket piled with balls of failed attempts: the first sounded smug, the second churlish, the third too saccharine, the fourth too personal, the fifth pedantic. . . . Into the early-morning light he'd written and finally gave up hope that what he wanted to say could be enclosed in a letter at all, considering that letters, as he remembered, had been Oscar Wilde's downfall.

Alexander tried to change the subject, suddenly looking around the garden. Almost three acres, he imagined. "You've really been taking care of all of this yourself?" he asked.

Atlanta'd told him Teenotchy was paid nothing for the mammoth task and Alexander was thinking "hypocritical bastard" of Mister Kleber, because Teenotchy'd said, when he'd originally begun, he expected it would be only for a few months, six at most. But Mister Kleber's stroke seemed to have had a permanent effect, three years on since he'd been bedridden.

It made Alexander too angry to want to hear more, so when the nine o'clock symphony of Germantown's church bells rang out in competition, Alexander was as happy as Teenotchy to use that as their work whistle.

By ten, both boys were laboring intently, Alexander a little the worse for his missed sleep, Teenotchy trying not to think about Geronimo and expecting Helga Kleber to swoop down upon them at any moment. But since he planned to give notice anyway, he was feeling smug that she couldn't really fire him.

Alexander heard Teenotchy say, "Oh my goodness, look at you, Miss," and rushed over to see who he was talking to.

It was a perfect rose, alone on a short, weak stem, and he thought it charming the way Teenotchy talked to wild things in a half whisper as sweetly as if he were talking to a child, though his presence in the garden was as commanding as a tree which had been growing for one hundred and one years.

Teenotchy chiseled land and bush with the care and compassion of a craftsman and Alexander felt inspired to tell him so. "You really are so clever. If only you believed it." And when Teenotchy blushed, Alexander was sure that a little more praise was needed. "Doesn't Mister Kleber tell you how brilliant your work here is?"

Leaping to his old friend's defense, Teenotchy said, "I only learned to garden following Mister Kleber around."

"How long have you worked here?" asked Alexander, though he anticipated it had been too long.

Teenotchy grinned, somewhat proudly, and said, "Feels like my whole life."

He had a few leaves in his hair, but Alexander knew better than to tell him to brush them off, disturbing Teenotchy's train of thought while he carried on. "I used to come with my mother," he said quietly. Somehow Alexander's silence always drew him out. "Didn't my sister already tell you?"

Alexander said nothing.

That Sunday morning was the wrong time to admit to all he'd discovered. From Atlanta. From Edison. From the Germantown Police Station the previous Wednesday.

Alexander's mind flashed back to his indignation when the police sergeant at the desk said he vaguely remembered the Dusty Simms's murder case, but produced a file with little more than her description and her five-year-old son's. Money jogged the sergeant's memory back to 1899, and he told Alexander that he seemed to remember that the boy had gone missing with his mother and was found in the woods by some Boy Scouts. But the sergeant didn't know why the child was released to Mister Kleber, nor why the case was never followed up, using the turn of the century revels as a possible cause.

Looking at Teenotchy in the Klebers' garden, Alexander was certain that to uproot what had been dormant for fourteen years was unfair since he was leaving. But that didn't stop him wondering whether Mister Kleber knew something about his housekeeper that might have helped to solve her murder.

"You were the one who said we'd never finish if we stopped to talk," he told Teenotchy, and hiked up his trouserlegs to get back to work. Though five minutes later he broke the silence, rolling a bit of Mister Kleber's dark-brown soil between his fingertips. "Wouldn't it be better to work in gloves?" he asked. "I've always hated getting my hands dirty."

"Shoes are bad enough. Arm sheaths . . ." sighed Teenotchy, like he was addressing the latter to Helga. He scooped up a handful of soil. "These are meant to touch the earth," he said, referring to his hands and looking at the small clump of soil as though he could see angels dancing in it.

"Say that again," asked Alexander, kicking aside a mound of weeds and squatting the way Teenotchy was. "Please. What you just said, say it again?"

Teenotchy was right to blush. "Naw . . . you heard me the first time. You're making fun." Only for Geronimo would he repeat a statement five times effortlessly.

"These are meant to touch the earth," Alexander said, tucking his hands into a spot he'd cleaned of weeds. Then, using the trowel Teenotchy gave him to dig up two fistfuls, he emptied the little pile in front of him, hoping to see what Teenotchy did.

"This stuff," said Teenotchy, taking a pinch, "can make a tomato or a rose or a great big ol' oak." He opened his palm and dropped a bit in, dusty top soil that sprinkled like gold dust. "Dirt's not dirty. It's magic."

Alexander wished against all reason that he could freeze them in that moment, with the sun showering them through the trees. He, Alexander Blake, and Teenotchy "Theodore" Simms.

Alexander watched him blow the earth from his hands and go back to pruning, not daring to stop to look up when Alexander's voice said quietly, "I want to tell you something. But first you must promise you won't run off."

That seemed too dangerous a promise to Teenotchy in the light of what had been said to him on the bench hardly more than a week before. He hoped that by clenching his teeth and saying nothing, no promise was implied.

Alexander'd decided to pull some weeds while he spoke so that Teenotchy would feel more comfortable. "I remember death," he began. "Nanny and the nurses liked to pretend their soups and cups of tea could protect me from it. Hot baths and nasty potions were supposed to protect me from this thing that I could see but they couldn't, because she hadn't come for them. 'Tight, tight, tight,' the day nurse would always say, tucking the bedclothes so I couldn't budge. And death was right there in the room, sitting on a large painted rocking horse that I had long before I got ill."

Alexander laughed, which startled Teenotchy, who hadn't heard him say something which deserved a laugh. In fact, had it been a story that, say, Atlanta was telling him, Teenotchy would have told her to shut up and stop being morbid. Instead, he tried to think about a new shape for the hedge along the meadow as Alexander's laughter subsided enough for him to carry on.

"It didn't seem funny at the time, of course. But when I think of myself too frightened to sleep, and Nanny imagining that her sitting by my bed made me feel safer, it's just . . . " He caught his breath. "Death was *always* in my room, sitting on my rocking horse or playing with my soldiers. Always touching my things so that I was afraid to touch them. And I don't know why I was sure she was female, because the cloak, the big, black, hooded cloak, had no face or feet. . . . The only time I ever recall my grandmother getting angry at me is when I tried to tell her about the thing sitting on my rocking horse which kept waiting. Watching. Playing with my things."

Talk of death disturbed Teenotchy. But it was safer than talk of love, so he listened, sorry that two dogs had begun to bark somewhere nearby, because Alexander had to speak in a normal voice and Teenotchy preferred his half whisper.

"My granny's idea of death was something invisible that could be beaten back with hot tea, when I knew that the only way to keep death away from me was never to sleep. So I tried never to sleep." Alexander laughed again. "Children are ridiculous! I believed I could keep myself from sleeping. And that was how I fought to stay alive. Refusing to say the prayer, 'Now I lay me down to sleep, I pray the Lord my soul to keep.' "

Teenotchy finished it. "And if I die before I wake, I pray the Lord my soul to take."

The dogs barked on. But Alexander needed to finish.

"It took me until recently to understand the reason I didn't want to say it. Death on the rocking horse and me afraid to sleep, that prayer seemed to me the opposite of what I thought my evening battle cry should have been. But I was too young to explain. I hadn't the words, although being unable to explain in no way altered the facts as I saw them. I was just bullied by the big people into silence and felt I had to stave off this thing in my room by myself."

Alexander stood to check his pocket watch. "Getting on for twelve," he said. "Aren't you famished?"

Teenotchy shrugged a yes, but wondered where the story was heading. He asked, "Why'd you want me to promise I wouldn't run off?"

Brushing loose dirt from his trousers, stained by grass, Alexander turned them back down. "I wanted you to know that I know what fear feels like, and that not being able to explain what lies at the root of it makes the thing feared the more frightening."

Teenotchy was praying Alexander wasn't going to talk about Geronimo. He thought perhaps that was the real reason Alexander'd told that story. Like Miss Sullivan, who used one thing to lurch straight into something worse.

But when Alexander said, "Reuben'll be coming soon, I'd better go," Teenotchy felt his prayer'd been answered.

"Maybe you ought to go out that gate back there." Teenotchy pointed to the small exit furthest from the house, hoping to avoid Helga Kleber. "Is that all to the story?" he asked shyly, curiosity having got the best of him.

"You never swore you wouldn't run off," said Alexander. "Swear, if you want to hear more."

"I'm not allowed to swear," Teenotchy said, because thirteen years working for the Klebers meant some Quaker dogma had stuck.

Alexander pulled a couple of leaves from a bush and chewed the tip of one. He'd begun telling that story wanting to explain that, in spite of his battle with death and his fear of it, he would die for Teenotchy. But recalling him bolting from the bench under Mister Kleber's oak trees, Alexander'd lost faith in the notion. He couldn't afford for that to happen before his departure from Holybrook. So he waved off the issue by saying, "I hope Ruth's given us some pie."

Having heard that Alexander was leaving, Ruth was pleased for him. "That poor confused child needs to be home with his own people," she'd said. But sure, in spite of that, that he had a good heart, she'd made extra effort to prepare a lusty feast.

He and Teenotchy found homemade bread, slivers of turkey and ham, and potato salad. Though it was her pickled melon rind that Teenotchy thought even outdistanced her sour-cream cake. Not that he had Alexander's craving for sweets and was surprised to see him forgo the gooey cake in favor of sleep.

Alexander was feeling breathless, but didn't want to admit it. So Teenotchy tiptoed off the minute he dozed off.

Waking some time later, Alexander was aware his chin itched, but he felt too exhausted to scratch, worried that the heaviness in his chest was more illness than heartache. But managing to stand up and shake off a bad dream, he concluded it was the combination of heartache, illness and nightmares, looking at his watch, refusing to believe he'd slept three hours.

Teenotchy was trimming a hedge when Alexander finally found him, the ache in his chest a signal that he should lie down, though he refused to listen. He hoped Teenotchy would agree to his last wish and asked, "I had Reuben leave Entelechy, thinking we might ride to Fisher's Hollow."

He was bowled over to hear Teenotchy's, "OK . . . but you look like you should go home to bed." Teenotchy couldn't help noticing how the circles under Alexander's eyes had darkened since his sleep. "Aunt Em does this tonic that the woman next door swears by," he added.

But the melancholy veil tainting Alexander's smile had nothing to do with illness or fatigue. He told Teenotchy, "I wish I had my Kodak here. I'd love to take a picture of you beside that hedge you're carving."

Teenootchy'd seen an advertisement for the newfangled portable. "They really work, huh?"

It was their moment shared before noon which Alexander wished to frame. But he knew the spirit of a moment couldn't be photographed. "C'mon on, then," he said, trying to sound American, frustrated their day together was about to end.

To see Teenotchy on Entelechy lifted Alexander's malaise. He laughed, laughter feeling so right whenever Teenotchy was within arm's reach. "You'll surely go down in history as the only person who's ever refused the gift of a racehorse," he said, thinking about how casually Teenotchy had told him that he didn't think accepting Entelechy was a good idea.

When Teenotchy took off his spectacles and stuck them in his overall pocket, Alexander could feel him missing his harmonica.

"My giving you my horse was far less magnanimous than you giving your harmonica. As I explain in here," he said, passing Teenotchy the letter. "But please don't read it until six. Six sharp. Not a minute before or after. You can judge by the church bells."

"Why?" Teenotchy asked, wishing he knew what mag-na-ni-mous meant.

Alexander couldn't say he wanted to be concentrating on him as he read. Instead he jibed, "One lesson in the art of conversation and you're all questions." He scratched at the stubbly five o'clock shadow on his chin. Sloppiness suited him.

They cantered to Fisher's Hollow without words, Teenotchy with the mud on his boots, a bit in his hair, and the long white envelope burning a hole in his overall pocket, although he pretended not to notice.

He'd never received a properly sealed envelope. In fact he'd never received an envelope addressed to him at all and it was too much to contemplate what it might contain. Big words probably, he was thinking to himself. One minute he was itching to force it open and the next scared that whatever it said would be beyond his understanding.

That Sunday in Germantown was glorious, the September afternoon vain in her best dress. The leaves had begun to turn and every shade of green surrounded the boys with splashes of wild pink, simmering to red here and there. Occasionally there was a dash of yellow or a splurge of purple color pulsating in the feathery breeze. Under a honey sun towering trees danced a last tango with summer. As if they could avoid that deadly waltz with autumn.

Teenotchy looked up as one blue jay flew past and then another. One cardinal and then another. One dove. Two doves, and a third. He took less notice of the sparrows and pigeons, which played like identical twins smitten with their own image. Teenotchy was intrigued when he said, "Birds of a feather flock together. . . . Wonder who said that?" he asked.

Alexander liked hearing him sigh, which he did loudly just as they approached that point where it was obvious he could manage to guide Entelechy back to the manor alone.

"Do you think that's why we have the expression 'bird-brained'?" quipped Alexander in response to what Teenotchy'd said almost two whole minutes before. But Alexander judged from Teenotchy's expression that this witty reference meant less than it was supposed to and he hoped Teenotchy would ask for an explanation.

"Answer me one thing," began Teenotchy, pleased he'd remembered not to say "please" or "sir."

Alexander was busy being a camera, his eyes staring hard at Teenotchy's profile as Teenotchy continued to speak. "You know when you were telling me that stuff about . . ." Teenotchy went on, scared to mouth the word death and scratching around for another. "You know . . . about when you were a kid . . ."

His scramble for words that didn't want to sit on the tip of his tongue made Alexander anxious for him, made him ache a little bit, like Teenotchy's painful shyness was his own burden. So, as usual, he rushed to the rescue, saying, "Teenotchy, I wanted to explain that I've faced death. Since I was young I've feared it and thought endlessly about the grave and Hell, of which I am more sure than Heaven." He smiled as Teenotchy smiled, the latter smiling out of discomfort at the intimate tone of Alexander's voice as he carried on.

"You thought that would make me run off?" Teenotchy asked, squinting. So Alexander shifted his position to shield his small, dark friend from the sun's rays. Sitting tall in his English saddle, Alexander was suddenly aware that he was so tired all the muscles in his shoulders and back ached. But he couldn't understand why. He drew a deep breath from what he knew to be his empty well.

Then he rubbed his eyes with the ball of his fist like a tired baby before he took off his hat to use it as a fan to swat the pesky flies from his stallion's nostrils.

Fatigue and frustration overwhelmed Alexander, who waited and watched closely as Teenotchy dismounted Entelechy. He noticed as he took the reins in his hand that they were still warm from Teenotchy's grip.

Feigning a smile which felt false and looked falser, Alexander doffed his hat and nodded goodbye, surprised when his temper spilt out in a sudden rage. "I would die for you!" he called over his shoulder as he led Entelechy away, expecting no reply from Teenotchy and getting none.

Teenotchy could do no more than sigh and shrug his shoulders and walk in the opposite direction, heading toward

town with that white parchment envelope and its stately red
seal flapping against the palm of his brown hand.

He wasn't prepared to deal with life's complexities and
couldn't understand why graduating from high school hadn't
changed that. He was still a bundle of nerves. He was still
lost for words. And still love and death flummoxed him.

Teenotchy knew it was possible that Alexander was that
wolf in sheep's clothing that Miss Sullivan tutored him to
guard against, especially when he got to Cleveland. But then,
Teenotchy was positive that it was unlikely he'd ever be expected to shake a white boy's hand again, especially in
Cleveland.

He eyed the envelope, wanting to sniff at the red seal,
which was as tempting as a ripe cherry. He struggled with
the polar pulls of his two minds. Was it good or bad? Was
Alexander good or bad? Was it his duty to throw away the
envelope unopened? The only person he suspected would
know the right answer was Mister Kleber and so Teenotchy
tried to wear the old man's shoes as he walked carefully along
the path strewn with broken leaves and heavy with the smell
of pine.

The seal kept taunting him. He sniffed at it with the
innocence of a puppy, deciding to open it in a secluded spot,
believing he could throw it away if it hinted at things not
meant to be said between men.

A mustache of hot sweat sprouted upon his upper lip
while he shifted from foot to foot under an elm as he waited
for the faint toll of the town's church bells, counting the
labored ring of each one as six struck just as he'd pouted his
lips to imitate Alexander's speech.

Teenotchy wondered if it sounded exact only to his own
ears and was feeling bold as he carefully opened the envelope, surprised he hadn't made a mess of it.

Inside, the weighty sheet of stationery was paler than its
creamier, beveled edge and Teenotchy leaned against the
stump of a tree to unfold its neat creases.

Finding two green bills, as crisp and clean as the stationery itself made Teenotchy gasp. "Holy moley," he breathed, taking his glasses off so he could put them on again. "Holy God! What the . . . ? Jeez, oh Jeez," he kept on until his shock finally silenced him. But he still couldn't completely take in the 100s printed on the money.

One slipped out of his hand and, bending to pick it up, he dropped the letter, so it was necessary to chastise himself in the voice of an old geography teacher he loathed, "Pull yourself together, boy," Teenotchy imitated. "Just read the letter."

His legs felt too much like jelly to hold him and he sat, noticing that Alexander's handwriting was nearly as precise as the U.S. Treasurer who'd signed the money bearing Benjamin Franklin's semibald image.

> Holybrook Manor
> 14 September 1913
>
> Dear T'notchy
> Apologies if I've spelt your name incorrectly. I considered addressing this "dear friend" but remember your once asking if I was a Quaker and wouldn't like to contribute to that false impression.
> I'm enclosing two portraits of Ben Franklin. Three others await you in a safe deposit box in the name of Theodore Simms at Cranford's Merchant Bank, Rittenhouse Square, Philadelphia.
> Having lectured you about entelechy, I feel it only fair and proper to help you realize your full potential. So don't think the enclosed is charity, because I've waged a bet with myself that with this minimal financial assistance, you'll do very well.
> Please don't refuse it.
> In any case, generosity is relative, and five hundred dollars is a pittance of the excess I'll soon inherit effortlessly by becoming twenty-one.

I never meant to offend you, but I have a right to my feelings, though no right to impose them. To commit more to paper would be unwise, but it may comfort you to know I leave tomorrow morning.

Also enclosed is a receipt for Geronimo's headstone. The stonemason next to the new funeral home on Bringhurst Street will deliver it to Miss Sullivan's next Saturday. He's been paid in full for materials and the labor required to mount it. I hope the inscription is acceptable to both you and Miss Sullivan.

Good luck.
                    Your friend,
                    Alexander

Teenotchy didn't know whether to stand or sit, walk or be still after he'd read it. So he did all four in a sudden flurry, his eyes watering as he examined first the bills then the letter. "Your friend," he said aloud three times as he finally decided to sit and read the letter again. But first he sniffed the bills, less interested in Benjamin Franklin than in the lavender water Alexander'd splashed on his cheeks to keep awake before handling them.

He had a simple signature, clear and exact, which Teenotchy fingered, picturing the fine dark hairs growing sideways on the back of Alexander's hands. Then Teenotchy examined one of his own. Brown. Hairless. Dirt caked under his fingernails as always from the Klebers' garden. He wiped both hands on his overalls before wiping his eyes.

"Big dummy," he said of himself, sniffing the bills again and grinning. Out of harm's way, it felt safe to think about how sad Alexander's brown eyes had looked when he had been unable to decipher Miss Sullivan's poem, and for some reason their sadness made Teenotchy laugh, imitating the way Alexander said his name, so had anyone heard they would have sworn it was Alexander himself saying

"T'notchy" in that way he had of hardly pronouncing the "T" and stressing the "not."

Teenotchy looked at the bills, front and back. He'd never seen one-hundred-dollar bills before and there was a lot to look at and think about. Only two weeks before, the idea of fifty had seemed crazy in one win.

The windfall of five hundred dollars allowed Teenotchy to see Alexander's lips, the smooth, dark-pink half smile, white teeth slightly crooked, bottom front.

The shock and excitement made Teenotchy want to pee, and he never enjoyed it so much as he did that moment when his water shot forth: instead of aiming it at the base of a tree trunk, he shot it into the air like a geyser. "Yahoody!" he hollered, before moving two trees along to sit in a drier spot. Unlacing his boots, feet unbound, he sprawled himself under the tall maple he'd chosen.

Then he looked at the letter again with his toes playing among some crispy fallen leaves, when jealous memories stole upon him to vie for his attention. . . . His mother's hands made shadow puppets, her bassy voice chanting, "Sister's heart."

But even her ghost couldn't compete with Alexander's gesture and letter, which Teenotchy read again, saying, "Thank you." A rush of tears streaked his cheeks, his nose running, though he sniffed and sniffed.

He wanted to laugh but couldn't stop crying, unaware that he'd just been drugged by that heady bouquet of aphrodisiacs: to be believed in, cherished unconditionally and trusted absolutely.

Not since Dusty Simms's injections of motherlove, her eyes assuring Teenotchy he was her angel, Heaven sent, had he felt as equipped to stay out of the poorhouse. He wanted to dance, though he'd never danced; he wanted to kiss, though he hadn't been kissed since his mother died.

So he did the most he could, giving himself over to the need to roll upon his stomach, to rub his impotence against the earth. Sure she wouldn't mock or tell what he never admitted to himself.

In Upper Germantown, Alexander'd sat himself at his desk as clocks throughout the house chimed six.

He was dented by the same feeling of despair he'd suffered after his grandmother'd died. But despite the temptation to succumb to a depression, he commenced his fifth thank-you letter, resisting the urge to walk, to run, to do anything but sit in that room surrounded by that wallpaper with pheasants in flight.

"Dear Colonel Fullerton," he wrote, grinning at what he really wished to say. "Dear Colonel Fullerton, you bastard, may you and your Confederate League rot in Hell . . ."

Even this small, innocuous fantasy made Alexander feel better. So he got up to grab his sraw boater from the bed, plopping it on his head, and collapsing onto his reading chair, wishing his uncle would enter, since Jonas Tewksbury regularly created a row any time he saw a man wearing a hat indoors. "Only heathens and niggers keep a hat on in the house," he was often known to say.

Alexander took it off, put it on, took it off, wishing he could break a window or set fire to the bed, since he couldn't challenge his uncle to a duel to the death.

Not that anything could really take his mind from Teenotchy.

Alexander's desire for him had harried itself into an obsession. He ached for Teenotchy, longing to save him, though he couldn't be sure from what.

A thousand times he'd imagined Teenotchy lying in his arms, gray eyes half closed as Alexander's lips brushed his brown cheek more gently than a butterfly tasting a rose. But it wasn't this fantasy which Alexander indulged in nightly in his easy chair once Teenotchy'd eclipsed his passion for the history behind the history of the Revolution. It was the memory of Teenotchy shirtless upon General, ebony nipples guarding that defined, hairless chest drenched in sweat, that titillated and tormented Alexander.

It was this image which swelled his soft penis to a reddish blue truncheon, hot and hard beneath his silk dressing gown. Nightly it had refused propriety, refused concealments, refused to lie down with Alexander slightly slumped, legs akimbo, as tingling started in his loins, worming its way to his lungs, until to scream seemed more rational than breathing, although he resisted the urge with the house asleep.

Night after night, "Break me, break me, Teenotchy," would rise up involuntarily from his throat, as seductive and romantic as a rhapsody between cello and oboe. Alexander begged to be tamed. But it also shamed him, because he hated his instinct to supersede good form.

His tingling was even more edgy than he remembered from occasions when a baby tooth had to be pulled: his grandmother would attach one end of a string to a doorknob, the other to his tooth, dislodging it by slamming the door. But beforehand, little Alexander's every corpuscle could have anticipated the sharp pain passing quickly to the ecstasy of their shared laughter and her applause.

But in his room alone, his last Sunday evening at Holybrook, Alexander sat gracefully in his reading chair. Head back, eyes closed, he concentrated, and heard himself saying, "Break me, Teenotchy, break me," as his thoughts caressed Teenotchy, a mile away at the edge of Fisher's Hollow thinking about him.

Teenotchy clung to the ground as Alexander's good intentions crawled over every inch of him, salving internal wounds; while Alexander's brave intentions washed the blood and pus from past humiliations, Teenotchy moaned and cried his relief.

The money was Alexander's faith in him ramming itself down Teenotchy's throat to feel around for a heart hurt and hurting.

Was it a dream or nightmare that Alexander's fingers had laced themselves around his slippery heart? Teenotchy couldn't decide.

"Jesus, five hundred dollars," laughed Teenotchy, "five hundred!" Rolling on to his back, he checked the letter again and sniffed the one-hundred-dollar bills. But reality nudged him to say, "You're gonna get me killed," before he whispered Alexander's name as one breathing the name of a saint.

Is that what brought Alexander screaming to his feet as he punched through the crown of his hat to stuff it back on his head? His was a primeval roar.

Ezekiel was the first to reach his room and sent the maid cleaning the stairs to mind her business, as he put it, after taking two steps at a time from Mister Tewksbury's dressing room where he was laying out Jonas's third change that day.

"Mister Alexander!" Ezekiel called, keen to make a showy rescue, imagining he'd find him on the floor writhing in pain. But when he unlocked the door, he couldn't believe Alexander was laughing, with a broken hat on his head. "You all right, Mister Alexander?" he asked, suddenly recalling Ruth's conclusion that the boy, viscount or not, wasn't all there.

Alexander's soul flip-flopped when Teenotchy called his name a second time to make him fling himself across his bed.

"You all right, sir?" asked the butler, who'd heard about fits but had never witnessed one and wondered if he shouldn't get the maid cleaning the stairs to come help. "You all right?" he nearly demanded the third time, having had no response.

Alexander felt drunk. "In love," he dared say, tossing his hat to catch it with the grass-stained, muddy toe of his white shoe.

"I know how that feels," Ezekiel smiled, somewhat relieved since he didn't want disgrace to fall upon the Tewksburys by way of madness in the family. "My Ruthie got me with her smile and then her pies got hold of my sweet tooth," he said, doing a crab step out of Alexander's room.

"Ruthie Mae," Ezekiel said, shaking his head going downstairs, as though she could hear, "that's nothing but a fool in love. Didn't shave, suit look like he's been brawling . . ."

Summoned from the dressing room by Mrs. Tewksbury, Ezekiel was quick to explain who had screamed, adding, "Wedding bells'll be ringing next thing we know. Bet it's Miz Melanie."

Having been party to Julia's various schemes to get those two together, Ezekiel expected Mrs. Tewksbury's face to light up and was anxious he'd said too much when she flushed her pinkest.

Worldly enough to suspect what she considered the unthinkable, she thought about Alexander fixated and sweating at the race. She tried to sound casual. "Was Atlanta's brother working here today?"

"Sorry, Miz Julia, I can't rightly say," admitted Ezekiel. "But I think I saw that old nag of his still here late last night."

Her cheeks reddened so, he hoped he wasn't going to have to run for the smelling salts. Not that he'd ever known her faint, but regularly Mister Tewksbury liked to imply she was carrying his child, an unborn many years in coming.

Julia pranced across the room in her sober gray dress, looking too matronly on Sundays for her light-footed gait. He was glad her voice was as even and calm as always when she said, "Tell Edison to make certain that Simms boy isn't here tomorrow. Or ever again for that matter." Her turned back dismissed Ezekiel, who gave a dirty look to the dogs, Georgia and Laura, sleeping on the table he'd French-polished only Friday.

"I'll see to it right away," he said leaving, unable to resist a smile since he liked to be right about things and assumed

Mrs. Tewksbury had heard Teenotchy'd been in the phaeton. In the passenger seat.

Julia looked out of her study window and put one thin, delicate hand to her mouth, thinking about what her sister'd said in the letter that Alexander'd so reluctantly delivered early on in his stay.

Even then Julia'd wondered what Irene had meant by "Jacques and Alexander are becoming too close," since it had once been Irene's great pride that the cousins had been raised practically as brothers.

Julia went to her drawer to retrieve the letter, reading it quickly to stop at the sentence which said, "Please encourage his interest in girls."

Georgia and Laura were jolted from their sleep when their mistress slammed the drawer. "Love," she said to their yawn. "It couldn't be possible. . . . Could it be possible?"

The dogs answered with a yawn. Having been spayed, love and sex interested them not at all.

Julia knotted her hands together, remembering how morose her nephew had seemed when they'd collected him from the port and how inexplicably he'd become near to starry-eyed. And how odd she thought it was that Alexander'd claimed he was leaving a down payment for a horse in a safe deposit box at the bank in the stable boy's name rather than in hers or Jonas's.

She shook her head, looking at her mother's picture in one of the modern frames Alexander had brought from England. Though Julia prided herself on being egalitarian, she always loathed her mother for her abolitionist causes and promoting equality between the races, which had alienated them socially from Julia's earliest memory.

"Happy now?" she had asked her mother's image, that stout face smiling in the photograph. "Abolition. Abolition. Abolition. And now look where it's got us! Love! Love, indeed!" Julia stamped.

Suddenly Alexander's departure couldn't come soon

enough and she was proud that she'd forwarded Jacques's letters on to Irene, only sorry that she hadn't snuck a peek into one.

Julia prided herself on being liberal-minded, and had Alexander been beguiled by an Irish immigrant straight off the dock at Ellis Island, she imagined she could have blessed their union. But a colored stable boy!

Perhaps Alexander was as mad as his father, who'd died from an opium overdose within a year of Irene marrying him, much to everyone's horror. Though all conceded it was the best thing, since a future in an asylum was equally shameful.

As the clocks struck the half hour, Julia realized she still hadn't changed for dinner, but thought she might feign a headache and dine in bed since the mere thought of having to be polite to Alexander suddenly offended her sense of decency.

From having wished she could find some excuse forcing him to extend his stay, his aunt couldn't get him out of her house fast enough. She gave a quick pat at her thigh to beckon the dogs, who took their time in coming. "Mother's little darlings," she said in her most pampering voice. "Your cousin's a . . ."

Her sixth sense told her to say no more as Marie Annette had been more than once caught eavesdropping.

Julia tiptoed to the door with the dogs at her heels and thrust it open, disappointed to find no one and deciding to continue straight to her room.

She sneered at herself in the gilt mirror in the hall. What had she done, she asked herself, to deserve a husband who was a cretin, a mother who'd been a crank, a brother-in-law who had been an opium addict and a nephew (or was it two) who was a sodomite?

"Nigger," she thought, as Ezekiel stood aside to allow her to pass him on the stairs. She smiled graciously, the wagging pups her foot soldiers. "Thank you, Ezekiel," she said aloud, always the lady.

He gave a slight bow, delighted to be in favor. Although he hated white people, he took immense pride in serving them well.

"I shan't be dining with Mister Tewksbury tonight," she told him. "Have Marie Annette draw my bath and bring my supper up."

Ezekiel guessed from her tone there was no point in reminding her how elaborate was the meal she'd planned, it being Alexander's last; he merely had her place setting removed from the dining room the first chance he got.

"Ol' man Jonas'll be eating by himself," sighed Ruth, who'd been cooking all day, " 'cause that boy already sent word he's too sick to eat. And me fixed him that Boston cream pie."

XXII

After maintaining a vigilant patrol all day, the sun was worn out and ready to let the moon take its night shift. Eight o'clock and the birds were still fussing over their dinner as Teenotchy made his way along the path under the towering trees, their leaves silent in the still air. So the sound of him dragging his feet past two squirrels and some sparrows seemed downright noisy, but he was in too much turmoil to make his usual effort to be neither seen nor heard.

The initial ecstasy of Alexander's letter had dimmed, and shame was like a ball and chain clamped around Teenotchy's right leg, while guilt had a strong hold on his left, making it impossible for him to be light-footed anyway. That money was burning a hole in Teenotchy's soul. It was a dead weight which his life made him too weak to carry, an offering so strange that it made him too aware of himself. He felt poor and small. He felt humbled and owned and dirty. Like somebody's nigger. Because in trying to give him everything, Alexander'd forgotten his grandmother's warnings about the care that must be taken when giving to those less fortunate than oneself.

But although the money had a damning effect upon Teenotchy, his back was straighter than it had been when he stole into the Hollow to read Alexander's letter. Maybe he even held his head a little higher as he sniffed that sweet smell of evening. Theodore "Teenotchy" Simms was dangerously rich with no place to go, especially with that come caked and drying inside his right pants leg, proof that he wasn't fit to live. He was practically limping with guilt and shame, and yet he felt a crazy boldness the moment he reached the meadow where the open sky was still painted the palest blue. He was scared to scratch his inside leg, sure that everything alive knew he couldn't get the picture of Alexander's hands out of his mind. He kept seeing the way the dark hairs grew in a swirled pattern against the pinkish flesh, those fingers as graceful as Dusty Simms's that used to pick the sleep from his eyes and rub a bit of grease on his knees.

He wondered if his mother knew what the birds cackling at him knew as he took one step then another with that letter and the two one-hundred-dollar bills folded neatly in his pocket that had once been a safe for his harmonica.

"Sister!" he called from out of nowhere, as surprised to hear his own voice as the wild things that galloped off. Birds. Hares. Squirrels. Hedgehogs. All racing for cover as Teenotchy's voice rapped back into the hollow of trees. "Sister!" he found the nerve to call again, since being rich made him as bold as it scared him.

Suddenly he knew what he was meant to do and he took the letter carefully out of his pocket, easing his fingers past the two bills as his feet took a turn that would lead him home. He had to tear it up but was afraid to stop, so he moved on, breaking tiny little sections off and discarding them here and there, tossing them to his left, then his

right to rid himself of the evidence before he reached Main
Street.

His heart was beating like a thief's caught in the act and
he was relieved that, it being Sunday night, he was the only
person about. Nobody to see the earth clogged between his
toes. Nobody to see through his pants leg and spy the yellow-
ish come flaking on his thigh and slightly caked on the hair
between his legs.

Teenotchy didn't dare look up as he passed the Klebers'
there at Schoolhouse Lane. He coughed a nervous cough
and broke off two more bits of the letter, small enough that
there could have hardly been a whole word in the two pieces
combined. What worried him was the red seal he was able
to tear from the envelope but which refused to bend or break
between his fingers, so he waited until he got to the gutter
at the curb in Market Square and carefully dropped it in.

"September," he said aloud. It had always been a bad
month in his mind. Not just because his mother'd died that
month, but because the promises of summer ended so
abruptly. Mister Kleber used to get excited about the leaves
changing colors and the days getting short, but Teenotchy'd
always felt a swell of fear and sorrow when the leaves began
to crunch underfoot, and he felt grateful that his plan would
allow him to avoid that.

As he rounded into their dead end, he swore he could
hear Aunt Em's voice before he reached the gate. Hers and
Atlanta's in another evening duel. Aunt Em's was the bowie
knife, a fat, brutal blade taking swipes at Atlanta's long, elegant sword, which made a swoosh as she cut Aunt Em to
size, yelling, "fat tub of lard."

The two women didn't draw breath as Teenotchy entered the kitchen, making his way to the one drawer, which
he opened quietly, careful not to disturb their Sunday night
foray so that he could stick that two hundred dollars in with
the clothes pegs and scraps of paper, matchsticks and broken
pencils that lived there with the hair grease.

"Heifer, don't you know I'll take and maul your head to that there wall," shouted Aunt Em, so that Tessie could hear as well as Atlanta, standing her ground in the kitchen, both hands on her hips as she'd seen Aunt Em do all her life.

They didn't even notice that Teenotchy'd come in and gone out and they were still shouting at each other as he made his way back down their little side street after leaving his shoes on the back steps, because he knew somebody would have use for them.

Within half an hour, just as the light dropped out of the sky and stars began twinkling over Germantown, he'd reached the woods beside Lincoln Drive. It made him pant with trepidation and excitement that he'd braved that place alone and in September too. So he broke into a little smile at the same time that his eyes welled with tears.

Not that he was actually crying when he climbed the bank to the Walnut Lane Bridge above the Wissahickon.

Teenotchy felt bold when he took off his spectacles and laid them on his cap, which he put on the arched brick wall that kept people from tumbling into the river. He had a sudden surge of power that people often get the moment they feel they are able to take control of their lives. And he was still almost smiling when he took the great leap, his small, compact body hitting the riverbank with a dull thud that hardly shattered the peace of that quiet September night, 1913.